T0158738

Kiss Her Goodbye

A Houston Cash Novel

Harvey Burgess

iUniverse, Inc.
Bloomington

Kiss Her Goodbye
A Houston Cash Novel

iUniverse books may be ordered through booksellers or by contacting:

iUniverse
1663 Liberty Drive
Bloomington, IN 47403
www.iuniverse.com
1-800-Authors (1-800-288-4677)

ISBN: 978-1-4620-2802-3 (sc)
ISBN: 978-1-4620-2803-0 (hc)
ISBN: 978-1-4620-2804-7 (e)

Library of Congress Control Number: 2011910175

Printed in the United States of America

iUniverse rev. date: 9/9/2011

For my mother and father, Pauline Stewart Burgess and the late F.R. Burgess, without whom this could never be.

CHAPTER ONE

I WAS PUTTING AN EIGHT of hearts on a nine of clubs when she came through the door. I looked up, smiled casually, pulled the desk blotter over the cards. Always prepared for times like these. Tucked a straggling two of spades under the bottom. Had to remember to get a bigger blotter.

It took a second or two for my eyes to focus on her, and I quietly reminded myself to replace those two dead bulbs in the three-bulb ceiling fixture. At least it was too dim for anybody to see the walls needed painting.

Auburn hair fell to her shoulders, parted on one side, coppery strands draped sensually over one eye, high-arching brow setting off the other one, gray with green flecks, easy to see even in the bad light of the office. Didn't somebody once say that people with gray eyes were never up to any good?

She was built like Jessica Rabbit, the hourglass cartoon in the movie that, with Kathleen Turner's voice, was an exaggerated sketch of every heterosexual male's dream. A feminine cliché in four-inch heels. Tall, sultry, perfect complexion, a little pale in the light.

"Mister Cash?" Her voice went with everything else. Low, husky. Lauren Bacall in *To Have and Have Not*. An old-timer would have called it a "whisky voice."

"That's what it says on the door." Already trying to be too cool. If Dawn had been in the room, she'd have kicked my shin for being a smartass. I wanted to take it back as soon as the words came out.

"Sorry. I just wasn't sure. It's this building. It's confusing," she said, gliding toward the desk. She was being kind, probably figured all private detectives were supposed to be smart alecks holed up in dingy offices, which wasn't that far from the truth. I'd rented this closet in a building not likely to be around in another couple of years. My cube was supposed to be nine hundred square feet, might even have been fancy once, nice dentil work. Now the old office building had three empty floors overhead and my ground-level suitemates included a bail bondsman, a debit life insurance salesman, and a Hindu tailor who always stuck his head out the door when anybody walked down the hall. Bet Mr. Thakur got an eyeful this time.

I stood, motioned to one of the brown fake leather chairs flanking my cluttered government-type, gunmetal gray relic of a desk. "Please sit down." Suave.

She flowed into the chair, I swear to God. Crossed her legs. I caught my breath, involuntarily sucked in my gut and tried to sit taller. The dress looked to be silk, green with subtle highlights. A good four inches above the knees. Clingy. Sharon Stone-ish.

"What can I do for you, Miss ...?"

"Devore. Priscilla Devore." She offered her hand. I wanted to kiss it but shook it instead. She had a firm grip, long fingers. Her palm seemed a tad damp, cool to the touch. Probably nervous at meeting such a famous private investigator. Her name rang a bell, but I couldn't remember from where at the moment. Maybe I was a little too preoccupied with my visual analysis.

"Well, Miss Devore ..."

"Please, call me Cissy. Everyone does."

"All right, Cissy, now where were we?"

"I got your name from Aaron Drake. He said you might be able to help me with a little, uh, problem."

Aaron Drake was a retired cop who ran security at the city's largest bank. Orbited in pretty high circles these days, but still dropped by Billy's Shamrock Lounge to smoke, lie, and drink with cops and people like me. We spent a lot of time together since his wife died, him helping me out whenever he could.

"Aaron and I go way back." Confirmation. Put her at ease, Houston. "What can I do for you, Cissy?"

"It's a little personal. I don't actually know where to begin, to tell you the truth." She crossed her legs again, and I tried not to be obvious, watching the green floral silk move, faint yellowish orchids merging in the folds.

"Everything you say here stays here, Cissy. Kinda like a lawyer-client thing."

She seemed to relax a little and reached inside her purse. Little patent clasp thing. "Is it all right if I smoke? I know that's so politically incorrect these days."

"Sure. Here." I fumbled my old Zippo out of my pocket and reached across, igniting the tip of her Virginia Slim, and slid a crusty metal ashtray across the desk. I'd quit a few years back but still kept the trappings handy, since most of the people who came through my door rarely saw the need to be politically correct. I could live with the cigarettes, but cigars did a number on my sinuses.

She took a long pull, blew the smoke out as she started talking. It just hung there. Maybe I should get a ceiling fan. "I think I'm being followed by a man."

"I wouldn't find that hard to believe." What an attempt at levity. I sounded like I needed a pocket protector. She smiled, a humorless grin really, punctuating that hint of tension. She kept talking.

"I don't think this man knows I've seen him. He tends to stay in shadows, but I know he's there," she continued. "At first, I thought I was just being paranoid. I felt silly saying anything to the police, so I asked Aaron for advice.

"He said if anyone could find out what was going on, it was you. Said you were a police officer once. A pretty good one."

"Aaron and I worked together." In fact, Aaron had been my training officer and, though he denies it, he was the one who got me put in investigations. I'd probably still be there if it hadn't been for that bastard Frank Malone, but that's another story.

"I know I've seen this man in my neighborhood, even though we have security, and I'm sure I've seen him following me at a shopping mall and at least one social function. When I told my husband, he just laughed and told me to look in the mirror. Carson doesn't take me very seriously sometimes."

"So Carson Devore is your husband." Bells started ringing. Chairman, CEO of the bank Aaron protects against the bad guys. Had to be a good twenty years older than Cissy. Money talks, bullshit walks, and apparently earns you a trophy wife.

"We were married four years ago, two years after his first wife died," she said, making me feel bad about the "trophy wife" thought. "I was a loan officer at a branch and we met at a company staff meeting. He asked me out and, well, it just happened."

"Does he know you've come to me?"

"No. Not yet, anyway. I mean, we talked about it, the possibility of kidnapping and all that, but he just says this is a nice town and things like that don't happen here. He said if I was troubled enough by it to talk to Aaron. I did, and here I am."

Reasonable assumption, I thought. "I'm going to ask you something I don't want you to take the wrong way, but before I ask it I need to know if you really want me to take this case. My fee's three hundred a day plus expenses …"

"Mister Cash, money is no problem. I simply want to quit looking over my shoulder every time I go somewhere." I got the feeling that she was holding back. Don't know why, necessarily, but the instinct doesn't usually fail me. I plunged forward.

"Would there be a reason why your husband would have you followed?"

She had to reflect a minute, though I had the odd feeling it was an act. She tamped out her cigarette. "No. I think when I told him about it, if he had anything to do with it I would have been able to tell. Carson's not a very good liar."

I wanted to say that's not what I'd heard, but I kept my mouth shut. Discretion, valor, and all that.

"You might have to let him know I'm working for you."

"I'd rather not just yet, if we can help it."

"All right, we'll worry about that when the time comes." I had no doubt she could pay me out of her pocket change, so I shuffled some papers on the desk. It always seems to impress people when you do that. Probably messed up a good solitaire hand in the process. I reached into a drawer and pulled out a narrow notepad. "I'll need your itinerary for the next few days." After patting every pocket, I settled on a chewed Bic in a glass thing on my desk. Somebody had given it to me when I opened the office. The glass thing, not the desk. Bought that at Goodwill for twenty-five bucks, scratches and all.

She told me where she'd be and when she'd be there. I scribbled furiously, hoping I could read it later. When she was through, we both stood. Before I could say anything, she stuck her hand back in the purse and pulled out a wad of bills straining against a gold money clip. She peeled off ten hundreds and handed them to me.

"Will this be enough to start?"

"I should think so. I'll give you a receipt …" I shuffled some papers again but she stopped me with a touch on the arm. If I didn't know better, I could have sworn a spark flew. Maybe the carpet and my crepe-soled shoes. Cheap carpet. Probably came from Goodwill, too, but it was here when I rented the place and I couldn't afford to replace it. Dawn said it gave the place character.

"That won't be necessary. You can total it all up when you're through, something like that. I'd just as soon keep this as off-the-record as possible."

"Fine. Well, I'll see you tomorrow at …" I looked at the notepad. "Fynwyck's. Actually, you might not see me. The best way to shadow a shadow is to be less conspicuous than he is."

She smiled again, clueless to what I was saying. Dazzling. Perfect teeth. Lucky Carson. I silently prayed my tie was straight, there was no spinach in my teeth from that lunch calzone, and my pants weren't too shiny around the knees.

"One more question, if you don't mind. Could you maybe give me a little better description of this guy who's following you?"

"Not really. I've never seen his face; just his, you know, shape. Average height, average build. I'm not very good at those things. I couldn't honestly say the man I saw would even be the one who's following me, I guess. But I've seen him twice and it seems like more than just a coincidence." Modifying her story already.

"Could you tell if he was white or black? That'd help some."

"Not really. You know, I hadn't even thought about it," she said, reflective. "I'd say white, I suppose, but I really don't know."

I had the odd feeling that she really had not looked at this guy at all. "That's okay, but if you happen to think of anything else, I can always use the information."

"I'm sure you'll do just fine." She turned to walk to the door, not a very long trip. She looked over her shoulder. "Aaron's a good judge of character," she said, and then she was gone.

A funny thing to say after only a few minutes of conversation, I thought, but what the hell.

I plopped back down in my squeaky, cracked black leather chair and exhaled loudly. Then I picked up the phone and called my answering service. The girl on the phone was popping gum between words. It was a cheap service, one of those deals where you got the first month free.

No calls, no cases pending. No real shock. Looked like Cissy was going to be a full-time job for a while, and it sounded easy enough. Find her stalker, rattle his chain. Maybe some poor stiff who'd defaulted on a loan, or some backroom computer geek from the bank who had the hots for the boss's wife. Cut and dried, but it would pay the rent.

Then the palooka walked in.

- - -

"This Houston Cash Investigations?" He had a prizefighter's nose, flat and kind of at an angle. He could barely squeeze into the chair. I took him to be about six-one, a shade over three hundred, gone to seed a long time ago. Mostly just fat pockmarked face, close-set, beady eyes, hair greased straight back, thinning a little.

"What it says on the door."

"Okay, wise guy. What kind of investigations? I mean, you look for stray poodles and shit like that? Peep on husbands and wives? What?"

"You got the dime, I got the time." I could talk easier with palookas. "What, your Shi Tsu strayed?"

"Shit what? You tryna be funny?" He leaned toward me, close enough to smell the garlic on his breath, mingled with a cheap El Producto, I'd guess. His sport coat tightened, and the bulge on his left side outlined probably a semi-automatic, nine-millimeter range.

"Shi Tsu. It's a kind of dog."

"Huh, well, I ain't got no dog." He fidgeted in the chair, acting like he didn't know what to say next, or maybe just didn't know how to say it. "You, uh, talk to a lady came in here a while ago?"

"I don't share information about my clients." I was beginning to get annoyed and wondered if my Glock ten millimeter was in the desk drawer where I thought I'd put it.

"Well, let's say for a minute that you did talk to this lady. You know Joe Trenton?"

Joey T. Small-time local hood with supposedly big-time connections. Started out in Brooklyn, headed south to flex more muscle among the rubes, drawn here by the arrival of big-league sports. The NFL and NBA don't always attract purity to places like Charlotte.

Joey T ran some numbers networks; did a little dope-dealing, marijuana mostly; loan-sharking. Always kept a layer of kids between himself and the streets, so the cops could never quite touch him. I knew him well from my police days. "Yeah, I know Joey T."

"Mister Trenton don't like to be called that."

"I'm sure you'll extend my apologies to him."

"Yeah, well, he's got an interest in this lady, see. Doesn't want to see anything happen to her or anything." The palooka fidgeted some more, groping for a vocabulary.

"Since I don't know what lady you're talking about, I can't address the issue, Mister …"

"Eddie. Just Eddie's all you need to know."

"Well, Mister Just Eddie, if you'd be a little more specific, maybe I'd know what you're talking about." I looked him over. No average height or build here. Somebody you'd easily be able to describe, somebody who couldn't hang around in anything but very large shadows. Little doubt that Eddie wasn't Cissy's stalker.

"Just think about it, smart guy. I deliver messages is all. I ain't got much else to do with nothin' else, see?" Didn't doubt that for a minute. He heaved himself out of the chair, startling me slightly until I realized he wasn't heaving toward me.

I stood up, didn't extend my hand. I had Eddie by a good four inches, he had me by a good fifty pounds. I felt better when he had to look up at me just a little, and it was obvious he didn't like it too well.

"You've delivered your message. Can't say it applies to anything I'm doing, but if it does, I'll give you a call. Got a card?"

Eddie looked puzzled, then his eyes narrowed and he started to speak, thought about it, and turned to walk out the door. "Like I said, I deliver messages. You have a nice day, smart guy," he added, with a surprisingly adept flourish as he waved his hand and walked out.

Looked like Cissy and I were going to have to have a talk.

CHAPTER TWO

THE SUN WAS MELTING into the horizon as I pulled my aging Sebring ragtop into the carport. A burnt orange hue dappled the trees in front of my house, defining shadows. One of the things I liked most about living in the South was the sunsets. They seemed to be made here, and I hoped to see as many as I could. Charlotte isn't a city of big shoulders or baked beans, more a thriving financial center that's beginning to give cities like Dallas and Atlanta runs for their money, figuratively and literally. As good a place to live as I could find.

I nearly tripped over the cat as I walked through the door. He offered no apology other than mewing at me for being late. I dumped some Cat Chow in a bowl and he was my friend all over again, cat-motor running full blast. I'd had Bogie for twelve years. Not much of an image-builder for a badass private detective, but women liked him.

The cupboard was bare, as usual, but I had a few vegetables in the crisper, some fresh fettuccine in the fridge. Didn't take long to whip up some "fettuccine y'allfredo," a home-grown specialty I created after scores of friends and a few slow-pay clients brought me bounty from their gardens. It was easy enough. Slice up some squash, Vidalia onion, bell pepper, and a few mushrooms; toss in a couple of chopped-up garlic cloves; sauté it all in olive oil; and dump the concoction on a pile of fettuccine; coat with Parmesan cheese. Voila. Damn good, too, if I say so myself.

As I scooped the food at the kitchen table, I tossed the day's pile of mail. Mostly bills, chances to win ten million dollars, a Fraternal Order of Police newsletter—persistent relic from my cop days. Nothing out of the ordinary. Here lately, not much of my life had been out of the ordinary, but I wasn't complaining. People like Cissy Devore helped pay the bills, and that had become enough to satisfy at least the fiscal part of my existence.

After dinner, I stepped onto the deck tucked up behind my modest suburban three-bedroom, two-bath concession to the middle class and looked out over the woods that snugged up to the yard. A pileated woodpecker and his mate had taken up residence on a decaying pine tree, and I watched them jump, peck, and cluck for a while until it was too dark to see. Birds have terrific lives when people leave them alone.

Back in the house, I spooled up the computer and punched Cissy Devore's initial stats into the program I'd concocted for the office. I still used the old-fashioned note-taking method of case tracking, but I was learning to log it all eventually on a disc or flash drive. If Dawn taught me nothing else before she walked out, she taught me how to work a computer.

That was bullshit, actually. Dawn Rayburn taught me a lot. I used to pray she'd drop that cheeseball she married and walk back into my life. Those hopes diminish with every kid. I'll reluctantly admit Jerry Kline isn't really a cheeseball. He's a pretty good guy and has tried his damndest to be friendly to me, even knowing that his wife is probably the only woman I've ever loved, apologies to my two ex-wives. Those marriages only lasted a combined three years, and I was already having trouble remembering the first one's name. Diane, I think, but I couldn't remember if it had an *e*. Number two, Mariel, was too clingy and whiny, but I'll admit I never was a rock for either one of them, and now both were married and living elsewhere; happy, secure, familied.

Like them, I suppose, it boiled down to Dawn wanting security and a guy who stayed home a lot, neither of which I could guarantee. Now she's got a family and I've got Bogie, an empty house, and people like Mister Eddie walking in my office door. Ain't life grand in the private investigation trade. Not that I'm complaining, but I'm complaining. One of those moods.

I was dumping the dishes in the sink when the phone rang.

"Somebody told me I could find a decent private dick if I called this number."

"Depends on what you mean by decent. Or dick, for that matter."

"Well, I know you're a dick. Decent I can't vouch for."

"How ya doin', Aaron?"

"A certain lady come by your office today?"

"Auburn hair? Brick shithouse with gray eyes, legs all the way up to her ass?"

"That's the one. Often wondered where those legs went."

"This time she had a trailer." I told him about Eddie and Joey T. "Any guesses on why the interest's there?"

"Not the first. Let's go lift one and try to figure it out."

"Sounds like a plan." I looked at my watch. "See you at Billy's in an hour?"

I hung up the phone, stripped out of my sweaty day wear, showered, and thought about the turn of events. Aaron knew as much about Joey T as I did and, by the tone of his voice, liked this odd connection even less.

Every ounce of gut instinct I'd developed in fifteen years on the force I learned from Aaron Drake. We'd become so symbiotic he could finish my sentences. After he got his thirty-year pin and jumped ship at the department, his wife, Belinda, up and had a heart attack. Died in the ambulance on the way to the hospital. They had no kids, so I became his de facto son, I suppose. It hurt him when I quit the job, but I redeemed myself a little when, after getting my private ticket, I solved a couple of high-profile cases. One of them helped make Frank Malone look like the incompetent prick he was, and Aaron hoped I'd be off Malone's case. Maybe when I die.

-    -   -

Billy's Shamrock Lounge is a throwback to the fifties, when cops had soft hearts, no college degrees, and carried truncheons. When Miranda was the last name of a singer with fruit on her head. Not necessarily better days, mind you, but days when cops relied on instincts more than textbooks and if they promised you something, they'd die trying to deliver.

His place was once a downtown fixture about two blocks from the police station until Billy Muldoon yielded to Chamber of Commerce yuppification and moved his saloon to a strip shopping center on Central

Avenue, about six miles from what the Chamber now liked to call "Uptown Charlotte."

But it was like Billy had gutted the old Weinstein Building and moved its insides into the concrete-block slot beside an empty A&P. You walked in the door and were propelled back in time. Lots of dark wood, exposed beams, a few round tables; unbalanced, plastic-cushioned pine chairs trying to look leather; a long, heavy bar with a brass rail and worn spots on the bumper; booths shoved up against the wall.

Most of the light came from neon beer signs and a few fake Tiffany lamps scattered around, green metal-shaded lights hanging over the booths. The air was thick with smoke, the stale smell of beer and the noises of a dozen or so off-duty cops competing with a forty-inch flat-screen that hung from a rack over one end of the bar. A basketball game was on but nobody seemed to be paying much attention.

Aaron was tucked in a booth, Della McGovern leaning toward him and laughing. Della was Billy's only full-time waitress; Billy, his own bartender for forty-odd years. He was wiping out a beer mug when I pushed through the stained-glass door. Aaron raised his hand and Della looked around and smiled. She must be fifty, but she stayed in good shape and filled out the black and white waitress costume well. Rumor had it she'd screwed half the force over those years. I wasn't in that number.

"Well, if it ain't Mangum, Pee Eye," Billy said, shifting a stubby cigar from one side of his mouth to another. He looked a little like a buzzard: gaunt, big nose; but he had a thousand-watt, store-bought smile he'd sometimes take out and flash around when he'd been tipping a bit himself, amusing the troops. Bless his heart; Billy, I believe, spent most of his life wanting to be a cop. Never quite made the grade, according to Aaron, no matter how many bananas he forced down his throat or how many tire weights his badge-toting friends slipped in his shoes. By the time physical size was no longer an obstacle, Billy was too old and the bar was too successful.

"Yeah, and you're David Fuckin' Letterman, and it's Mag-num, not Mang-um," I shot back, grinning as I negotiated the crowd of familiar faces. Some smiled or nodded, others looked away. Some cops don't like private detectives, even if the PI used to be a cop. It's like you suddenly went to Internal Affairs and ratted everybody out. Whistling past a graveyard, afraid your former compadre was looking at you through those binoculars.

"Aaron's ordered for both of you," Della said as I slid onto the bench across from him. She leaned over and kissed me on the cheek, more for cleavage display than familiarity, proud of those puppies, which she frequently informed inquiring minds had not a gram of silicone aboard.

She walked back to the bar, hips swaying like a panther about to strike. Aaron and I both watched appreciatively.

"You oughta give that girl a tumble, Aaron."

"Again?" He grinned. In his thirty-five years with Belinda, I knew he'd never strayed. Since she died, as far as I knew, he was still faithful. Put roses on her grave every week, a hometown Joe DiMaggio paying homage to his lost Marilyn.

We started out with small talk until Della brought Aaron's Miller Lite and my Amstel, plopped the bottles down with one hand, set two heavy, ice-filmed mugs on cardboard coasters with the other, and sashayed off.

"So, Cissy Devore and Joey T. Damn. I've been studying on that one since you told me."

"Me, too. How much you know about the bank boss's missus?" I stared at Aaron in the half-light. Lines were getting deeper, but he still had that chiseled, Dick Tracy look. Square jaw, skinny neck, Adam's apple bobbing whenever he talked. He'd stayed in fairly decent fighting shape. Still pounded a bag down at Planet Fitness when he could, worried he'd go to seed like so many retirees.

"When she married Carson, I dug up her resume. From a small town in the eastern part of the state, went to one of the local colleges, got a job on the teller line at First Southern, worked her way up to junior loan officer. Seemed on the up and up. I don't have a clue where she mighta run into Joey T."

"Maybe into a little betting? Needed some money in the leaner years?"

"I doubt it. Pretty solid family background, no apparent financial trouble. One of her former coworkers told me back then that she'd graduated near the top of her class, went to school on a scholarship. Kinda naïve, way I understand it. Wouldn't know an inside straight from a poker machine, I shouldn't think."

"Think there's a connection between the stalker and Joey?"

"I suppose there could be. Maybe this Eddie guy is keeping an eye on her for Joey."

A big man walked up to our table and we both looked up. Yancy Frederick. Four-year hotshot who'd just made it to the plainclothes ranks.

"Gentlemen," Frederick said. "You guys hear about Frank Malone?"

I looked at him, trying to decide if he was rubbing salt, maybe knew about my feelings toward Malone, but his broad, Slavic face bore the innocence of youth; perhaps vacated a little, courtesy of his favorite brewery.

"Did he go and die and we didn't know about it?" Aaron replied.

"No such luck." A brother in the cause. "Got promoted today. Deputy Chief of Detectives. They had a big ceremony and everything. My damn luck. Get a gold shield and the king of the assholes becomes my boss. I'm putting in for a transfer back to the squad."

"Smart move, Yancy," I said in a flat monotone.

"Maybe I'll even go private," he added, his words slightly slurred, a silly grin on his face. Probably had a few celebratory drinks to honor Malone.

"You could do worse."

"Hey, you guys hold it in the road. Just thought I'd spread the good news." He walked away, swaying a little.

"Another member of the Malone fan club," I said, looking at Aaron.

"Yeah, well, fuck Frank Malone and the horse he rode in on. Best you forget about that son of a bitch and add a few years to your life. Anyway, as I was sayin'. What was I sayin'?"

"Senility. Happens to the best of you old farts. Eddie. Cissy."

"Kiss my ass. What I was sayin' is that I think maybe Eddie doesn't fit. From what you say, he's too clunky. Not the creep-around type. Also not very astute, if he's keeping an eye on Cissy, for not seeing the stalker himself."

"I suppose so. He's looking *at* her, not *around* her is what you mean."

"Probably just a straight tail. No frills. What you told me about her shadow, it sounds more like the slinky type. Slips around. I doubt Eddie slips," Aaron said with a grin. "Like old Clarence Kuchenbrod. Sumbitch couldn't stake out the symphony orchestra. He could quick-draw that thirty-eight, though. Fast as lightnin' with his arms, slow as thunder with his feet. Remember that time he shot himself in the foot?"

"Let me get another beer before you start in on the old days." I motioned to Della, held up two fingers.

We talked through a couple more; a few straggling old-timers in the bar joined us. As Aaron held court, I made my apologies and ducked out, telling him I'd see him tomorrow.

When I pulled onto Central Avenue, a pair of headlights jogged loose from the parking lot behind me. Eddie, more than likely. Clumsy. I'd have to talk to him about that.

I eventually turned onto my short cul-de-sac and the tail, an old Cadillac, drove on past. I waved, but couldn't see if Eddie waved back through the tinted windows. Probably offered a single-digit salute at best.

I fumbled for my keys at the door. More buzz from the beers than I expected. When I pushed the door open, I saw a slip of paper on the floor. As I bent over to pick it up, something hummed over my head and the Sheetrock on the wall in front of me popped and flaked abruptly.

I kept going down, rolled on the floor, and scuttled down the short hall to the kitchen, pulling the Glock from the holster in the small of my back, glad I remembered to carry it this time.

Nothing. Total darkness, no noise. Because no sound preceded the shot, probably silenced. Definitely Joey T's style, but why the hell would they be shooting at me? Warning, maybe? Eddie making a point? My brain working overtime, nothing making sense.

In the distance, I heard a car revving up. Didn't sound like a Cadillac. Older muscle car, maybe. The engine sound diminished and all I could hear were the katydids chirping.

After a few beats, I crawled toward the door. The storm door had closed behind me, undamaged. The shot had been fired as I was leaning over, butting the storm door aside. I bellied up to the Plexiglas, raised my head slowly, and looked around. The porch light kept me from seeing too well in the darkness, but I could see enough to know nothing stirred.

I rolled to the right, reached up and switched off the porch light, and dropped back to the floor, my right hand sweaty on the pistol, maybe shaking a little. When my eyes adjusted to the moonlight, they only confirmed that the street was empty. I reached over and pushed the door shut, then crab-walked to the back door, looking around the yard through the uncurtained window. I eased the door open, side-stepping out onto the deck.

No shots, no shouts, no movement. A breeze lifted the honeysuckle coating the woods.

With the Glock pressed lightly against my leg, I moved around the south side of the house, back toward the front yard. Going to the right wouldn't have been an option, since an old dog lot I inherited, now overgrown with weeds, would have been too difficult an approach for any intruder, with or without skill. Too much noise, too little forward motion.

After circling the house, walking up and back on the street, and checking neighbors' yards, I felt reasonably sure I could holster the gun. No faces in any windows, just darkness; though I'd bet Mrs. Konarski next door was watching. My neighbors knew what I did for a living; shouldn't have been particularly shocked to see me trudging around with a gun in my hand.

I went back inside where Bogie waited, looking curiously at the damaged Sheetrock. He wasn't hiding, so no one had been inside, but I checked each room anyway.

Back in the entrance hall, I looked at the hole centered in the broken wall. It hit between studs, so the bullet was probably in another wall or under the house. Couldn't tell the caliber because Sheetrock gives too much, but it had to be bigger than a .22. My left foot swept across the note and I bent over to pick it up.

"I don't know what you are or who you're from, but you apparently saved my ass," I told the sheet of paper as I unfolded it. The note was in a feminine script, smeared slightly from being pushed under the door: "Sorry we missed you. God bless you and your family."

It was signed "The Missionaries of Calvary Baptist Church." Probably saved 'em a soul today and won't ever know it.

I walked into the kitchen and thumbed on the light, reached for the phone, and dialed Billy's. No answer. I hit the kill button and punched the programmed number for Aaron's house. After a few rings he picked it up, still awake but groggy.

"Things just got serious," I told him, outlining what had happened, adding that I saw no point in calling a squad car.

Aaron agreed. "You wanna sleep over here tonight?"

"Nah, figure it was a one-shot calling card. I'll be okay. Sleep with the Glock under my pillow."

"It might be the kinda bullshit thing Joey would do, but I don't know. Too big of an alarm too early in the game, don't ya think?"

"Yeah," I said. "But who?"

"Beats the shit out of me. Talk to the lady tomorrow, see what you think."

"Maybe we'll get together for dinner, hash it out."

"Sounds good to me. Be careful, Houston. Looks like there's something bad in this woodpile."

Going to sleep was easier than I thought it would be, seeing as I was still shaking a little when I stepped out of the shower. Adrenaline brings you up fast, lets you down completely. I felt like I'd been on a long, serious drunk. Weary.

What had I gotten myself into this time?

CHAPTER THREE

Fynwyck's is a little bistro on the edge of one of Charlotte's wealthier communities. Back when the city was a town, it was an all-night waffle house frequented mostly by third-shift cops and newspaper carriers after midnight.

But the gentrification of Myers Park prompted somebody with a lot of money to buy it, add some wood, brass, and ferns, and turn it into a "chi-chi" eatery where lunch cost twenty bucks, the wine bottles had corks, and *y*'s got substituted for *i*'s on the menu. I had a hard time imagining consumption of a bowl of chyly. Glad I wasn't a yuppie.

I parked in the lot in front of an old strip shopping center a block south that housed a couple of shops, a drug store, and what was now the city's main art-house movie theater. Aimed the car toward Fynwyck's and made sure I had a full view of the place. A couple dozen cars in the parking lot this time of day, so I didn't draw any stares. Just another midday browser.

Lot of people going in and out of the restaurant, mostly women in designer dresses, high-dollar jogging suits. A few with sweatbands I'm sure didn't stink, a couple with cashmere sweaters tied around their necks or waists—in May, for cryin' out loud. An old guy with a sweet young thing, him holding the door, running his fingers through a dark Hair Club for Men creation as he scooted inside behind her, nudging her along with a hand patting her tight jeans.

When Cissy Devore pulled up and got out of the green Mercedes 560 SL, a couple of heads turned. One older woman walked up to her; they air-kissed and walked inside together, chatting. The other woman in one of those ridiculously baggy culotte numbers, Cissy resplendent in a white blouse and black jeans, big sunglasses. Casually elegant. She paused a second, looked around. Maybe for me, maybe the tail.

The glass entrance door closed behind them and I eased out of the car.

For this stakeout I'd chosen a proper neighborhood disguise. Tan Dockers, light blue button-down shirt, no tie, navy sport coat unbuttoned so it wouldn't inhibit access to the Glock, a pair of limber Rockports in case I had to run. One pocket of the jacket hung a little heavy. I'd brought along an old pair of handcuffs, just in case. Snappy but prepared, that's Houston Cash.

I crossed the street and walked beside a row of tall boxwoods, just another Myers Park stroller out for a lunchtime break. A half-dozen students from nearby Queens College were trotting in formation on the sidewalk. I was a head higher than the pack, but I blended in well enough. By the time I got to the funeral home directly across from Fynwyck's, I'd scanned every corner, holes in the shrubbery, the tables and chairs outside the Ben & Jerry's that shared the bistro's parking lot. Two or three couples licking cones of Cherry Garcia or Chunky Monkey, nobody paying particular attention to the restaurant. Nouveau riche imbibing in nature, glancing at the funeral home, probably wondering how big a crowd they'd draw when the time came.

I passed the grim black Cadillac hearse parked in the circular drive, then turned to retrace my steps when I saw him.

He sat low in the driver's seat of a dark blue Camaro in the parking lot of a dry cleaner about thirty yards north of the restaurant. Occasionally putting a pair of binoculars to his eyes, aimed at Fynwyck's. Not real slick, this guy. The tinted windows were rolled up; engine running; small puff of smoke coming from the exhaust.

Some traffic passed, and I crossed the street a block farther north of the dry cleaner. He could have seen me if he'd looked in the rearview mirror, but I was betting his attention was the other way.

I walked toward the car, trying to maintain an even pace. No irregular movement, fast or slow, to catch the corner of his eye. I think I could have been wearing cowbells and riding Rollerblades for all the difference it would have made. The guy was riveted on Fynwyck's; didn't even see me jerk the door open. He'd been leaning against it; fell flat on his back on the pavement, binoculars clattering across the asphalt, threw up his hands to protect his face.

"Hey, man! What the fuck!"

He was small, maybe five-six or -seven, skinny but wiry, wearing a Harley-Davidson T-shirt and blue jeans with holes in the knees. He'd taken off his shoes, and a toe stuck through one of the dirty white socks. Not from the neighborhood.

I reached down, got him by the hands, and pulled him up and around, pushing his acne-scarred face against the side of the Camaro, a somewhat scratched '78 model with several gray primer spots, rebel flag bumper sticker, Grateful Dead decal on the back window.

"You stand there nice and easy, sport, and everything'll be just fine." I held one hand on his neck under a mat of long-unwashed, stringy hair, patted him down, pulled out a heavy lock-blade knife, nothing else.

"You a cop or something? What the hell have I done?" He was starting to whine; something of a contrast to his biker look, I thought.

"What's your name?" I wasn't quite ready for him to discover I wasn't a police officer.

"Buck. Buck Skinner. Hey, man, what the fuck is this all about?" He tried to turn around and I gave his neck a little jolt, held his face toward the car.

"Why are you following the lady?"

"What lady?" Jolt again, a little harder, spittle flying.

"You mean Mrs. Devore? Shit, man, I'm working for her. Look, you need some ID? My wallet's on the passenger seat, man." I turned him around, facing me. His dull, brown eyes said he was telling the truth, but I didn't want to be fooled just yet.

"Reach across, unlock the passenger door," I ordered, spinning him around, holding him now by his woven leather belt.

"It's unlocked, man."

"All right, turn the ignition off, give me the keys, then stick your right arm through the steering wheel." He went through the motions like he'd actually done it before, dropping the keys in my outstretched left hand while I held on with the right.

I cuffed his arms through the wheel. He sat awkwardly in the seat while I walked to the passenger door, opened it, and retrieved the big leather wallet; one of those models with the chain and belt loop, probably tooled by the finest craftsmen of Central Prison. I opened it up, and his driver's license showed through a clear plastic rectangle. Buford Aloysius Skinner, white male, date of birth June 23, 1976. Really goofy picture, like he was startled they had a camera. I tossed the wallet in the back and slid into the passenger seat.

"Tell you what, Buford …"

"Buck."

"Whatever. Why don't you tell me about your employment arrangement with Mrs. Devore?"

"She knows my sister. Works in the vault down at the bank." He was beginning to calm down a little, didn't seem as interested in whether I was a cop anymore. "Mrs. Devore said she'd seen me come pick Debbie, that's my sister, up at the bank. Asked her what I did. Debbie said I was between jobs, and Mrs. Devore asked her if she thought I'd like to make a little money.

"I thought it was kinda weird, but, hell, I needed the cash and she paid me a thousand dollars up front. Said somebody was following her, thought she might need a bodyguard but didn't want to make a big deal of it. Asked me if I could keep my mouth shut." He rolled his eyes. "I didn't expect this kind of shit, though. Look, man, you gonna lock me up or what?"

"You just sit here for a little bit and I'll go have a chat with Mrs. Devore. Everything you tell me's straight, then you go about your little way."

"I ain't gonna have to give her the money back, am I?" Anxious. Probably already spent a good chunk of it on crack or some kind of dope, judging by his eyes and general aura.

"Probably not. Just sit tight. I'll leave the windows down so you don't roast."

"What a guy." Buford was getting his courage back. I took a couple of minutes, looked under the seats, in the back, tossed the trunk. A rusted Stevens single-barrel shotgun, crudely cut down and unloaded, was wrapped in some dirty newspaper. No pistol. I doubted Buford was sharp enough to follow me home, take a shot. He watched me through the rearview mirror, eyes telling me he had no idea what I was looking for.

I closed the trunk, pocketed the keys, and walked toward the restaurant wondering what the hell was going on.

- - -

I'd never been inside Fynwyck's, but it was the kind of layout I expected. Lot of plants, brass rails, polished oak tables with cute scenic inlays under acrylic, people engaged in the kind of rustly, whispery conversation that marks these places. As soon as I got through the door a cheerful, fresh-faced girl walked up and asked how many were in my party.

"Actually, I'm looking for someone who's already here," I said, trying to play the reserved Myers Parkian.

She told me I was welcome to look around, and I started through the tightly-packed tables and booths, scanning heads and faces. I saw the woman Cissy had met outside the door, sitting alone in a booth under a giant fern. The bench across from her was empty, a salad plate barely touched and a half-drunk glass of water indicating her boothmate was either in the ladies' room or gone. I walked up to her.

"Pardon me, but I'm looking for Mrs. Devore …" I started. The woman looked at me like I was from another planet.

"Oh, well, Cissy left just a few minutes ago. She had a call on her cellular phone and said it was some kind of family emergency, I think. Sorry."

Up close, the woman was the image of a neighborhood blueblood, but her faded blue eyes had a sort of glaze and I noticed the half-gone bottle of wine. I thanked her and walked back outside, several dozen eyes following my progress. I sometimes think these people have some kind of radar that detects an intrusion of someone not their kind, alarms probably going off all over the place.

I walked out onto the parking lot. The Mercedes was gone. In my rush to go inside, I'd forgotten whether it was there before.

Back at the cleaners, I unleashed Buford, told him Mrs. Devore wouldn't need his services any more, but got his phone number in case I needed to call him. I doubted he'd call her to find anything out, worried about having to forfeit the grand.

As an afterthought, I asked him about the shotgun. Said it was to protect him from bikers in case he pissed anybody off. I told him that, in its condition, if he pulled the trigger he'd probably blow his own head off. He looked at me funny, gunned the rust bucket, and sped off, tires squealing. Buford's last shot.

By the time I got to my office I recalled an old Southern phrase that matched my mood: Fit to be tied.

CHAPTER FOUR

"I'M SORRY SIR, BUT Mrs. Devore has no return from her luncheon appointment," a woman with a slight Hispanic accent informed me. The housekeeper, I suppose.

Not sure what kind of message I should leave, I just told the woman I wanted to talk to her boss about a political fund-raiser and promised to call back.

I punched up the bank's security number and went through two people before Aaron came on the line. I told him what had happened at the restaurant. He agreed something wasn't kosher about all this; asked me if I'd made any headway on the shooter.

I told him no and that I'd try to locate Cissy; asked him to keep his eyes open around the bank.

"Let me know if you find anything," Aaron said. "I'll see if I shake something loose from the company grapevine, then we'll get together for dinner. Come on over to my place."

We decided to meet at seven and hash it out. As I hung up the phone, I quietly thanked God again for an anchor like Aaron Drake.

-   -   -

Checking the list she gave me, I made a half-dozen phone calls to Cissy Devore's haunts. She hadn't been seen today at any of them. Manicurist, an exclusive women's clothing store in Dilworth, a Nautilus center on the southeast side, the Mercedes dealership. Each time, I made up what sounded like a legitimate excuse for the call, not wanting to raise any suspicions about a strange man trying to find the wife of the city's most prominent banker. Even disguised my voice a couple of times, trying to sound effeminate. The clothing salesman tried to make a date.

Then it dawned on me that I should dial up her cell number, which she'd given me the day before. Always save the most obvious for last. That's why I'm a detective.

"The party you are trying to reach is either out of the calling area or the unit is not in service," the mechanical female voice said. "Please try again later."

If she wasn't in the car and not at any of the places she told me she'd be, where could the elusive Mrs. Devore be? Hiding? Had I stumbled on something she didn't want me to know? I found it hard to imagine she wouldn't expect me to find Buford.

Or was that what she wanted me to do?

— - -

"I didn't want to call after her hubby came home. Don't want to raise any eyebrows on the home front just yet," I told Aaron as we stood on his flagstone patio, smoke encircling us from the barbecue grill. "She said she didn't want him to know about me."

"I know," Aaron said, poking at a couple of New York strips with a long-handled fork. "That's why I've got the security service guy going by to do a station check."

"You old dog."

"We do 'em every now and then. Makes Carson happy. The guy will do a walk-through, then call me to let me know how everything is." He looked at his wristwatch. "Should be hearing from him in the next thirty minutes or so. Bub Crowell. You remember him?"

"Bub the old desk sergeant? He's on your payroll?"

"He's on the bank's payroll. The house system's actually an ADT setup, but Devore likes us to do our own check. Makes him feel like a big cheese or something, I guess. We humor him. He signs the checks."

As if on cue, Aaron's cell phone chirped. He picked it up from the patio table and punched the *talk* button. He nodded and grunted a few times, shared a joke I couldn't hear over the sizzle, then put the phone down.

"The Devores are the happy hosts tonight. Entertaining that guy who owns the football team and his wife. Bub said he did a Stepin Fetchit routine for the boss, then slipped out the side entrance like a good servant."

"So Cissy's back home, safe and sound."

"Looks like it."

"Not a care in the world."

"Wouldn't seem so."

"Aaron, I'm thinking she's got something going on here. The only thing that doesn't seem to fit is the gunplay."

"A logical conclusion, but I still wouldn't rule out Joey T on the fireworks. It would be his style. Let's eat some steaks and talk about possibilities." He skewered the meat, tossed the steaks on a platter, and we headed inside.

A bear loomed in the kitchen as we walked through the French doors.

"Well, ain't this Ozzie and fuckin' Harriet," said the bear. "Or is it Ozzie and Ozzie? You two guys a coupla fags?"

I tried not to look startled and pissed off, both of which I was.

"Aaron, meet Mister Eddie. Eddie, Aaron."

"Pleased ta meetcha, Officer Drake." He didn't extend a hand, nor did Aaron.

"So how's our pal Joey T?" Aaron asked casually, placing the meat platter on the kitchen table.

"Ask him yerself."

"Gentlemen," Joseph Trenton said as he walked into the kitchen from the den. "Have a seat. You should lock your front door, Drake. This city ain't as safe as it used to be."

"As I recall, it *was* locked, Joey," Aaron replied. "I think we'll stand."

"Have it your way," Trenton said with a flicking motion, like he was shooing a fly.

"To what do we owe this visit?" Houston Cash, man of few words, polite bon vivant.

"I know we have a mutual interest, figured you'd be looking me up, decided I'd save you the time," Trenton said, taking one of the kitchen chairs and nestling his short, thin frame into it. Joey T looked bad: face drawn, cheeks hollow, flesh on bone that a tanning booth (one of his fronts) couldn't burn to a healthy glow. Eddie walked around beside him, kind of looming. I moved to Eddie's left, deciding to do a little looming of my own.

"Anyway, this lady," Trenton continued.

"Cissy Devore." I figured we might as well put a name on her, quit dancing.

"Yeah, Mrs. Devore. Okay, first of all, I do some banking with her husband, legit stuff as all my stuff is." He squinted at us, waiting for a reaction. When none came, he rasped on. "Anyway, I was in the bank one day. The big one downtown. This Devore lady, she comes up to me outa nowhere, says she knows who I am, wants to talk to me."

"You'd never met the lady before?" As if he'd tell me.

"No, Cash, I never met the lady before. Swear to God, if that'll do you any good. Anyway, she says she wants to talk, but not in the bank. I say okay, let's meet over at the hot dog stand in that big—whadda they call it, Eddie?"

"Atrium, boss," Eddie said, surprising all of us.

"Yeah, the atrium. I get a hot dog, sit on a bench until she comes up, starts talking. To make a long story short, she says some guy is following her around, wants to know could I help her out." Joey starts to cough, a deep, phlegmy cough.

"Need a glass of water?" Aaron said, speaking for the first time in a while.

"Yeah, if you don't mind." Aaron got a glass, filled it, handed it to Joey. I'm watching all this and feeling kind of strange, not knowing exactly where this is heading. Joey sipped on the water, the cough subsided.

"So anyway, I tell Eddie here to help the lady out. Figure it can't hurt me to be nice to the big shot banker's wife. Might pay off some day. Hell, you boys know me, I don't mind telling you I do favors when there's a chance it can come back. Who doesn't?" He didn't wait for an answer.

"Eddie goes and follows this lady a coupla days, next thing he knows she's going into Cash there's office. That's why Eddie paid you a visit." He looked at me. His dark eyes said he was telling the truth. "Eddie being Eddie, he thinks Cash has something to do with the problem, but he comes back and tells me no, he don't think so."

I looked at Eddie and saw a sheepish grin, almost a blush. The day's surprises continue to mount.

"Then Eddie tells me he sees you grab that guy in the Camaro over on Providence. He follows the guy after you let him go, finds out that guy, too, is working for the lady. I'm wondering what the hell's going on, so when Eddie tells me you come over to Drake's place, I figure it's time we all need to talk." He stopped, looked at both of us, opened his palms like "What's next?"

"My health ain't been too good here lately, and I don't need you two on my case. Got too much shit on my mind. Drake, I swear your front door was open," he added in an almost pleading tone. "I don't need any more crap with the law, even ex-law, if you know what I mean.

"Neither one of you's gonna believe me, but I want to get my stuff straight. You probably already heard, but I got cancer. Started in the prostrate." I didn't want to correct him. "Makes you think about things. I know I'm no angel, but I've, uh, kind of retired from the old stuff, if you know what I mean. Eddie, here, he's got nowhere else to go so he stays with me."

I could have sworn a tear was working in Eddie's eye, and though I was more confused than ever at the moment, I figured we had heard at least some truth, though I doubt Joey T was out of action completely; just getting somebody else to handle it.

"What I want to do is give you Eddie to help you out. I don't know if this lady's trying to drag me into some shit I don't need, so I'm doing it for me more than you, but whatta ya say?"

Eddie didn't exactly look like the eager assistant, and had probably argued with Joey about this idea. I think Aaron was getting the same read. I also noticed, at this point, that no mention had been made of gunshots at my house. I didn't want to bring it up just yet, and gave Aaron a look that I hoped relayed the message.

"Tell you what, Joey," Aaron said. "Let me and Houston do some checking around on this. If we need Eddie, we'll let you know. But if you want to help us now, then just pull Eddie off."

Eddie looked relieved and Joey T nodded, thoughtful.

"Okay, I'll buy that …if you keep me posted." Joey still wanting to be in control. Old habits die hard. "I don't mean like reports and shit like that, just let me know what the hell this is all about. Nobody needs to know, if you're worried about that."

"I'm not worried, Joey. Oh, and one other thing. Eddie." The palooka looked at Aaron. "What kinda piece you carry?"

Eddie looked at Joey, who nodded. Eddie reached under and behind his jacket, pulled out a Beretta nine, dropped the clip, held it out to Aaron by the barrel.

"Nice. Why doesn't it surprise me that it's Italian?" Aaron hefted it, held it to his face, close enough to smell. "You keep it clean."

Eddie actually smiled, proud. Aaron racked back the slide, looked down the barrel, handed it back to Eddie. Trenton watched, his face unmoving, but he'd no doubt seen a cop check to see if a gun had been fired; knew what was going on but asked no questions.

"I'm sure you've got a permit," he said, smiling.

"Yeah, I do," Eddie half-mumbled, shoved the clip back. "Even got a carry permit. Sheriff's a nice guy."

Joey and Eddie left with about as much ceremony as when they'd entered. We stuck the steaks in the microwave, heated them up, talked about the turn of events.

"That gun's not been fired anytime lately," Aaron offered. "Not threaded for a silencer, either, but I expect Joey's got a few of those around."

"You think he came completely clean?"

"As odd as it sounds, I believe if Eddie had tried to pop you or warn you, he'd have told Joey and Joey would have told us. Nah, it's not his way."

I agreed. We finished eating, burned out on the situation for now. I drove home, feeling like Alice falling down the rabbit hole.

It was time to add a different perspective to the game. Dawn, I knew, could give me that.

CHAPTER FIVE

Dawn Rayburn Kline and I stayed in touch, and I still wanted to think there was some kind of sexual tension between us, despite her three kids and adoring husband. We still swapped body function jokes and she still touched me when we talked, let me touch her back, all in a proper, non-sexual way, though it still gave me a jolt. I hadn't dated anyone more than twice since her; just couldn't get into the groove. I felt like it was a case of well, I've been in love and there's not much chance of that anymore so I'll work and sleep and play with my cat and live like a monk. She told me I was full of crap and somebody would come along.

Dawn was the perfect one to talk to about Cissy Devore, maybe give me some input on the female psyche, guide me toward what kind of situation I was dealing with. I wanted to talk to her before I chatted with Cissy again. We had agreed to meet at the Treehouse restaurant on the south side. I offered to pop for day care because we didn't need the distraction, but she said the kids were going with their father to the zoo. I noticed lately she was referring to Jerry more often as "their father." Maybe trouble in paradise, though more likely just the language of familiarity after a few years and kids. For all I knew, they called each other "mother" and "father," but I really didn't want to think about it.

The Treehouse wasn't as trendy as Fynwyck's, and the food was probably better. I'd been there enough that a couple of people knew me, so when I asked for a quiet booth I got it.

I saw Dawn come through the door before she saw me, and a waiter pointed her in my direction. She still took my breath away. Dawn is one of those people who ages well, at least in my eyes. Even across a room, she gives me the kind of feeling you get when you hear Beethoven's Ninth Symphony for the first time, or when George Bailey finds Zuzu's petals. Chills. I didn't know I was losing her until she was gone, and a part of me's been missing ever since.

"Hey, Beast!" Her wide-set, azure eyes glittered even in the dim light, and when she leaned over to give me a peck on the cheek I ran my hand down her arm, fired. Dawn had stayed in shape despite the kids and, though a little larger than Cissy, would have drawn all the stares on a runway.

"How's tricks, Beauty?" We'd called each other that on occasion ever since we both saw the Disney movie *Beauty and the Beast* and I likened the association to us. Her oldest, a girl, was hip enough now to think it was weird, and Jerry at first thought it too intimate, until she explained that it didn't mean anything; but I knew better. Or thought I did.

I had already gone over the rough details of the Cissy Devore situation with Dawn on the phone, so after we ordered and chatted briefly about families and lives, we homed in on the topic at hand.

"So you think La Devore is pulling some kind of scam on you?" Dawn asked as she picked at her Caesar salad.

"It would seem so, if for no other reason than she didn't tell me about the whole cast of characters." I'd ordered a house salad, vinaigrette dressing, hard to eat without being sloppy and worrying about greenery in your teeth except when you were with somebody like Dawn.

"Maybe she thought it'd scare you off, planned to tell you later or something." In the past, Dawn's role in conversations like these was the devil's advocate. Sometimes it irked me but it was usually effective.

"I suppose. I had the feeling when she was in the office that she was holding something back, and it could be that this was it, though I thought it was something more important."

"Is there a possibility she hasn't played out her hand yet?" Dawn paused while the waitress took away the salad plate and deposited a heaping platter of baby back ribs. She was one of those people who could eat you under the table and never gain a pound. She even lost weight after her second pregnancy.

"That's what I'm afraid of. I don't know if I should show my hand right now or ride it out, see what happens." I reached across the table, pulled off a rib section and plopped in on my plate beside the veal chop I'd ordered. She reached over, sawed off a piece of veal, and popped it in her mouth. Some of the barbecue sauce from a rib clung to her lower lip and I couldn't take my eyes off it for a full minute.

"What does Aaron think?"

"He's left it up to me. You know how he is. Keeps most of his opinions to himself."

"He's always confident you'll do the right thing, and he's usually right."

"Except when it came to us. He told me I was an idiot and, of course, he was right."

"Smart man."

"Before I go making any more mistakes, I thought maybe you'd help me set something up."

"I kinda thought you'd get around to that."

"Actually, it just came to me, watching you eat those ribs. The way you suck on the bones."

"You want me to suck on her bones?" She erupted into giggles, eyes sparkling. I couldn't believe how much she still made me ache.

"Nah, something a little simpler." I handed her a slip of paper with the name, address, and phone number of Cissy's hair stylist.

"So you just now thought this up but had the details handy? How convenient." Eyes merry. She knew me better than I knew me.

"Maybe I thought about it a little bit, but I did just decide."

She stared at the paper. "The banker's wife goes to a relatively middle-class stylist, judging by the address. That surprises me a little."

"What I thought is that maybe you'd make an appointment, be there about the same time, engage in some woman chat."

"Talk about babies, husbands, stuff like that, right? The little woman picking up a few pointers." Dawn wasn't a hard-core feminist by any stretch of the imagination, but in our days together she made it clear she abhorred typecasting.

"Hey, we all have to make compromises in the detective trade. You know what I'm talking about. Feel the woman out, see what you think. You're perceptive, maybe you can tell me something I don't see."

"What if I can't get an appointment on the same day, at the same time?"

"I'm going to take care of that, if you'll agree. Frustrated husband setting something up for his wife before they go on a trip to Europe. I've got the day and time for Cissy's appointment. Tomorrow at three. She had one yesterday, but it was for the manicurist. This time it's the hair."

"The kids'll be at kindergarten and day care, so I should be able to swing it. You'll owe me for this one, bucko."

"I can think of no more pleasant task in my life than repaying a debt to you." Truer words were never spoken.

"Simmer down. I'm a married woman." Emphasis on "married," clipping my wings.

"I figure if you ever change your mind, I won't make the same mistake twice." I knew this encounter was winding down, and I didn't bring up the shooting incident. No use spreading that around just yet.

"Nice to know I've got somebody in reserve," she said, almost sounding like she meant it. Or was it just me?

We finished our dinners; Dawn ordered and consumed a chunk of Oreo cheesecake and, after another spate of small talk, she went home and I went to the office, called Hairkutters, and had less trouble making the appointment than I expected. I called Dawn and told her it was on, then checked with the answering service.

Cissy Devore wanted to talk to me. I called her, told her to meet me at the office. I wanted to see her face when we talked.

- - -

Cissy walked in, cool as a cucumber, this time wearing a black knit number. She liked short dresses, had the equipment for them. We said our hellos, she slid into the same chair, pulled out a cigarette; I lit it.

After a short pause, she asked me how things were going on the case. Acting maybe a little nervous, though it could have been my imagination.

"Saw a guy outside Fynwyck's, talked to him. Dead end."

"Did you by any chance come looking for me inside the restaurant?"

"As a matter of fact, I did. The lady at your table said you had to leave in kind of a hurry." Playing the game. She was doing well at avoiding spillage of any beans.

"I'd completely forgotten that Carson and I were entertaining, had to head out. Mrs. Gladstone described you as a tall, good-looking gentleman, by the way." She smiled. Flattery will get you everywhere, I thought. Unconsciously sucking my gut in.

"Lady needs glasses. The lighting wasn't so good." She hit the target, though. Ego jacked up a couple of notches. "So where do we go from here?"

"You've got my schedule for the rest of the week? I guess you just keep following me around, right?" Buford must have, indeed, not said anything. Or it was Buford pulling my leg, which I didn't think he had the creative energy to do. Cissy seemed innocent, or was it the compliment?

"I guess that's the game plan. So how're you holding up? Got anything else you need to tell me?"

She paused, maybe startled. Could she know that I knew, and was that part of whatever plan she was devising? I thought I was pretty good at reading faces, though Dawn was better. Or my paranoia was making me translate every twitch, every hiccup in our conversational fabric as some kind of ploy, diversion.

"No, I honestly can't think of anything else," she said, recovering a little. "Have I given you the whole week's schedule?"

She leaned over as I pulled out the notepad. I tried to place her perfume. Black Pearls?

I read the list back to her, she made a few additions, adjustments, thankfully not eliminating the visit to the hairdresser. Maybe I was imagining things, because she did seem genuinely afraid of whatever phantom she believed was following her. Maybe Buford and Eddie were, in fact, backup. Maybe I didn't see someone else because I spent too much time on Buford; maybe Eddie was spending too much time on me.

Too many maybes.

She leaned back in the chair, looked at me kind of odd. Blushed a little.

"There is one thing I probably ought to tell you."

Here it goes.

"Before Aaron told me about you, I didn't know exactly where to turn, so I … well, I talked to a couple of people, asked them for help. Paid one of them, as a matter of fact."

"Let me guess. Buford 'Buck' Skinner and Joey Trenton."

"You know about them?"

I gave her the details of my encounter with Buford, most of the conversation with Joey T, but didn't mention that it took place at Aaron's. No use making him look like my co-conspirator just yet. I left out the suspicions we'd all shared, partly because they were still there.

"You must think I was up to something." More a statement than a question.

"The thought crossed my mind. If you hadn't told me, I'm not sure where I would have gone from here, to be honest."

"To Carson, I suppose?" A touch of anger creeping into her voice.

"No, not to Carson. I told you the contract between you and me is just that." I decided to turn up the heat a little. "But you should have told me about those guys up front. Right now, you're the boss and I'm the employee, but if we're not going to be honest with each other, well …" I let it sit for a minute, waiting for her to take the next step. She stayed quiet, eyes dewing a little.

"Tell you what, where's your next trip?" No point in waiting around.

"The hairdresser tomorrow, I guess."

"You go on to that, I'll do a little watching. This time it'll just be me, you understand."

"I understand."

"Nobody else hanging around I ought to know about?"

"Nobody, I swear." She cast her eyes down, then looked up at me. "I'm truly sorry."

"No sweat. Let's catch this guy." Now we were a team. Go, team, go.

I was sure she was still holding something back.

CHAPTER SIX

THE HAIR SALON WAS on the first floor of one of those old Dilworth houses that had sometime back been converted into shops. It was in what had become the city's gay district, more or less, and instead of raging against stereotypes most of the shopkeepers had painted their establishments in pinks and pastels, giving them cutesy names like "Boy O'Boy" and "Good Vibrations," a lesbian accessory boutique. It was intended to be clever, I'm sure, but served in my mind only to reinforce some people's notions. To each his own.

Hairkutters was a five-chair operation that once flourished as an old-fashioned barbershop. When the gays moved in, the owner sold it, name and all, to a guy named Paul Whitstead. He brought a few upscale clients with him, and it became all the rage in some quarters to say that "Mister Paul" cut and styled your hair, but the nouveau riche and bluebloods weren't enough to keep a business going, so he added two more stylists from the west side and had a huge middle-of-the-road clientele, according to Aaron who, to my surprise, kept up with such things. His wife had used Paul and told him all about it.

Though I didn't know the man, I had to admire Whitstead for not looking down his nose at ordinary people. The bottom line can often temper even the most severe snobbery.

It was easy enough to park at a good vantage point to watch the place, but not as easy to blend into the surroundings, which was not to say gays looked any different from me. I guess maybe I just felt self-conscious.

Since I only had one door to watch, more or less, and Dawn was doing all my inside work, I brought a book this time, trusting my peripheral vision enough to catch any movement that might draw my attention; though, honestly, I didn't think I'd see anybody following Cissy.

I was getting into the third chapter of Robert B. Parker's *Walking Shadow* when I saw Cissy's Mercedes pull into the gravel driveway beside Hairkutters, watched her sashay in, then saw Dawn's Volvo wagon bounce into the driveway. As Dawn walked in she cut a glance my way, and I could see the smirk from across the street. I'd swear the woman was radar-equipped.

Then I saw the other car with a guy sitting in it. It was a Dodge Charger, black with smoked windows that weren't so dark I couldn't make out the profile of a man sitting low in the seat. I didn't remember seeing it when I parked and don't believe it had been there then; could have pulled up when my attention was drawn to Cissy or Dawn.

Just for the hell of it, I eased out of my streetside parking space, pulled past the Charger, went down about two blocks and turned around, drove past the salon, U-turned and eased into a space about thirty yards back from the Dodge. I climbed over the hump and slipped out on the passenger side of my Chrysler.

The guy in the Charger must have seen me, because the car rumbled to life about the same time my feet hit the sidewalk.

I ran around to the driver's side of my car, jerked the door open, jumped in and hit the ignition. By the time I was pulling out, the Charger was moving fast, maybe a little too fast, down East Boulevard. I knew I'd never catch it on the open stretch past the next two traffic lights, and since I'd blown any cover I floored it, the V-6 whining as my old '01 ragtop worked up a head of steam.

I made both traffic lights on yellow, maybe just turning red on the second one, and the Charger got caught in some traffic. I closed the gap to about two car lengths. I strained to read the license plate, then saw that it was one of those cardboard temporary tags. No way to trace that baby, even in this computer age. Damn. Had to catch him or I was SOL, as the old boys often said. Shit outa luck.

While I turned all this over in my mind, the Charger suddenly took a hard left, cut in front of a city bus that nearly went sideways when the driver locked the brakes down; shapes of passengers spilled into the aisle. I had to go around the bus and cut right behind the Dodge, by now topping the rise on Kenilworth behind the hospital, getting nearly airborne, like one of those *Streets of San Francisco* chases. Would have been cool to watch if I wasn't the one doing the chasing.

By the time my Sebring topped the rise, he was gone. Two side streets to the left, one on the right that led to the Emergency Room entrance at Carolinas Medical. If this yahoo was a local, he wouldn't have taken the right, so I headed down the second street on the left, remembering that it eventually crossed over to the other one.

I crossed Scott, the one-way that doubles back on Kenilworth, barely missing a '76 Ford pickup likely helmed by a cussing farmer come to see his mama in the hospital, now pissed off at another city slicker who couldn't drive worth a damn.

I went screaming into the next intersection and saw the Dodge to my left, a block over. I kicked the Sebring sideways, cut across, and hung a quick right as the sleek, black speedster rounded a shallow curve beside the Catholic church, hit Dilworth West, fishtailed right, and smoked its tires toward Morehead Street. He had spread the distance a good three blocks and I knew there wouldn't be a chance in hell for me to catch him, but I had to give it the old college try.

I gunned it through a four-way stop as the low-slung Charger got smaller in the distance, then topped the rise myself just in time to see the Dodge get airborne on the curb at the Holocaust Square monument, flip at least three times, slide on its roof into the back of a Jack Willis Paving Company tar truck, and explode.

- - -

"Houston Cash, as I live and breathe," Sergeant Rich Brady said as he walked toward me from the slag heap that used to be a thirty-thousand-dollar sports car.

"Rich." Brady and I had gone through rookie school together, partnered briefly in the same squad before I went to investigations. He'd made sergeant right after I left the department. We hadn't really stayed in touch beyond a drink at Billy's, but we passed for friends. Every now and then he helped me with the odd background check and I'd slipped him a few bucks.

"Lady jogger says you were in hot pursuit of that crispy critter in there," he said, poking a thumb in the direction of the melted Dodge.

"More or less."

"Well, there's more of you here and less of him, so I figured I'd ask."

"This is the first time I even knew it was a 'him,' which is about all I know of the guy at this point," I replied, then filled him in briefly on why I was behind the Charger, "involved in a surveillance," leaving out any attached names, of course. Most particularly Cissy Devore's.

"Yeah, well, bystander says it was a man. Listen, I know you didn't break any laws." He rolled his eyes up at me from under his watch cap. "By any chance, did you get a tag number?"

"It was a temporary paper, more'n likely ashes by now."

"Interesting thing about that. Serial numbers look to have been cooked off, too. They don't build 'em like they used to. Right now all we know is what kind of car it was. Hopefully, we'll find out who the driver was when they find enough teeth to send off."

"I notice you called in the homicide boys," I said, watching a couple of plainclothes officers I vaguely recognized poke around the smoking hulk, occasionally picking up things with surgical-gloved hands and dropping them into clear plastic baggies.

"New general order on fatals from your friend and mine, Deputy Chief Frank Malone. Says it's a backup in case an accident ain't no accident." Brady was about as fond of Malone as I was, since he probably would have made sergeant earlier, maybe even captain by now except for Malone giving him a bad evaluation. Funny how the department had divided into two clear camps, Friends of Malone and Foes of Malone; the latter having the larger membership.

"Frank's wasting no time exercising authority." Extending that long arm, I thought, putting his finger in more pies than Jack Horner at a bake sale. What an asshole. Is it any wonder why I hate this man?

"Yeah, well, since your car ain't involved in this directly, don't see where he needs to know you were around. Not officially, anyway. One of his boys might say something but ask me if I give a shit."

"I appreciate it. Got a case I wouldn't want Frank screwing around with."

"I know what ya mean. Look, we get anything on this, I'll slip it to you or Aaron," he said, knowing of my association with the retired, revered detective.

"I'll do some checking, too. Let you know if I find anything." We shook hands, mine palming a folded fifty he carefully extracted and put in his pocket. Not a bribe, mind you, just my way of saying thanks. "How'd the truck driver do, by the way?"

"Jumped out before the tar tank blew. He's at Carolinas Medical and they say he'll be all right, a coupla burns is all. Scared the shit out of him."

"Thanks again, Rich. Whatever I can do, you know how to get me."

"Yeah, well." He turned back to the wreck.

I got in my car and headed back to Hairkutters. It had been almost two hours, so I expected Cissy and Dawn to be gone, which they were. I checked the answering service from my cell and gum-popper said I'd had a call from Aaron. Since it was almost quitting time anyway, I pointed the Sebring toward the house.

Things were definitely getting curioser and curioser.

CHAPTER SEVEN

A RED 3 BLINKED AT me as I punched the answering machine. The first was a credit card company wanting to sell me theft protection; the second was Aaron asking me to call him at home; Dawn was number three.

"Had a nice chat with your friend. You're not going to like what she did, by the way. I'll be home about seven and Jerry's working 'til midnight, so it's safe to give me a call," Dawn said, hint of a smile in her recorded voice, playing with me.

I looked at my watch. An hour until she got home. I found the cordless and poked out Aaron's number. Had one of those speed-dial setups where all you had to do was program a number into a single digit, but I didn't always use it. Figured it'd make you forget the number, and punching a *1* or a *2* at a phone booth gets you nowhere.

Aaron answered on the second ring, said he'd heard about the "little wreck" and did I want to talk about it. It amazed me how the grapevine still functioned so well and so fast. I told him I'd come over and fill him in after I phoned Dawn, and that he might hear something from Rich Brady. Aaron said he knew all three Dodge dealers in town and might make a couple of calls himself. I told him I'd bring Chinese, since neither of us had eaten yet.

I cleaned out Bogie's litter tray, took a shower, put on some Sears casual and looked at myself in the mirror. The years weren't wearing too bad, I thought. Still had all my hair and teeth, which was a plus when you topped forty. Could use a few months back at Nautilus, though. Maybe a little less Amstel at Billy's. I sucked in, profiled, a silly grin that looked more like a leer. *Cosmo* photographers would never beat a path to my door.

The big hand crept past the twelve as the little hand nudged the seven, and I dialed Dawn. She was on a cordless, scrubbing a kid in the tub that sounded like he was trying a new breaststroke in the 400 meter.

I told her about the chase and the wreck, leaving out a few unnecessary details. I could hear her take in a little breath; didn't know if it was Jerry Junior popping a freestyle or if maybe she was a little worried about me.

"Let me get these rounders in bed and I'll call you right back," she said.

Fifteen minutes later the phone rang and I grabbed it. Dawn started right up before I could even say "Hello."

"Cissy got about half that hair cut off, sport." Triumph in her voice? Maybe a little hair envy at work here?

"That the part you said I wouldn't like?"

"Yeah, I know how you feel about hair. She talked some, too, while we were both waiting. Is she, like, on edge all the time or was it just me?" Dawn could affect a Valley Girl mode with panache.

"The woman's a tad wired, I'll admit. I wanted your take on that, too." Some of that female radar, I didn't say.

"Nervous as a kitten. Talks about her hubby in the third person a lot. Seems to be proud of who he is, but maybe a little detached."

"I don't think she's got any pretensions about being a trophy. She say anything of substance?"

"I tried to nudge her toward the insecurity thing, about how the wife of a big shot probably has to slip around with sunglasses, that kind of thing. She didn't seem to think it was a problem. Said she was 'just like anybody else, I suppose,'" Dawn trying to husk up her voice a tad, not doing it very well.

"So she didn't act like somebody who's got three men watching her back?"

"Not to me, Beastie Boy. I'll tell you what, though, this girl's got something going on. I don't know exactly what, but she's working something." The woman could read minds if given time, I was sure.

I still didn't think it was time to tell Dawn about the potshot, if such a time ever came, but I had a creeping feeling that something was, indeed, rotten in the state of Denmark.

Dawn didn't pick up anything else, information-wise, but I'd gotten what I was after in her character study. My doubts about all this were taking substance, bit by bit.

After we hung up, I flipped through the Yellow Pages, punched up the Wan Fu. They had a half-dozen warm cardboard containers waiting when I stopped by on my way to Aaron's.

When I got to his house I noticed he'd forgotten to pick up his paper, so I juggled the take-out boxes and worked the paper under my arm, stabbing the doorbell with my elbow. Aaron opened the door, expertly extracted the newspaper, and grinned as I toted the remaining cargo inside.

"Talked to Ed Johnson down at Independence Dodge about that Charger," Aaron said as I plopped the carryouts on the kitchen table and started unfolding the tops. The man knew everybody in this city. "Throw those damn chopsticks away. I'll get a couple of forks."

He sat down across from me, tossed me a fork, took his, and stabbed at the egg foo young.

"Ed was the third call, by the way. They're the only ones who've sold any Chargers lately. Turns out it's now a special-order model, and it just so happens one of the three they unloaded was black. He remembered it because he thought it was an odd customer for the car."

"Odd?" I asked through a mouthful of mu shu pork.

"You don't see many churches buying Chargers. Generally tend toward twelve-seat vans, Ed said. Two weeks ago they leased a souped-up Charger to the Primitive Church of the Redeemer, one Reverend Charles Satchley."

"The television evangelist?"

"Same guy, Bible network and all."

"This Ed talk to the cops yet?"

"Nope. I told him if anybody called to try to be a little vague until you and me checked this deal out. Might cost you a fifty."

"Let's go see Ed in the morning, if you've got the time."

"Better still, how about if Ed comes by here tonight with a copy of the bill of sale?"

"I'd kiss you if you shaved better."

43

A sweaty, polyestered Ed Johnson brought a copy of the bill of sale just as we were finishing the takeout. We exchanged a few words, I slipped him a fifty, and he was quickly on his way, looking from side to side like he'd just made a drop in a Robert Ludlum spy novel. The agent for the church was listed as one Claude L. Farnsworth, who Ed described as tall, skinny, bad complexion, pretty nervous. "Didn't look like any deacon I'd ever seen" were his exact words, I believe. Paid the down payment and first lease payment with a cashier's check. I bet Aaron a twenty it was probably Claude's teeth the forensics boys were checking out right about now.

"Sounds like he could have been the one behind that tinted glass, sure enough," Aaron agreed. "Especially when Ed likened him to a hawk or a vulture."

"A pillar of the church, I'm sure."

"I expect the homicide boys will be zoning in on the Dodge dealership in the next day or so, and Ed won't be uncooperative," Aaron surmised.

"I'll check out the church angle first thing in the morning, maybe call Rich Brady and see where they're at in the case." What I didn't express was a fear that Frank Malone's fingerprints were probably all over the report by now. Aaron must have been reading my mind.

"If Malone's involved, don't try to get into a pissing contest." Aaron knew that if Malone smelled my presence in anything, he'd attack it like a starving fly on a cow patty.

We had a couple of beers, Aaron headed for bed, and I drove to the house, going in the back door this time, mindful of front-door surprises, though the most recent turn of events suggested it might have been somebody like Mr. Farnsworth who'd paid a call the other night.

Cissy Devore was running in some strange circles, and for the life of me I couldn't figure out what the hell was going on. I had a nagging suspicion that some kind of setup was in the works, but nothing seemed to fit a pattern. Cissy's shadowy entourage could, I suppose, be some kind of elaborate way to get her husband to pay more attention to her, or maybe she was the bored housewife, creating a mystery for lack of anything better to do.

Trouble is, when people start weaving webs with potential spiders in them like Joey T, Eddie, Buford, and now Claude Farnsworth and the

Reverend, it's more than just an adventure. I made a mental note to check Farnsworth's rap sheet, which I was sure probably existed, and I really wanted to talk to the televangelist.

I'd never paid attention to Satchley's channel, not being what you would call a real religious kind of guy. No more than I watched his predecessor, Jim Bakker, but just for the hell of it I tuned in the Primitive Church Bible Network when I climbed into bed, watched what I figured to be a taped show featuring him and his wife begging and crying, a toll-free number flashing on the bottom of the screen. Stylish, not as blatant as I would have thought, I suppose, but tawdry in a reverential kind of way.

Satchley was a good-looking man, blazing blue eyes, lots of swept-back blonde hair. His wife, I think her name was Andrea, was a slightly more attractive Tammy Faye with less makeup, and they seemed to clutch each other sincerely as a choir sang "Just a Closer Walk With Thee." He seemed more a Lexus type than a Charger, but the Lord works in mysterious ways. I thumbed the remote switch and Bogie leaped between my splayed legs, ready for sack time.

It seemed I had barely gotten to sleep when the phone rousted me out of a dream I think involved Dawn, a fast car, and a gospel choir.

"Houston?" Aaron sounded as bleary as I felt.

"What's up?" I looked at the clock on the nightstand. Three a.m.

"Carson Devore just called me. Cissy's missing."

CHAPTER EIGHT

AARON PICKED ME UP on his way to the Devore manse, both of us deciding it was time for Houston to come out of the closet and let Carson know what I'd been up to.

I agreed, but on the condition that I played it by ear. Carson might not need to know everything just now.

"He called me first, I told him to wait on any call to the police until we talked it over," Aaron said, rubbing his eyes with one hand while piloting his company-owned Ford Crown Victoria with the other. I've always believed, given the proper equipment, cops could shower and drive at the same time and never miss a lick.

"How'd he sound?" I sipped from the Styrofoam cup Aaron had shoved toward me when I got in the car. Seven-Eleven coffee tasted like tobacco juice, but the caffeine was pushing into my veins faster than a wide-open IV drip.

"Pretty damn distraught. I could have sworn he'd been crying, but Devore's an ex-Marine and they don't cry, if you know what I mean. Tried to cover it by saying he had a cold."

"No doubt about his sincerity?"

"None. He's a tough bastard, but I've always known him to be honest. He's been pretty good to me and I believe the man's a straight arrow."

I had no reason to doubt Aaron's assessment of his boss. Aaron rarely pulled punches in public, much less with me. He was probably the only guy I'd ever completely trusted in my entire life, family included. Of course, I never knew my mother; and my father, a two-fisted drinker, abandoned me when I was sixteen. I had no brothers or sisters, so that narrowed the field.

Aaron looked at me and grinned half-heartedly. "So what've we got here, sport?"

"First impression? Cissy has been setting up a kidnap scenario. I probably should have spent more time checking out her status with hubby, but she's kept me running from the get-go, which may also have been part of the plan."

"She's not likely to make any demands on your schedule now, but I don't get it. It's too damn obvious, even for somebody who would have been too naive not to tip her hand," Aaron said, rubbing his eyes again. "She and Carson looked like the perfect couple to me. He's smart, rich, and decent-looking; she's smart, beautiful, and at least acts like she really loves him. Kind of like the Howells on *Gilligan's Island,* only she's a hell of a lot better looking than Lovey.

"Course, I can't ever figure out these damn rich people. The money and the good life never seems to be enough. Shit, they've been married four years and still act like newlyweds every time they're together."

"Well, something is definitely out of kilter here." I didn't want to question Aaron's instincts. He'd been right more often than me; it's just that the jigsaw lines in this puzzle seemed to be going all over the place.

Carson Devore's sprawling, stucco neo-classic mansion was lit up like his sixty-story bank building downtown. A camera eyed us at the gate, which ratcheted to the left a couple of seconds after we stopped in front of it. The Ford's tires thumped on flagstone pavers as we looped around the big circular driveway to the front of the house. Devore was standing in the huge double doorway when we pulled up.

"Come on in the house. Who's your sidekick?" Devore's face was tight with concern under his graying Marine brush-cut. I'd never actually met the man face to face and was slightly surprised at how short he was, five-six in shoes, maybe. Even Cissy probably had him by a couple of inches.

"Carson, this is Houston Cash. A private investigator and someone I've known for quite a few years."

"I've heard the name, I think. Hell, maybe from you, Aaron. You're a former police officer, I believe? Glad to meet you." Devore extended his right hand and pumped mine. I doubted he knew me from Adam's housecat, but people like this, bankers and real estate salesmen, always want you to think they're all-knowing, all-seeing. He had a solid, military grip. To Aaron: "Probably is a good idea to go the private route until we figure out what the hell's going on here."

"Actually, there's a little more to Houston's being here than that," Aaron said as we walked down a hallway, past a winding staircase and into a high-ceilinged, cherry-paneled study straight out of *Citizen Kane*. Devore walked over to a wet bar tucked between two huge, loaded bookcases.

"Can I get you fellows anything?" he asked over his shoulder, unstoppering a crystal carafe and pouring a smoky liquid into a large glass. I think his hand shook a little. Glass clinked. He was doing his level best to appear cool under fire, not entirely succeeding.

"Nothing for me," Aaron replied, settling onto the large, black leather couch.

I declined, too, though a fresh cup of coffee would have hit the spot.

"Got a pot of coffee on in the kitchen," Devore said, looking at me with a kind of half-grin. I found myself warming to him, wondered if this was how he closed billion-dollar deals.

"I'd go for that," I said. Devore walked out of the room and returned a few minutes later with two steaming mugs on a tray beside a little pitcher and a bowl stuffed with sugar and Splenda packs. I took one, tilted in a touch of cream. Aaron grabbed the other mug. I didn't know how this was going to start, so I jumped in.

"Mister Devore …"

"It's Carson."

"Okay, Carson. First thing I need to say is that your wife hired me a couple of days ago. Thought she was being followed."

"She told me about being followed," he said, pulling a hand across his face, blue eyes squinting. "I didn't know she'd bothered to actually hire anybody, though." He looked at Aaron. "Your idea?" Aaron nodded. "I won't ask why you didn't tell me." No anger, just a statement.

I told him about the afternoon at Fynwyck's, the Buford encounter, and what I thought about it. I neglected to mention Reverend Satchley, the

Charger at the hairstylist, or the subsequent chase; but when I told him about Eddie and Joey T he looked like I'd slapped him in the face.

"Joey Goddam Trenton? The hoodlum?" Devore exploded, jumping to his feet and nearly dropping his drink. I had an odd image of a Tex Avery cartoon character, eyes popping.

"He said he does business with you," I carefully pointed out, watching his face.

"He's got some accounts at the bank, that's true, but they're legitimate businesses I didn't know were associated with him at the time. I've been trying ever since to decide how I could get him to move his business elsewhere. Couldn't see any alternative. I don't make it a practice to do business with people like that, but the damn court system won't give you an out unless you catch 'em up to something."

It surprised me a little that he'd shun what were likely big accounts in Trenton's network. I'd always figured that with bankers, money was money and that was all they were interested in.

"If it means anything," I offered, "I think Trenton's intentions were noble when it came to your wife. He was, for lack of a better term, smitten by her, I think."

Devore couldn't stifle a grin. "A lot of people are smitten by Cissy. She has that effect on you. Okay," he appeared to calm down, back to business. "So you two think you can rule out any involvement by him or his kind?"

"Yes, and I'll get to the reason why. But my first question to you is—and please, don't take any offense—why you're reacting like this so quickly? The police'll tell you to wait twenty-four hours on a missing person."

"It's a fair question," Devore said. "With a simple answer. I can recall no time in the four years, three months, and eleven days we've been married that I haven't known, within an hour or two, where Cissy is and what she's doing. She's never failed to call, leave me a message, or tell someone to let me know where she is and what she's doing.

"It's just our routine. Always has been," he said, eyes pooling a little. "I always make it a point to ask her if she feels suffocated, guarded, just to make sure, but she's always told me it was nice to have somebody who cared that much. Hers wasn't a particularly emotional family, so we've tried to compensate, I guess. Maybe I've overcompensated, I don't know."

I nodded, tried to look studious. Still seemed a little obsessive to me, but I'd never had much of a family life either, so I imagine something in me understood. Devore continued.

"She left the house about seven last evening to visit a friend, called me when she got there, called me when she left and said she was on her way home.

"That was about eleven and the friend's house isn't more than thirty minutes away. At midnight, I figured she stopped by the grocery store or something. At one a.m. I worried she might have had car trouble, so I tried her cell. Got a recording, then I remembered we had been having trouble with it lately.

"At about two-thirty I'd run out of options. I was panicking, and called Aaron."

"She took the green convertible?" Never know when there's more than one Mercedes in a barn like this.

"Yeah, it's about the only car we've got that she'll drive. Hates the big ones, as she calls them."

I didn't bother asking what the big ones were.

"First thing we can do, I suppose, is backtrack her route." Nothing that had happened up to this point bothered me much except the Charger incident, and with it melted, likely along with Claude Farnsworth, I wasn't too worried about that angle for the moment. "You might not want me to, but at this point it probably wouldn't hurt to ask a little favor from Joey Trenton."

"I'd rather not," Devore said quickly.

Aaron leaned forward. "Carson, the best thing we can do right now is get whatever resources we've got out and about, blanket the area, look for clues. At this hour, our resources are limited, to say the least. I agree with Houston, in that I think Trenton's on the up and up about this. We can make it clear to him that we just want to use his guy, Eddie, for a little legwork. He offered. I'll make damn sure there are no strings, you can bet."

Devore studied both of us carefully, looking tired. "All I'm thinking is Trenton thinking I owe him some kind of favor as a result of this. The repercussions …"

"I understand, Carson," said Aaron, trying to placate him. "If Trenton's doing anybody a favor, it's me and Houston. Like I said, I can spell it out to him."

Devore sighed, nodded. "Let me get you the cordless."

Aaron punched Joey T's number from the business card Trenton had given him the night he and Eddie paid a visit.

"Thought you threw that thing away," I said, grinning.

"Never throw anything away except garbage. Hello? Trenton? Aaron Drake. Yeah, it's about four. I'm taking you up on your offer."

After a brief conversation during which Aaron made it clear Joey T was helping only us, he arranged for Eddie to meet the two of us at a strip shopping center about two miles from the Devore house. Carson was to stay by the phone.

Twenty minutes later, Eddie pulled into the parking lot in the big Cadillac, a '91 Sedan DeVille. It fit. He pulled up beside Aaron's Ford and powered the window down.

"Gentlemen." Except for the five o'clock shadow, Eddie looked like he'd been up for hours. As properly dressed as somebody like Eddie could be. We told him Cissy was missing and, for a brief moment, he looked genuinely surprised. Aaron gave him Cissy's route from the night before; we swapped cell phone numbers and agreed to meet back at the shopping center in an hour. Eddie pulled off, eager to participate.

"I hope this isn't a mistake," Aaron said.

"Doubt it. Let's go get my car and spread out."

I took the farthest edge of Cissy's last known journey, Eddie took the middle, and Aaron ran the roads closest to the Devore house. I was driving down Providence Road on the southeast side when my phone chirped.

"Found her car," Eddie said. "You might wanna come on over."

Aaron and Eddie were standing beside the Mercedes when I pulled up on the dead-end street in an upscale Charlotte neighborhood known as Eastover. Huge houses and massive oak trees were being etched in the pink, damp light of dawn. I got a flashlight from my trunk and joined them.

"Parked and locked," Aaron said, peering through the driver's side window. He produced a set of keys. "Carson slipped 'em to me as we were leaving. 'Just in case,' he said." He thumbed a small button on the keychain and the car's security system chirped once. He took a handkerchief out of his pocket, palmed it, and gingerly pulled the door handle.

I crouched beside the open door and pointed the Kell light on the tan leather seats, checked the floorboard. Nothing out of the ordinary. Aaron had walked around to the passenger side, opened the door, and was scanning with his own light; popped the glove compartment, fished around with the tip of a pen.

"Can't see anything over here."

"The engine's cold," Eddie declared.

While we scanned the car, a man appeared from the shadows. Lean, fortysomething, graying hair, in a jogging suit. He slowed down as he approached the Mercedes, looked at us, and kept jogging. Like it was an everyday sight to see two guys and a gorilla in a pinstriped suit shining lights around a parked Mercedes at dawn in the city's most uppercrust neighborhood. Struck me as a little odd.

"Eddie. Stop that guy."

In a few seconds, Eddie was guiding the jogger back, holding onto an arm. The man looked none too happy.

"Are you people police officers?"

Dodging the answer, I asked him where he lived, if he'd seen anyone park the car here. You can act like a cop and people just assume you are.

"This is the first time I've seen it. It wasn't here when my wife and I came home last night, about eight." He was a little nervous and Eddie hadn't released his arm yet. I looked at Eddie and he released his grip, backed up a couple of steps.

"It may have been stolen last night, and we're trying to figure out how it got here," I told the man. "Belongs to Mrs. Carson Devore."

At the mention of the banker's name, the jogger brightened. "Carson Devore? My goodness." I'll bet Eastover bluebloods were the only people in Charlotte who still said "my goodness." Said his name was Elliott Brighton the Third and handed me a business card, which I thought was an unusual thing to be carrying while jogging until I saw that he was a real estate broker. Probably ran into a few prospects from time to time. Aaron came up behind me, whispered that the car was clean.

"Thanks, Mister Brighton. Can we give you a call if we need any more information?"

"By all means. My home and office numbers are on the card. Anything I can do." He jogged off, Eddie watching as he swung wide around him.

"Think anything's printable?" I asked Aaron.

"Possibly. I'll get one of my boys over here later this morning, dust it."

"You realize if we mess with it, we could be screwing up a federal case."

"I'll take good notes."

We secured the car and Eddie volunteered to stay and watch it until Aaron's freelance forensics pal could look it over. Somehow, I doubted we'd find anything usable. We went back to Aaron's car and dialed up Devore, told him we'd found the car but no Cissy, and that we were headed back.

At almost the moment we walked in Devore's door the phone rang. He punched the cordless, listened for a minute, and motioned us to an extension. I picked it up.

"I'm sorry, could you repeat that? I'm on a cordless and didn't hear the last part," Devore said.

It was a man's voice; calm, sophisticated.

"I said I believe you and I need to talk about your wife. I'll call you back when you don't have company."

The line went dead.

CHAPTER NINE

"HE SOUNDED PRETTY CALM to me," I told Devore as we drank coffee in the kitchen, munched on Bojangle's biscuits, and watched the telephone, now rigged with a recorder courtesy of First Southern Bank's security department, a private police agency in its own right, populated largely by ex-law officers and with more bells and whistles than any taxpayer could afford.

"Didn't sound much like the thug type, either," Devore observed.

"I noticed that. Couldn't pick up any background noise, either." We'd checked Devore's phone company caller identification device after the man hung up. It had registered a number block, which didn't mean a hell of a lot. They hadn't perfected those things yet. I tried one for a while at the office, but it hit on a number about once in every ten calls or so and I sent it back. No techno-clutter around the Cash household, at least none that cost something a month.

We were waiting for Aaron to come back from the Mercedes sweep; then I was going to visit the Reverend Charles Satchley, who I was beginning to think might be playing a major role in the Cissy Devore case. Not having told Devore about Satchley, I just told him I was going to "chase some leads" and left it at that. Detectives chase leads all the time. Part of the job description.

Since it appeared we had some type of kidnap scenario going on, we'd all agreed to keep it to ourselves for the moment, as much for Cissy's safety as anything else. Aaron and I had dealt with the local and FBI boys on kidnap cases before, and despite their vaunted reputations, it often wasn't a pretty sight and we weren't ready to lose control of the situation just yet. That and the fact that Aaron and I weren't completely sure it wasn't bogus; a theory we still weren't ready to share with Devore.

I'd put my car in Devore's four-bay garage, between a huge Mercedes Maybach sedan and a midnight blue Bentley; the "big ones," I guessed. But if the caller had been monitoring the house, he probably knew I was there. Still, the absence of police swarming the property should be a sign that we were waiting, and if he did have Cissy (and Aaron and I were wrong), he may very well already know about my involvement. At the very least, were he astute enough, he would know I wasn't a cop and probably wouldn't care whether I was there or not. One possibility after another after another.

Devore had phoned his office, canceled his appointments, checked Cissy's daybook—I couldn't believe these people kept daybooks on each other—and canceled two stops she'd planned for the day: one a hospital auxiliary meeting, the other a gown fitting for a former coworker's wedding. Devore told each that his wife wasn't feeling well, and probably felt that might actually be the case. He'd also sent his housekeeper, a pleasant, chubby Mexican-American woman named Rosario, home after she arrived, making some kind of excuse, then telling me she didn't know about the absent Mrs. Devore. She may not have known, but she'd have to be blind not to suspect something. No one else was scheduled to come by. He used a gardening service that came once a week, wasn't due for a couple of days. I thought about asking him if any of his hired help had any grudges against his wife, but that would have been too obvious and, based on assumptions to this point, unnecessary. Filed that thought for future reference, though.

I'd finished my second biscuit when the phone rang. Devore picked it up on the second ring and the voice-activated recorder Aaron had hastily rigged started humming. He reached over and hit the *stop* button.

"Aaron." He handed me the phone.

"My guy tells me the car's been wiped," Aaron advised, sounding tired. "I'm going to bring it over. Only odd thing is there's absolutely no trace of Cissy Devore anywhere in it. No papers, no tissues, not even a pack of gum."

I told Devore, who said Cissy always had odds and ends in the car so someone must have cleaned it up. I relayed the information to Aaron, who said he'd have his ID man and Eddie sweep the block and give us a call if they found anything else, sounding doubtful.

After I hung up, I asked Devore to show me the bedroom, any of Cissy's closet space, bathroom, wherever she went around the house.

In the hallway leading upstairs was a full-length oil portrait of an attractive woman, her features almost impishly cute in the flowing ball gown, the artist's severe brush strokes doing little to alter her apparent charm. The portrait was alone on the wall, no other art to detract from her beauty.

"My late wife," Devore explained without being asked. I wondered how Cissy must have felt being watched over daily by the woman she'd replaced. Maybe running away was more of an option than I'd first believed. Ghosts from the past.

In the bedroom, Devore didn't ask any questions, but watched me as I lifted, touched, moved, and poked around all traces of his wife, occasionally offering advice on whether anything was missing. Nothing was, though he said he couldn't tell about the lingerie drawer, which I hated to toss in his presence. Even in cases like this, you feel a little dirtier having to pick through a woman's underthings, afraid you'll find something kinky, which I didn't, by the way. Could have just as easily been Snow White's wardrobe. Another conflicting image as I remembered Cissy in those slinky, short knit dresses.

"I don't want you to think I believe Cissy has any part in this," I told him as we finished the last dresser drawer. I did think she did, but, as I said, I didn't want to tell him just yet.

"I understand," he replied. "I'd probably think less of you if you didn't check every angle, to be honest."

We went back to the kitchen, one of those spacious, island-in-the-middle setups, copper-clad pots and pans hanging from a rack over the island, which held a range of suitable size to feed Patton's Third Army, one of those fancy Jenn-Air deals with the barbecue grill built in on one side. A real *Southern Living* setup in shades of dark green and cream. A nook set into a large bay window off to one side, about the size of my entire kitchen, had become our command post, the table holding a phone, the recorder, note pads at each of the four chairs. We sat in two of them.

"Where do we go from here, Houston?"

"We wait, Carson. About all we can do." Which described ninety percent of private investigation. Sit and wait. Only part of this profession that bugged the hell out of me.

His face was a mask of fatigue, impatience, and concern. I found myself feeling sorry for the man, regardless of the outcome. If Cissy was scamming her billionaire husband, this guy didn't deserve it. If she'd really been kidnapped, neither one of them deserved it.

I couldn't wait to see the reverend.

─ ─ ─

By the time Aaron got to the house I was making mental notes for my interview with Satchley, trying to figure how I was going to go about it. Charging right in and making accusations probably wasn't the way to go, but that's what I really felt like doing, maybe catching him off guard since he'd probably already worked an angle in the wake of the Charger explosion. So many "what ifs," so little time.

No, probably the best way to deal with Reverend Charles was to act like nothing was particularly out of the ordinary, especially since he'd probably have no idea I was the one who'd chased the Dodge into the tar truck.

Devore forced Aaron to go upstairs, take a nap. He said he'd take the first shift, then in a couple of hours try to rest a while himself, let Aaron mind the phone. I promised to be back later in the day, figuring I'd take a nap myself if the opportunity presented itself. I'd been so juiced up to now, the fatigue I knew would be coming hadn't hit yet, and I figured I could fight it for a few more hours. Too bad they didn't bottle adrenaline so you could load up when you needed it.

I pulled out of the Devore driveway, looking in all directions. The house was in a smallish development that showcased the city's best-heeled citizenry. The owner of the local triple-A hockey team lived in a thirty-room French Provincial next door, a former Cuban immigrant who'd made millions in electronics lived across the street in an antebellum-style two-story. The neighborhood, called "Soaring Eagles" on the gates flanking the lone entrance street, consisted of maybe a dozen five-acre lots, houses situated in the middle or toward the rear of each, all with secured and monitored gates, brick or iron-spiked fences surrounding the mini-compounds, all of the homes partially or completely hidden from the street by all manner of oaks, shrubs, and expensive landscaping. It looked like America was shifting back to the feudal era, walled castles separating the rich from the poor; class division. Made you think at some point we'd be calling people "Baron This" or "Lord That," depending on income level.

I didn't see many opportunities for covert surveillance of the Devore property and wondered if the caller was just making a wild guess, though I suppose he could have driven by or been prompted by Cissy. Soaring Eagles had a security guard at the main entrance; one of those rent-a-cops who'd been sleeping when Aaron and I had entered in the wee hours. The Ringling Brothers and Barnum & Bailey elephant parade could get past most of those guys, though I did know a few who were decent, usually retired police officers or moonlighting deputies. Twentieth century guns for hire in cheap cotton uniforms.

I poked out the number of the Primitive Church on the car phone, got a cheerfully reverent operator who, to my surprise, patched me directly to Satchley's office without a single question. Satchley's secretary said the reverend was in but with someone. I asked if I could drop by to talk to him about a personal matter and, second surprise, she took my name and said he'd be free in about thirty minutes, if I cared to come then. The Reverend Satchley, she said, always tried to avail himself to the public. Score one for the preacher. Praise the Lord.

- - -

The Primitive Church of the Redeemer was housed in what wasn't much more than a tight collection of metal, industrial-type buildings on a service road parallel to Interstate 77 south of Charlotte's business district. It was surrounded by some office complexes, a couple of trucking companies, and three low-end motels on a street aptly named Bible Boulevard. A remarkable contrast, opulence-wise, to the former Reverend Jim Bakker's once-grand Heritage USA farther south. Bakker's federal conviction and the multiple scandals that surrounded Heritage had apparently taught the electronic evangelism world a few lessons in humility.

I pulled into the Primitive Church parking lot and there wasn't a Rolls Royce or Mercedes in sight. Mostly Tauruses, Toyotas, and other nondescript sedans. The Lord works in mysterious ways.

The center structure in the five-building complex had a wide, glassy entrance, so that's where I headed, walking past a garden of six or seven huge satellite dishes. I found myself in a maroon-carpeted lobby where a woman wearing a headset sat inside a large, circular desk. Madonna without the cone bra, blonde hair drawn back so severely it made her face look tight, demurely dressed but savagely made up. I told her who I was; she ran a finger down a notebook, smiled, and directed me to Satchley's office at the end of a long, narrow hallway. Portraits of Jesus and assorted reprints of Sistine Chapelish paintings flanked my path, hidden track lights shining on each work of art.

I pushed through an unmarked wooden door into a small reception area, where another woman, also wearing a headset, looked up and smiled. More the Wynonna Judd type; a little chunky, but a magnificent head of red hair.

"I'm here to see Reverend Satchley. Houston Cash," I announced.

"Yes, sir. He's waiting for you," she said, pointing to another nondescript wooden door to her right. I walked in, expecting another institutional layout, only to find myself consumed by an almost cavernous office, richly paneled in light pine.

The man I had seen on the television screen a few hours earlier stood up behind a massive oak desk, walked around it, and extended his right hand.

"Mister Cash, Charles Satchley," he said, pumping my hand with a firm, seemingly friendly grip. Dry palm, no nervousness.

"Reverend Satchley."

The preacher was dressed in a well-tailored, dark blue pinstripe suit that brought out the blue in his eyes; blonde hair perfectly coiffed in a sort-of pompadour, a style I believe they must have required at all theology schools and no small number of used car institutions. I felt like a street urchin beside him, self-conscious of the state I must have been in after hours of no sleep or grooming.

"What can I do for you?" Not impatient. Inquisitive was a better word.

"I'm involved in an investigation," I said, handing him a card. I kept a few for the more important visits. He looked at it, then looked up at me, calm, curious.

"Mr. Cash, I have a confession to make," Satchley said, walking back behind the desk, tossing the card on a large, green felt blotter. "I know that you're a private investigator, and I know that you're working on a case involving a member of the church."

I'm not sure if my mouth was hanging open, but it should have been.

"Priscilla Devore, am I correct?"

"I can't really talk about cases or clients …"

"I understand completely and I'm not asking you to do that. But Priscilla—Cissy—came to me recently and told me of her fears and that she had hired you."

I didn't have a response. Cissy had said nothing about her involvement in the Primitive Church, Devore never mentioned it and, until this moment, it had never been a factor until we traced the Charger.

"Perhaps I'd better explain," Satchley said, sitting down in the large leather swivel chair. "Please, have a seat."

I plopped heavily in the green cloth wingback to one side of the desk, still speechless.

"I have actually been thinking about hiring an investigator myself in the past few weeks," Satchley began. "My wife, Andrea, had received some rather unusual calls and messages that we took to be somewhat intimidating.

"As a result, three weeks ago I hired a bodyguard, a man recommended by a member of the church, an ex-convict by the name of Claude Farnsworth." It took all my energy not to raise an eyebrow. "Now, before you go wondering why I would hire a former criminal for something so sensitive, let me say that I got my start in prison ministries and have seen the power of the Lord work in His most mysterious ways in the lockup.

"Mr. Farnsworth found the Lord, Mr. Cash, and I trust him implicitly. The church member who recommended him was himself a former convict who now runs a successful trucking company, and I had no reason to question his judgment."

My head was spinning. This wasn't even close to what I had been prepared to face. Wheels were turning all over the place, gears shifting in my brain.

"Reverend Satchley, I'm afraid I have some bad news for you," I think I stammered. "I'm fairly sure Claude Farnsworth is dead."

Hitting the preacher in the face with an axe handle wouldn't have had a more stunning effect, I don't think.

"What ..." he swallowed, tears welling in his eyes. "What do you mean by 'fairly sure'?"

I told him about the Charger wreck, naturally leaving out the pursuit part. "It would be reasonable to assume, I think, that Mr. Farnsworth was behind the wheel, since I learned that he was the one who had leased the car."

"I ...I don't know what to say. Excuse me for a moment, if you don't mind." Satchley got out of the chair, picked up a small, tattered-looking book off the desk, moved shakily to an illuminated picture of Jesus on the wall, knelt, and bowed his head. After a minute, he rose and returned, face pale, hands shaking. If this was an act, it was the best I'd ever seen. No matter how dapper, this man was rattled to the bone.

"I can see this has upset you. If you want, I'll come back," I offered, suddenly uncomfortable and definitely confused.

"No, no. I'll be fine. Really," he said, somewhat unconvincingly. He punched a button on the desk phone. "Ellen, could you bring me a glass of water? Anything for you, Mr. Cash?"

I shook my head.

"Just a glass of ice water, Ellen. I would appreciate it." He looked back at me. "So that was why you came? To tell me about Claude?"

"Actually, I've got a few questions, if you think you're up to it." He was in the dark after all, it would appear.

"By all means," he said, producing a handkerchief and wiping his eyes. "Please. Go on."

The sequence of events had me off my stride, but I sucked it up and pressed on.

"I guess the first question may be a little obvious, maybe even seem incongruous, but why would a church lease a car like that Charger?"

"When we hired him, Claude told me he might need a car, possibly a somewhat fast car, for his job. I authorized him to get one. In all honesty, a car is a car to me, and all I knew was that he'd signed a short-term lease for the kind of car he thought he needed."

Reasonable assumption, I suppose. A Dodge is a Dodge.

"You said you hired him to protect your wife. Is there any reason that assignment would have him following Cissy Devore?"

"I don't understand."

"The last time anyone saw Mr. Farnsworth, he appeared to have been watching Cissy Devore," I said, avoiding any details.

"Mrs. Devore and Andrea have become friends over the past year or so, which I suppose could be the reason. I couldn't honestly say."

It actually made sense, and Cissy's relationship with Andrea Satchley and the Primitive Church might very well be the thing I felt she'd been holding back. From Carson, too, apparently. The question now was, had Farnsworth been sandbagging the preacher, maybe working his own operation on the side with someone else, an operation that resulted in Cissy Devore's kidnapping? I saw no other option but to tip at least part of my hand.

"Reverend Satchley, Cissy Devore is missing."

"Dear Lord, man. Do you think Claude had something to do with that?"

"At this point, I'm not making any assumptions, and I would also appreciate your discretion on Mrs. Devore, since the police aren't involved yet."

"Oh, sweet Jesus!" Satchley exclaimed abruptly, eyes widening. "Hold on just a minute."

He punched a number on the phone as his secretary walked in with a pitcher of water and two glasses. He nodded to her as she placed it on the desk and withdrew. He listened intently, then hung up the phone, paling even more.

"Mr. Cash, my wife flew to our house in Palm Springs last night," he said, punching another number and pressing the phone to his ear. He listened again, then hung up. "She should be at one of the two telephone numbers I just called, and I'm getting the answering machine at both numbers."

"I wouldn't jump to any conclusions ..."

"You don't understand. The last person she met with yesterday was Cissy Devore, then she was going to the airport and said she would call me today. I hadn't heard from her yet, but just assumed she was settling in."

The man appeared genuinely afraid. Then his phone chirped and Ellen's voice came over the speaker.

"Reverend Satchley, there's a gentleman on the line for you who says it's urgent."

Satchley pressed a button, engaging the speakerphone.

"Charles," the caller said. "We need to have a little talk about Andrea. Can't say anything right now, but I'll be calling you back."

The line went dead.

"Do you recognize that voice?" I almost shouted.

"No, I can't say that I do for sure. Maybe vaguely familiar, but I'm really not sure."

"I'm afraid I've got a second bit of bad news for you, Reverend. That's the same man who called Carson Devore this morning."

CHAPTER TEN

The last thing I had expected to have on my hands after my visit to the Primitive Church was a double kidnapping, but it was beginning to look that way.

And the two biggest fish in the suspect pond would have been Carson Devore and the Reverend Charles Satchley under normal circumstances, but instead of two prominent men sweating out suspicion, I had a pair of devastated husbands who, I believed, had no earthly idea what was happening to their families.

I decided at the church, on the spur of the moment, that it was time for a Victims' Summit at the Devore mansion, and Satchley, rapidly draining of emotion, agreed to follow me over.

It didn't take long to bring Devore and Aaron up to speed. Aaron and I left the banker and the preacher to commiserate for a few minutes while we had a conference of our own in the study. Devore was initially shocked that his wife had been freelancing an extra religion, since the two of them had been faithful, regular members of First Presbyterian. The only thing we could figure is that she'd done some creative scheduling in her daybook and had probably gotten some of her acquaintances to cover for her. Devore speculated that she didn't tell him because she would have been afraid he'd balk at any association between the first lady of First Southern Bank and a televangelist's TV network, something he admitted he might have done.

"What the fuck is going on here, Houston?" Aaron, never at a loss for words, asked as we collapsed on a couple of chairs in the study. My head was spinning, and I could look at Aaron and tell he was wearing down. Creases in his weathered face deepening, eyes getting a little hooded.

"The first and obvious thing is that Cissy hasn't been honest with any of us," I said, rubbing the increasing stubble on my chin. "Odd for a person going to two churches, but now an established fact. Granted she might have felt she had plenty of reasons to keep the secret, but her credibility's shot to hell at the moment."

"Carson said she's always been a sucker for attention and affection," Aaron said. "He told me about her family life, says she was raised by a couple of cold fish who thought it improper to even hug their little girl in public or private. I suppose I could see where she'd take to anybody who'd offer her a smile and solace, and I could also see where she might not think she was getting enough affection from a husband twenty-six years her senior."

"Twenty-six, huh? Could possibly cramp their love life a bit."

"I figured you'd ask. Him , too. We've been talking a little, personal stuff and all that, because he knew it would come up at some point, what with you searching through her panties and such—not his words, mine— and said he'd be more comfortable telling me."

"Must be an age thing." Aaron ignored my weary attempt at levity.

"He said everything's fine in the bedroom department, but what's considered fine for a fifty-eight-year-old might not be anywhere near fine for a thirty-two-year-old, if you get my drift. How long's Viagra good for? I didn't say that to him. Said she's never complained, but I could see where she wouldn't want to hurt his feelings, either.

"Houston, I'm satisfied these people love each other, but if Cissy's looking somewhere else for attention and not telling him, I'm not sure she's satisfied, if you know what I mean."

"So what do we make of the current situation? Andrea Satchley's been helping Cissy find a boyfriend?"

"Either that, or Miss Andrea may be the boyfriend, times being what they are."

"I think I need to have a personal chat with the reverend."

- - -

I walked Aaron back to the kitchen and looked at the husbands. Two leaders of big operations, one ecumenical the other economical, sat there starting to look a little disheveled; Devore in a jogging suit needing a shave, Satchley in his Brooks Brothers beginning to show some fraying around the edges. Him, not the suit. Under different circumstances, it would almost be comical; a picture I could sell to a tabloid for a small fortune. But this situation was, as Aaron was prone to say on occasion, "serious as a heart attack." I motioned for Satchley to follow me, and we trudged back to the study.

"Carson's a fine fellow," Satchley said, breaking the ice as he sprawled onto a leather wingback. "A good Christian man. I don't mean to get personal, Mr. Cash, and if you think I am, stop me, but do you consider yourself a Christian?"

"I believe in God, if that's what you mean. Do I go to church regularly? No. Do I welcome Jehovah's Witnesses into my house? No again. No offense, but I feel that some people try to force their brand of religion on others, and I don't particularly care for it." I also didn't tell him that my daddy blamed God for everything bad that had happened in his life, and that before he took off, he seemed to consider me one of those bad things. Kinda soured me on religion in general.

"No offense taken. I've been known to duck Witnesses myself." A small grin. "Do you pray?"

I had to think about that for a minute. "Not every night. Probably just when I'm in a jam or a friend tells me to pray for them." I shrugged, smiled. "If God keeps a list, I'm probably way down there somewhere." I prayed my father would stop drinking, prayed for my mother, prayed Dawn would come back. For a lottery win once or twice. No answers yet.

"God has gotten me out of a lot of jams in my life, Mr. Cash."

"It's Houston, and God probably has helped me, too, truth to tell, because I've been in some tight squeezes where He's the only one who could have done it." Might as well give God a little credit, especially when it's a preacher you're getting ready to interrogate.

"Do you believe God will see us through this squeeze, as you call it?"

"You're probably the one who'd be able to find that out, not me."

"Maybe so. I've got what I want to believe is a personal association with my Savior, but even my faith has been tested at times."

"Well, Reverend Satchley ..."

"Please call me Charles." First-name basis with two giant personalities in less than twenty-four hours, and I couldn't savor it. My luck.

"Well, Charles, until God sends us some kind of message, we've got to work with the facts we have, and part of what I've got to do is ask you some very personal questions."

"Remember, I started in prison ministries, so there isn't much I haven't heard over the years. Ask away, Houston."

"Do you and your wife have what would be considered a close relationship?"

"We've been married fifteen years and she's been by my side all the way."

"Jim and Tammy were married for a long time, too."

"Point taken." He tried to smile. "If what you're asking has to do with the bedroom, I'd say we've been okay there. We have no children. Andrea can't have them. But we have made each other happy, physically and spiritually."

"You said 'okay.' Could you elaborate?"

"We make love regularly and completely, Houston."

"Ever had to deal with the temptations of the flesh? Either one of you?"

"Speaking for myself, I will confess to you as I did to Andrea at the time, there was one occasion when I lusted in my heart. It was a brief and non-physical affair and the woman left the church." Hallelujah. Something.

"Did your wife forgive you?" Knowing in advance she probably didn't.

"We're still married, so I suppose she did."

"Just suppose?"

"I think a man goes to his grave wondering if his wife would ever forgive him for such a thing. We stopped sleeping together for a few months, then we resumed what was, ah, our regular schedule, I guess you'd call it." He loosened his tie, stood and removed his jacket. Maybe discomfort from the line of questioning, more likely just plain stuffy. He sat back down with a sigh.

"To your knowledge, did your wife ever succumb to the passions of the flesh?" Starting to sound a little preachery myself, trying to talk his language. Sounded stupid coming from me, I thought.

"She went to a therapist once, long ago. About the time we learned she was barren. I went with her on the first few visits; she kept going about a year. All she ever said to me was that she needed to come to grips with her sexuality, I believe were the words. I never pressed the issue." He was maybe holding back a little, but the answers rolled out with an honest timbre and I didn't savor the thought of getting too pushy too early in the game.

I took a deep breath, glanced at my wristwatch. Almost five o'clock. It had been a long twenty-four hours and a mind-numbing experience for all of us.

"Tell you what, let's take a time out. I might have to ask you some more questions, but right now some of us could use a little rest." Not to mention the fact that every bone in my body was aching, my head hurt, and I couldn't remember when I'd had something to eat.

"I've already asked Carson if I could stay, and I've alerted my staff that any personal phone calls should be forwarded to his number," Satchley said, standing. "Will that be all right?"

"I've got no problems with it and I'm sure Aaron would agree. Let's go make a plan."

We walked back to the kitchen; a trek that seemed longer with each circuit. Aaron and Devore were at the table, both looking as bad as I felt. The group agreed that a rest break was in order. Satchley would bunk with Devore, and Aaron volunteered to babysit the two while I did whatever legwork could be done.

I told them to call me immediately if anything developed, and promised to check in regularly.

A song was playing on the oldies station as I drove to the house. Lionel Ritchie. "All Night Long."

'Fraid so, Lionel.

- - -

My answering service actually had a message. Bubble Gummer told me Deputy Chief Frank Malone wondered if I could give him a call as soon as possible. I checked the paper to see if hell had frozen over. It hadn't, so Frank could wait. He was probably reviewing the Charger case, one of the plainclothes guys maybe telling him they saw me there. Rich had said I wouldn't be on any reports, so there was no other way and no other reason Malone would be calling his least favorite person in the world.

Just to be sure, I called Brady's pager number. In a couple of minutes the phone rang.

"Rich. It's Houston. Anything new?"

"Nope. No ID on the driver, but they did track down the Charger, I think. From a local dealer. One of the homicide boys is going to pay 'em a visit tomorrow."

Twenty-four hours ahead of the police department. Not bad, but I've done better. I told him what I'd already learned about the car, and that Claude Farnsworth was likely the name they'd be sticking on the box of ashes and teeth. No harm in letting someone at the department in on at least part of what I was doing, in case it came back to haunt me, and I felt Brady wouldn't betray any confidences at this point in the game.

Naturally, I stopped short of the kidnapping scenario. Also didn't want to make him an accessory after the fact.

"I always knew you had your shit together, Houston," Brady said, boosting my faith in him. "I'll make a note and watch Malone squirm another day or two. They sent the teeth to the state medical examiner's office, so you know that'll be at least a month coming back."

"Can you slip behind the wall in the radio room and run Farnsworth on the NCIC for me?" The National Crime Information Center was always a good clearinghouse. Might as well get some paperwork on him even if he had found the Lord.

"No problem."

"He's probably going to have a record, but I'm more interested in anything outstanding or recent." No way of knowing yet whether Farnsworth was involved in the kidnapping, though the fact that he was dead probably meant if he had been, he sure as hell wasn't now.

"Gotcha."

"Gimme a buzz at the service when you find anything, I'll call you back." I didn't wear a pager and my cell service was lousy most of the time. Hated the damn things. One of my last holdouts in the electronic age, even if they had become fashion statements for drug dealers and sixth-graders. Maybe that was why, actually. "Any reason, by the way, that Malone would be calling me?"

"Not unless one of his suit boys saw you at the scene, dropped your name. Malone's one cat curiosity would definitely kill."

"I figured as much. If he puts any heat on you …"

"Forget about it. Frank wants to talk to you, he can find you just like anybody else. What do I look like, Ma Fucking Bell?"

"Thanks, Rich."

I hung up, stocked Bogie's dish, made sure the water was up to the rim, stopped short of kissing him goodnight. He just looked at me, gave a half-hearted yowl, and padded toward the bedroom. A better world will be ruled by cats. Feed 'em and they're satisfied, pet 'em and they're yours forever.

About all I could find in the kitchen to stock my own dish was a frozen burrito. I popped it in the microwave, and the smell actually made my mouth water. I don't think one of those things ever tasted so good.

A long, hot shower followed. I'm not sure how I got to the bed, but I nudged Bogie out of the way, and didn't even remember my head hitting the pillow.

- - -

It could have been the burrito or the weariness, but I dreamed I was chasing Cissy Devore down a rain-soaked street that led somehow to the Primitive Church. We ran inside and the preacher, dressed in a tuxedo, smiled at me as Cissy and Andrea Satchley embraced. Then a phone started ringing.

I woke, shook out the cobwebs, and realized the phone part was real; reached over and picked it up, looking at the bedside clock. The digits showed 11:45, but I didn't know if it was a.m. or p.m. Still dark, so it must be night.

"We got a call," Aaron declared. I rubbed my eyes, fighting off the vestiges of sleep as best as I could.

"What'd he say?"

"Oh, not much," Aaron said, not sounding like he'd gotten much of a nap. "The girls are fine, they won't be harmed, they're in a safe place. He didn't seem surprised that Satchley was here. Oh, and he said to see if we can scare up ten million or he'd start sending fingers and toes."

"Ten million? That's a Wal-Mart price for the goods he's got."

"The price of fame, I guess."

"How'd the boys take it?" Not sure why we were so nonchalant about it, except maybe we'd been expecting this.

"Carson's ready to write a check, and the preacher tried to get the guy to pray with him but the guy hung up."

"They must not be in the room with you."

"Nah, I'm on my cell outside. Told Carson and Charles I needed to discuss a few things with you."

"Did the caller give a deadline?"

"Said he'd call back with the details, and said he's calling from different phones each time. Probably figures we're trying to trace. And caller ID is useless for something like this, as you well know."

"Are you tracing?"

"Is there a damn cow in Texas? Doesn't everybody have one of these things now? Shit, Houston, I've got night vision stuff if we need it."

"How soon? I mean when he'll call back."

"Didn't say. About fifteen hours between calls one and two, so it's anybody's guess."

"Did you get any kind of read on him?" Aaron's powers of perception often overrode such piddly things as phones.

"He was on the phone maybe ninety seconds. Didn't seem nervous, but wasn't what I'd call cool, either."

"Nobody recognizes the voice, I guess."

"Nah. I'm thinking he was trying to disguise it. Sounded kind of mush-mouthed, fuzzy. Surprised he isn't using one of those electronic things."

"Interesting." I sat up. "He could be disguising it because somebody might recognize it."

"I suppose so, or just because he thinks it's the right thing to do. Amazing what movies do for a criminal."

"I might as well come over."

"Don't worry about it. Get some more sleep. You gotta pound some pavement tomorrow."

I told him about my conversation with Brady and the call from Malone. He agreed with Brady on staying away from Malone as long as possible, didn't comment on my sharing some facts with the police sergeant. Aaron never hesitated to correct me, but always stopped short of second-guessing. Barn doors, cows, all that.

We hung up and I rolled over, tabulating the score. The guy disguised his voice for a reason, I thought. Maybe part of tomorrow should be spent checking on connections to Devore and Satchley.

Bogie nosed my shoulder, his motor running.

"Got any ideas, pal?" I asked him. He looked at me, turned his back; I ran my hand from ears to tail, then he curled into a ball and plopped up against me.

Getting back to sleep was easier than I expected.

CHAPTER ELEVEN

THERE ARE FEW SOURCES better than the public library for information about people. I Googled computerized newspaper clippings for articles about Devore and Satchley, figuring I could get more history on them here than sitting around Devore's house half the day.

Most of what they had on Devore involved mergers, charitable donations, corporate announcements, and such. A few contained cursory biographies. Born in the little town of Chester, South Carolina, the only son of a peach farmer. His sister died when she was only sixteen, a year after he graduated from the Citadel with honors. He spent four years in the Marine Corps; started out at Charlotte National Bank as a junior executive; rose to the top, became president, and started the merger machine that built what was now known as First Southern National Bank, Incorporated, the country's second-largest financial institution, with branches or some kind of operations in forty states and eleven countries around the globe. Both parents dead; a ninety-year-old uncle still living on the farm in Chester; a couple of cousins had become successful businessmen in their own right, one living in Columbia, South Carolina, the other in Raleigh.

Devore's first wife, Elizabeth, died of cancer about six years ago. The woman in the painting. They'd married while he was still in the Marines. No children. She came from a big Georgia family, met Carson at a Citadel-USC football game. She was a Gamecock cheerleader at the time, which fit the face I remembered from the painting; he was a running back for the Cadets. Judging by her picture in the Sunday newsmagazine article, Elizabeth had been a looker, even more attractive than the artist had been able to capture. A tough act for Cissy to follow, I had no doubt, though Cissy at least possessed the looks. My take on the second Mrs. Devore's character was diminishing by the hour.

I saw nothing in the banker's lineage that would raise a flag, so I tapped a few keys and plunged into Charles Satchley's past.

He and Andrea Satchley were childhood sweetheart; both ministers; both went to Duke Divinity School, where Satchley had gone on a basketball scholarship and where Andrea had apparently dropped out before graduating. Seems he was a good point guard in his day. I read about his prison ministry, noted that he'd spent a lot of time as a Presbyterian chaplain on death rows in several states, which would put him with the wrong people a lot, though most of them were likely fried by now, even as slow as justice's wheels turn. He founded the Primitive Church two years after Jim Bakker was trundled off to a federal pen in Minnesota, one reporter wryly noted. It seems the two men never met, never knew each other.

Satchley's parents were still living, both in their eighties and in a condo in what used to be Bakker's Heritage USA complex. He had a mentally handicapped brother in a nursing home in Fayetteville, North Carolina. Not much to be found on Andrea except a superficial reference to a brother.

Then something jumped out at me. The Satchleys, about eight years ago, had adopted a little boy who, the news clipping said, "died tragically in an accident at their home." No details. Funny that the reverend wouldn't have mentioned that to me in our little talk. I'd have to remember to ask him about that.

Rather than printing out the files, I took prodigious notes and tucked them in my dilapidated briefcase, where the Cissy Devore case had started swelling against the dividers. It was going to take me a long time to type this into the computer.

My next stop was the office, now looking strangely unfamiliar after being away for only a couple of days. The last bulb had burned out in the fixture, and I did a balancing act on a chair and screwed two replacements in the three-socket fixture. I jumped off the chair just as the phone rang.

"Houston Cash Investigations."

Nothing. The line wasn't dead, just nobody saying anything.

"Hello?"

Whoever it was hung up, one of the most singularly annoying things I can think of.

"At least breathe heavily or say a few dirty words," I said into the receiver before putting it back on the cradle. Could use a heavy breather right about now, as a matter of fact. Diversification.

It rang again.

"Leo's Delicatessen."

"I would have expected as much," Frank Malone said. "You subletting the place?"

"I'm a busy man, Deputy Chief Malone. What can I do for you?" Wondering if it was Frank the first time.

"I'm sure it couldn't mean anything, but one of my investigators said you were at that crash the other day on Morehead."

"Wrong place, right time."

"He said you spent some time chatting with Sergeant Brady."

"Old friends, Frank." I wanted to say more, like it was none of his business who I talked to, but didn't.

"I figured since you were there and you're such a crackerjack detective and all, you might be able to shed a little light on the situation."

"Want me to come in? Rubber hose? Bright light?" Frank Malone knew exactly how I felt about him.

"Nah, Houston, just any help an old friend might be able to offer. Got what's left of a body and a car I'm now told was leased by a church. Wouldn't happen to know where the Reverend Charles Satchley might be, would you?"

"Who?"

"Look, Cash. I've got better things to do than get in a pissing contest with a former subordinate. Your name's not on any reports, but I've got a feeling there's more to your being there than coincidence. All I'm saying is, you help me, maybe I can help you."

"Tell you what, Frank. I'll do that. You've got my number and I've got yours."

I hung up, maybe a little worried that Frank's interest might increase, but I also knew if I told him anything at all, he'd be watching me like smoke on you-know-what.

I punched Devore's number, got Aaron on the phone, and told him I'd crossed swords with Malone, if briefly. Aaron said no call yet and advised me again to stay the hell away from the deputy chief. I promised to drop by later in the afternoon.

Rich Brady was next on my "to call" list, so I dialed his cell; he picked it up on the first ring. I told him he was right about Malone.

"I've got your sheet on Farnsworth. Pretty long up to about two years ago, then seems to be clean, nothing local. Longest stretch was six years on a Florida manslaughter conviction. His probation would have run out three days after the wreck."

"That fits what I've been told. Thanks, Rich. Save me a copy."

"It's all tied up and anonymous. I'll drop it by your house, slip it under the newspaper or something."

I told him I owed him yet another favor. He said he was keeping score, laughed, and we promised each other a beer at Billy's before hanging up.

I sat down behind the desk, pushed the blotter off the cards still dormant after Cissy's visit, shuffled and stacked the deck, contemplating. A knock at the door startled me out of my musing and Eddie walked in, looking like death warmed over.

"Got some bad news," he said without preamble. "Mister Trenton's in the hospital, and it don't look good."

— — —

If you'd asked me the last place I think I would have been on earth on a given day, I could probably have said without hesitation at a mobster's bedside in a North Carolina hospital, but that's where I was, Eddie looming beside me.

He was right. Joey T didn't look so good. Tubes running into an arm, oxygen cannula under his nose, eyes appearing more bruised than usual. After a minute, the eyelids fluttered and he looked up at us.

"Cash," he rasped. "Eddie, leave us alone a minute."

Eddie didn't like it but shuffled out the door, probably lumbering down the hall, wordlessly intimidating nurses and orderlies. Eddie was a world-class lumberer.

"I don't think I'm gonna be leavin' this place upright, Cash," Joey T said, voice sandpapery.

"Oh, you'll be okay, Joey." Knowing better.

"They got me pumped full of some kind of pain-killin' bullshit, but my mind's clear, you understand? What's the score?"

I told him about Satchley, the caller, and whatever else I could think of at the moment, knowing it wouldn't be stored for long; uncomfortable at the thought.

"I kinda thought some weird shit was in the works when you and Drake called me the other night." He started coughing, a sound like his lungs were coming out next. After a few spasms and wheezes he continued. "Here's the deal. I'm gonna tell Eddie you're his boss until this shit blows over." He blinked, looked at me with what I guess he thought was a hard stare but was more like a watery glimpse. "Don't argue. You can use the legs, I know. Maybe the muscle, too."

Maybe he was right, but I hoped not.

"I ain't helped enough people in my lifetime. You know that, I know that. I want to help this lady." Joey finding religion, perhaps, or just scared as hell he'd flunk the SATs at the pearly gates.

He closed his eyes, chest rising and falling slowly. I thought for a minute he'd gone to sleep, then he was looking at me again.

"Eddie might not seem too bright, but he's smarter than he gets credit for. I've looked out for him, money and all that, but he needs somebody to look out for him every now and then. Look out for him, Cash. He ain't got nobody else."

Guardian angel to a king-sized criminal didn't seem like a good career move right now, but I felt myself nodding.

"Good," Trenton said. "Now get the hell out of here and send Eddie back in. I'll tell him to stay in touch. He'll do what I tell him now, what you tell him after."

I turned to go, but Trenton stopped me with a touch from a startlingly frail hand.

"Thanks, Cash."

I walked out, Eddie standing by the door looking like he was afraid of what I might say.

"He wants to talk to you, Eddie," was all I said, suddenly feeling very sorry for a guy who probably once broke bones just to hear them snap. Me soon playing George to his Benny didn't seem like something I'd want to put on a resume, but what do you tell a dying man? "Kiss my butt" seemed a tad inappropriate.

I figured I didn't need to say or do anything else, so I left the hospital, went home. I wasn't supposed to be sad. Joey Trenton was once a very, very bad man, but death was a great equalizer, and I knew that he wasn't far from answering for his crimes.

The answering machine showed a *1* and I hit the button.

"Mister Cash, oh, please be there, please pick up the phone," Cissy Devore's anxious voice said, then the line went dead and a dial tone hummed for a few seconds before the machine cut off.

CHAPTER TWELVE

I CURSED THE DAY I didn't spring for the four dollars for dial-back service when the phone company first offered it, but even Dawn told me she thought it was a waste of time, probably didn't work half the time.

I played the message back, listening for any kind of background noise. I thought I could pick up what might have been footsteps right before the line went dead. Hard-soled shoes on a hardwood or tile floor, maybe. A man's step?

I punched it again, turned up the volume, and put my ear close to the speaker. Definitely footsteps. Maybe a faint rustling noise mixed in. Answering machine tapes aren't known for quality. Should have long ago gotten one of those hard-drive jobs, but, like I said, me and electronics.

A spare tape was in the nightstand drawer under the machine. I pulled it out of the plastic wrap, popped out the tape with Cissy's message, and inserted the new one; waited until it rewound and set. Used the point of an old Cross pen to snap out the little tab on the back of the tape so Cissy wouldn't get erased.

Pocketing the tape, I checked Bogie's food, got in the car, and drove straight to Devore's house, too preoccupied to enjoy what had blossomed into a beautiful Southern spring day. At a stoplight a kid in a beat-up Ford Escort pointed toward my top and shouted something about why didn't I have it down. I shrugged, smiled, and pulled off when the light turned green. Didn't have time to tell him that the top wasn't down because the seams were pulling apart and I didn't want to sacrifice it to a semipermanent open-air state just yet. That and I wasn't exactly in a top-down mood.

At Devore's house I noticed a new car in the driveway. Dark green Corvette, new model. Not, I hoped, another new surprise.

The front door opened before I could knock and Carson stood there, maybe a little more refreshed than the last time I saw him. He shook my hand, and we walked into the kitchen where Aaron and Satchley sat at the table, flanked by a young, crew-cut guy in a red North Carolina State University sweatshirt. He would have looked more at home in the glare of a computer screen that at the wheel of a Corvette.

"Houston, this is Denny Samples. Denny, Houston Cash," Aaron said.

Denny had a somewhat limp, sweaty handshake, and peered at me through Coke-bottle-thick, horn-rim glasses. Bright, intelligent eyes magnified by the lenses; maybe a twinkle of mischief.

"Denny's our electronics whiz in the bank security department. Rigged up the tracing hardware. Figured we could use him. He's okay," Aaron added, meaning he'd survived the Drake background check and all-around good guy consternation.

Denny apparently didn't talk much, either. Sat back down at the table and fiddled with an assortment of metal boxes with dials and gauges. I noticed one of the boxes appeared to be a microcassette recorder, so I pulled out the answering machine tape and tossed it to him. He bobbled it, surprised. I guess that someone still used tape.

"Put that in the player, if you don't mind," I told him. We all sat, silent, and listened to Cissy Devore's plea. Carson blanched, looked at me through worried eyes.

"How good are you at cleaning up a tape, picking out background noise?" I asked Denny.

"I've got some stuff," he said. All that microchip magic boiled down to "stuff."

"How long would it take you to set it up?"

"I can go get it in about thirty minutes. It's at my apartment."

"We'll be here when you get back."

Denny made his exit; we heard the 'Vette rumble, tires chirp. Denny

Samples, the Green Hornet. I sat down at the table and looked at the assemblage. Carson was the first to break the silence in Denny's wake.

"When did you get that?" he asked, a slight edge to his voice.

I filled them in on most of the day; going home, listening to the answering machine. Occasional nods. Left out the Joey Trenton episode for now.

"I have no idea when it came in, but it had to be between when I left the house this morning and maybe an hour ago," I said, wrapping up the dissertation, hating that my antique machine didn't have a time stamp.

Aaron reached over and hit the *play* button on the recorder again, Cissy's voice repeating the message. Sounded exactly like it did the first time.

"Unfortunately," Aaron said, "phone service is so good now, it's hard to tell whether a call's long distance or local."

"We can't call the phone company for incomings to my house without tipping our hand," I noted. "Feds could find out in no time, but I'm guessing we still want to keep them out of the picture until we know a little more." Face it. We wanted to keep them out of the picture entirely. Dawn had told me I needed caller ID on all my phones. Never got around to it at the house.

"She didn't sound like she was hurt or anything," Satchley offered, glancing sympathetically at Devore. "Just kind of like she was in a hurry." His deductive abilities must not have had anything to do with getting a college degree.

"Best I can figure is that she sneaked to the phone wherever she's at, then got caught by the kidnapper," I said, picking up a little on Satchley's wavelength. "No point in trying to speculate beyond that."

And we didn't. A short period of small talk, a quick glance at the evening news (no references to the Charger crash or the police investigation), and the Corvette rumbled to a stop outside.

Denny lugged in a couple of boxes. Devore directed him to the study and, in a few minutes, the electronics whiz had a bank of machines set up in a row, like Dr. Frankenstein's stereo set.

Without comment, he hooked up some wires from the cassette recorder to his bank of gizmos, then tapped on a keyboard. A multi-colored, complicated-looking set of graphics appearing on the monitor screen.

"What I do," he finally said without turning around, "is record the tape onto this hard drive," he gestured to the box on the left, "play it back into the program, fiddle with a few things, then re-record it onto this one." A hand flipped toward the box on the right. "I'd go into detail but it'd just bore you." Bore you computer-uneducated weenies, I'm satisfied he wanted to say.

He did what he said, finally turning around as the machines started doing their work.

"First take, I'll wipe out the voice, enhance the background, then we'll take it from there." Flip. Punch. Spin. Tap. A blur of science, and I couldn't help but marvel at his dexterity.

After a couple of minutes, he tapped something on the second machine and hit *play*. There was a distinct hum, then footsteps that sounded like a horse's hooves on pavement, then a rustling noise, then dead air.

"Taps," Denny said. "The guy's wearing taps on his shoes. Likely leather soles, leather heel. You don't wear taps on rubber or crepe." Fine points for resolution, not much help for case-solving.

The rest of us looked at each other. I shrugged, watched Denny work.

"I'm going to run the cleaned audio back through the program," he said, punching, flipping, tapping some more. A regular PC magician, this guy.

Shortly afterward, he played it again, this time without the walking sounds. A distorted, clacking rumble filled the room; then the rustle, louder this time; then nothing.

"I figure the rustle's the guy's clothes when he reached for the phone line, maybe jerked it out of the wall," Denny said, matter-of-factly. "The other noise I can't quite figure."

He played it back.

"My money says it's a train of some kind," I said to no one in particular. "It's got some kind of cadence to it. Not heavy-sounding, so maybe light rail of some kind, a subway or an el."

"I'll clean it again, this time leaving only that noise," Denny said, sounding a little impressed at my speculation.

He played it again and it sounded even more like a train. Maybe even a little brake noise added.

"I think you're exactly right, Mr. Cash," Denny said, triumphant.

"So they're somewhere near a subway or elevated line, maybe even a light rail system," I said. "That rounds it down to maybe only a couple dozen cities. We've got the CATS Blue Line here, but I think it's quieter."

"Atlanta?" Satchley offered. "The MARTA system?"

"I suppose that's a possibility. Or Washington DC. They're the two closest," I said.

"There's another noise in there, too," Denny interrupted. "Lemme run it a couple more times."

Apparently the rest of us weren't auditorily sharp enough to pick up what Denny had heard, and when he produced the final cleaned tape, we were all more than a little impressed.

It was a radio or television playing, faint even on the enhancement, a little staticky but definitely understandable. It was an announcer identifying station WATL.

It looked like our girls were in Atlanta.

— — —

"A hacker I know figured out a program to bypass the caller ID block. Used to work for AT&T, got fired, got pissed off, got even," Denny said as he wired another box and a computer into the telephone line. "Beats the hell out of traditional traces.

"The old way, you'd have to tap into the phone network, do all kinds of line plotting, extrapolation, even GPS stuff to zero in on a phone number. But when the Bells broke up, they had to come up with a system they could control, and that meant every damn telephone in America sent out a signal identifying its number.

"You could block a receiver from getting your number, but that didn't mean the code wasn't still there," he explained. "Todd, my friend, came up with a logarithmic system to descramble the block."

He flipped a lever, tapped in a code, and a screen popped up showing a grid map of the United States. Turning around, he flashed a somewhat crooked smile.

"Give me at least thirty seconds on the line and I'll have the number wherever he is, guaranteed."

These guys were eventually going to replace detectives, I was sure. I patted him on the shoulder.

"Whatever Carson here is paying you isn't enough, Denny."

Devore grinned. "He's on the same scale as a senior vice president, gets bonuses and stock options. Denny could own a piece of the bank if he wanted it."

So that's how he affords the Corvette.

"That's how I afford the Corvette," Denny said, beaming.

"Last year, he caught some computer chicanery in the Texas division, saved the bank about twelve million," Devore said. "Whenever he does that, he gets a piece of the savings."

"Five percent," Denny said proudly.

"A cool six hundred grand," Aaron marveled. "I'm in the wrong line of work."

"It would have cost the bank ten times that to recoup the loss through normal channels," Devore added. "Not bad for a twenty-two-year-old, huh?"

"Pull some meat out of the freezer, Carson," I said. "I want to make this boy a steak he'll never forget."

"I'm sort of a vegetarian," Denny said meekly. "Most of the time."

"Not tonight."

-   -   -

"Now the last thing we want to do is tip our hand, let this guy think we know anything about his whereabouts," I said after dinner.

We had assembled in the kitchen. It was still fragrant from the ribeye feast.

"It's likely that our caller is somewhere else and the girls are tucked away, so tracing him may find just him, not the girls. Keep that in mind," I told them. "Nailing the caller could be just the first step. We might still have a ways to go."

"Either that, or he's with our wives and has some kind of plan. Don't forget the train," Devore said.

"There are scores of possibilities, I suppose," Satchley mused.

"I'm just saying that to make you understand that finding the caller may not solve anything right away," I said. There were dozens of MARTA stations in Atlanta, all of them with pay phones.

"Yeah, taking things a step at a time and all that," Denny contributed, his adventure with meat turning him into a gumshoe.

"I suppose so," Devore said. "He did seem to know Charles and I weren't alone when he called."

"More than likely, that was just speculation on his part. I saw no sign that anyone could have been watching either place," I offered, looking at my watch. "Look, it's time to start the waiting game again, only this time we're loaded for bear, thanks to our home-grown Bill Gates here."

Denny grinned; a high computer-era compliment to liken him to the Microsoft god.

"I'm going to go back to my house, on the outside chance Cissy calls again. Got a few things I want to ponder, too, and—I apologize and don't mean to say the company's not good—I need to do it alone," I said, beginning to pace a little. Things were starting to boil in my brain, like a lightbulb went off all of a sudden; adrenaline kicking back in again.

"Go on, Houston. We're fine here. We'll give you a call if anything shakes loose," Aaron said, studying my face. He knew something had hit me, and he knew me well enough to know I was itching to act on it.

By the time I got to the house, my thoughts were racing. I found Rich Brady's packet under the newspaper, right where he said it'd be; I took it inside, tossed it on the kitchen table without looking. I already pretty much knew what it said.

I went to the bedroom, glancing at the answering machine along the way. No messages. I grabbed the phone beside the bed and punched Dawn's number.

"Kline residence," Jerry said, dry. He wasn't happy, and was made less so when he learned who the caller was; reluctantly took the phone to his wife.

"Dawn, think back a minute to the hairstylist's," I said without preamble.

"Okay. Let's see, stylists, women, me, Cissy Devore, hair. That's about it." She sounded a tad agitated but there was humor in her voice.

"Was there anyone else there you'd have recognized? Maybe somebody fairly prominent?"

"Let's see, an overweight brunette getting highlights, a woman with a little kid she couldn't control. Oh, yeah. That television minister's wife, what's her name?"

"Andrea Satchley."

"Yes! That one! How'd you know that?"

"Can't say right now, but I appreciate it."

"Now that I think of it, Cissy looked at her like she knew her, but they didn't talk …"

"I'll fill you in later. Gotta go."

I punched another number, one I hadn't used in a long time. An old acquaintance at Southern Air I'd given a speeding ticket to in my early patrol days, then went easy on him in court. He'd said he would help me anytime I needed it. He'd been helpful a couple of times in the past, and I definitely needed him now.

"Dale?" I said when the phone was answered by a sleepy-sounding man.

"Yeah, who's this?"

"A voice from your past who really, really needs a favor."

Dale McDonald had been elevated to reservations supervisor since I'd met him, lo those many years ago, and was able to get the information I wanted in what seemed a matter of minutes. When he called back, he confirmed that Andrea Satchley boarded Flight 223 for Los Angeles two days ago.

A one-stop red-eye with a connection in Atlanta, and she had a female traveling companion. A "Mrs. P. Smith," according to the reservation. Creative.

"Reservations also says she and her friend didn't reboard in Atlanta," McDonald said.

CHAPTER THIRTEEN

IT APPEARED CLAUDE FARNSWORTH had died for no reason at all, or for the wrong one at best. He was at Hairkutter's watching Andrea Satchley, probably thought I was somebody from his past, took off, and is now defending himself in the most final of courtrooms.

It didn't seem right at the time that he had fled in such a panic rather than trying to talk his way out of whatever brought me there. I doubt he had any idea who I was, probably took me for a cop or parole officer. Still had the old "criminal jumps," and saw flight as the best alternative.

Satchley wouldn't have said anything about the hairstylist's, because I didn't. Wouldn't have seemed significant, considering the rest of our initial conversation.

So here was the scorecard so far: my information had taken care of the Farnsworth mystery, and had put Cissy and Mrs. Satchley on a plane together to Atlanta. Now all I had to do was find out who snatched them. Someone who apparently knew when they'd be together. Maybe Cissy's original stalker. Andrea Satchley's too, it appeared.

No explanation of how Cissy's Mercedes wound up where it was, but that may have just been a meeting place for the two women and, it struck me, about halfway, geographically, between the Devore house and Satchley's home up around Lake Norman. Probably left it in Eastover because it fit better than a truck stop parking lot on the interstate.

Yet with all this first-rate crime-solving, something still stuck in my craw and I couldn't quite pluck it out. I still didn't know who took the shot at me, and Claude Farnsworth was looking less and less like the candidate for that little incident.

Could it have been the caller? Is there someone else involved in this ever more complicated situation?

Much as I wanted to be in control of this deck, I had to admit I just didn't know.

-    -   -

I consider myself to be a fairly average guy. Decent looking, in pretty good shape, good sense of humor, and all that. I was no Tom Selleck (couldn't get the hang of a moustache, though I tried it a while; too itchy) but I seemed to be able to get a date when I wanted one. Trouble is, I couldn't quite extract Dawn Rayburn Kline from my mind, which kinda kept me preoccupied and, apparently, unable to find a new love in my life.

Among the reasons Dawn was so inextricable, if that's the word, was probably what I saw coming up my sidewalk at the moment.

Juggling her youngest in one arm, a grocery bag and her purse in the other, clutching what looked like a handful of mail with a free hand, she came toward the front door looking like an *I Love Lucy* episode in the making. I'd watched her pull up in the Volvo; opened the front door to greet her.

"A little help here," she said, trying to placate an obviously upset child whose name I couldn't remember at the moment.

I met her halfway, grabbed the grocery bag and mail. Even in this situation, she still took my breath away. I really need to get over her.

"Now, Jay Jay," she told the toddler, putting him down, "you be nice to Mr. Cash here and don't touch anything you shouldn't." At least I wasn't "Uncle Houston" to any of her kids. Yet.

The kid bounced into the house and Bogie took off like a shot, Jay Jay in pursuit. The cat ought to keep him occupied a while.

Dawn gave me a peck on the cheek and brushed past me into the living room.

"Lasagna in the bag," she said. "I figure when you're on a case, you don't eat well."

"Correct me if I'm wrong, but I've got a feeling this isn't just a lasagna trip."

"Exactimundo. You're quite the detective."

Something thumped in the area of the bedroom, followed by a giggle.

"Jay Jay's cornering Bogie, I imagine," I said.

"Honey, don't touch anything!" To me, "There's no telling where this guy's been and with whom." She flashed a thousand-watt smile. Dawn was everything I considered to be perfect in a woman except, of course, that she wasn't mine any more.

It would probably seem ridiculous to the average bystander that I would still lug a torch for a woman who not only left me but got married and had three kids, and I would not only not admit that I still loved her, but also wouldn't mount the pointless task of trying to explain why.

Her cerulian eyes bored into me.

"So what's the connection between Cissy Devore and the preacher's wife?"

"Right now, it appears they've both been kidnapped," I said.

"I'm listening." No expression of surprise, no "You're kidding."

I caught her up on everything that had happened since the day at the hairstylist's. She listened, rapt, jarred out of her concentration only once when Jay Jay came in, looked at me and grinned, handed her a can of shaving cream he'd gotten from God knows where, then toddled back toward the bedroom to search for the cat.

"So," she said when I'd finished.

"So."

"Carson Devore, Aaron, this computer kid, and the television evangelist are camped out at the Devore house waiting for a call. Sounds like a *Spenser* episode to me."

"That's about the size of it."

"Bet that's a pretty picture. Kinda like the Last Supper for bazillionaires with Aaron as the hired help."

"Think there's a Judas in the group?" Trying to get that image, all of them in robes passing wine around.

"Not from what you've told me. At least not in that group."

"Meaning?"

"If I were a betting person, I think you might be dealing with someone who knows someone in the group fairly well."

"And what leads you to that conclusion?"

"Surprised you didn't get it yourself. This caller knows Satchley is going to be at Devore's place, in fact called Satchley right after calling Devore, more or less, then calls Devore's house again when Satchley's had time to put one and one together. Not trying to keep them apart, it appears. Maybe even using you to be the mixer."

"Matter of fact," Dawn continued calmly, "Looks to me like he was maneuvering to get them together."

"Kinda like Cissy setting me up for this kidnapping scenario."

"Kinda. You got the tape?"

I plucked the original out of my pocket, stuck it in the answering machine, and played it.

"Could be acting," Dawn said afterward. "Play it again, Sam. I've always wanted to say that ever since I've known you."

"Okay, Ilsa." So you can get on that plane and fly off with Jerry, I wanted to add but didn't. And Bogart didn't say "Play it again, Sam," but we weren't into finer points at the moment.

Maybe it was Dawn's power of suggestion, but listening to the tape again made me hear it a little differently, like Cissy wasn't as frantic as she sounded before.

"I'm betting that if you'd picked up the phone, she'd have cut it off anyway," Dawn said. "I don't really know the woman, but I know women, and she didn't sound like she was in any serious trouble to me."

"Well," she announced, standing abruptly. "Jerry took the kids to a movie and should be getting home shortly, so I've got to get packing."

I stood, too, and we walked back to the bedroom where Jay Jay had curled up on the bed, Bogie snugged up to his back, both of them snoozing to beat the band. Dawn picked him up like a sack of potatoes and slung him over her shoulder. He grunted, snuffled, and stayed out of it; the slumber of innocence. Bogie looked up sleepily, tucked his head between his hind legs, and continued to doze.

"So I should consider the angle of Cissy continuing her little play here," I said, walking her to the Volvo.

"That, or she's just a person who can't show emotion and she's really in a pickle," Dawn said, unloading Jay Jay into his car seat and strapping him in, head lolling to one side. "If it were my money, I'd say Cissy's playing a bigger part in this than it appears. Your reservations guy didn't say anything about her being handcuffed, bound, or gagged when she got on the plane, did he?"

"Nope. Mrs. Smith was obviously a willing partner, but the actual kidnapping might have happened somewhere else, remember."

She studied on that for a moment; made no comment. "Does Mrs. Smith know how deep her husband's technology well goes?"

"I doubt she'd have any idea about The Great Denny and his computer tricks."

"Then you might solve this one with another phone call, so to speak. Catch 'em all by surprise."

"And Claude Farnsworth?"

"I think your take on that one's accurate. The overzealous bodyguard thinking the jig was up on his parole, him being out of state, possibly packing, takes off and gets fried." Dawn was not one to mince words. "Gotta go."

She stood on her tiptoes and gave me a sisterly kiss on the mouth. At least I guess it was sisterly. No tongue. Sparks did fly, though, at least on my side of the storm.

I watched her pull away; still wished things had been different between us when it counted, wished I'd been willing to commit. But those wishes were horses I'd never be riding again.

She was on her way home to a real life. I was going back into a house with a cat, an unsolved kidnapping, and a hunk of cold lasagna.

The phone started to ring; I picked it up.

"Bells are ringing for us and our gals," Aaron said. "Better come on over."

CHAPTER FOURTEEN

"HE SOUNDED A LITTLE more straightforward this time," Aaron said as we walked to the Devore kitchen. "Denny's working his stuff on the number trace."

By the time we got to the room, Denny was grinning, gesturing toward the computer screen where a ten-digit number blinked. Beside it, the identification. The Ritz-Carlton Buckhead. About two or three blocks from a MARTA station, as I recall. A short hop from the pay phone, also near a bus stop, definitely a place where a kid with a jam box would have been tuned in to WATL.

"Our refugees are being held first class or he's in the bar," I said. "Let's hear the tape."

The man's voice, a little crisper than before, saying how he wanted the money, small bills, in one of those silver-sided briefcases. He'd call back with a drop site. Click. End of conversation.

"Should we call the hotel?" Carson getting anxious.

"That would be a sure way to tip our hand, drive them deeper underground. No, we don't want them to know the technology we've got." I looked at Aaron. "You up for a trip to Hotlanta?"

"I haven't been there in a while," he said. "They still pick peaches, drink mint juleps?"

His humor was lost on all but me, nobody smiling or laughing much in Chateau Devore.

"Carson, with you, Charles, and Denny here on the phone and us in Atlanta, you may have to try some stalling techniques if he calls, at least until we either tie things up down there or get back here for the next move," I said. "The bank got a corporate jet?"

"I can have it fueled and ready by the time you get to the airport. It's a forty-minute flight there and if you want, I can have a car waiting at the airport," Devore said.

"I want. Somebody you can trust, somebody who knows the shortcuts and can get us to the hotel quickly."

"I know just the one. I'll call while you two pack."

"No packing," I declared. "We need to move right now and it's not that long a trip. Can you arrange to get us past the gate, too? Aaron and I will, well, you know, have certain equipment that would take some time to explain to the TSA."

"No problem."

Aaron and I boarded the First Southern Gulfstream on the private tarmac just east of the main Charlotte terminal. We were in the air in minutes, nestled comfortably in large leather seats, two of us not taking much space in the twelve-seat jet.

The pilot and copilot tried to be chatty, but I wanted to talk some things over with Aaron and politely closed the cockpit door after a couple of jokes about jet jockeys.

This was my first opportunity to tell Aaron about Joey Trenton, the news raising an eyebrow.

"So you're going to inherit Eddie?"

"Looks like it."

"I always figured you'd be a father someday."

"We'll get him christened, make you the godfather."

"I'll have to buy a new suit." More seriously, "Joey T looked pretty bad, huh?"

"Wouldn't be surprised if they were already rolling him out."

"Think Eddie will honor the wish?"

"Eddie's like a big kid. Of course he will. If he starts hanging around,

I'll give him something to do that'll bore the hell out of him, then maybe he'll think about heading back up north, go to Florida, or something."

"You got a plan for when we get to Atlanta?" Aaron asked, sensing it was time to change the subject, focus on the task at hand.

"Not really. We probably shouldn't charge up to the front desk and start asking questions," I said. "Don't see why we can't get Devore's driver to go to the desk for us; we'll sit in the car until we know something."

Aaron pulled out his old Charlotte badge. "I can use this if we encounter any problems."

"Suits me. I'll just be the silent partner." I didn't have my old badge, seemed to recall throwing it at Frank Malone's door, something like that.

I shared Dawn's observations with him regarding Cissy's phone call. He thought a minute, then agreed with her assessment, which he almost always did.

"You were an idiot for lettin' that girl go," Aaron said, probably for the thousandth time. "Shoulda married her when you had the chance. Maybe she could come back to work for you."

"Her husband would never go for it," I replied, avoiding any observations on the letting go part.

"You know," Aaron mused, "If Cissy's down here on her own accord …"

"She might not want to come with us," I finished the sentence. "Any way you cut it, we don't have a kidnapping and the case is closed. It'll be something Carson and the preacher'll have to work out on their own."

We felt the slight shift of the plane dropping in altitude, and the pilot's voice came over the intercom.

"On approach, gentlemen," he said.

The plane landed smoothly, taxiing to a private apron where a silver Lincoln waited, a dark-clad figure standing beside the driver's door.

"Cross your fingers," I told Aaron.

"Toes, too," he said.

- - -

Devore's Atlanta escort turned out to be Aaron's equivalent at First Southern's Georgia operation, a retired fed with not much enthusiasm for escorting a couple of snoops from the home office. Small talk was difficult and one-sided, but I think we convinced him we were tracing a wayward employee and not here to evaluate his job.

His name was William Baynes the Fourth, and he agreed to go to the desk for us to check on the registry of two women, one possibly under the name Satchley, the other Smith. Andrea Satchley's name didn't raise any hackles, so I had to assume he wasn't a regular watcher of the Primitive Church network. Not too many Bibles get thumped in law enforcement at any level.

It took about forty-five minutes for us to get from the airport to the cobblestone, semicircular driveway in front of the Ritz Carlton in Atlanta's fashionable Buckhead district, situated on a corner of one of the Peachtree streets and overlooking the mammoth Lenox Square mall complex on one side, the trendy Phipps Plaza on another.

Baynes parked the Lincoln in a slot opposite the driveway, putting us in a position to watch the hotel entrance. Cop habits die hard and we thanked William the Fourth for positioning us just so. He shrugged and said it was the only available parking space.

Still a bit sullen and distrustful, but ever the obedient servant of Chairman and CEO Carson Devore, Baynes lumbered through the brass, wood, and glass portico and disappeared from view. None of the doormen offered to hold the door for him, obviously pegging him as a cop the moment he hit the sidewalk and assuming there'd be no tip.

I told Aaron the hotel had a side exit that emptied toward Phipps Plaza, offered to cover it. Aaron said he would, needing to stretch his legs a bit anyway. He eased toward the corner and I watched the door, where Baynes emerged about the same time Aaron disappeared around the side.

Baynes walked to the car, approaching on the passenger side as I popped open the door.

"Two women registered in room 833, open-end stay, checked in night before last. Signed in as the Wilson sisters. The clerk who was working when they checked in is off duty now. This one couldn't say if anyone was with the women," he said, handing me a rectangular piece of plastic with some holes perforating one side. "He gave me a spare key after I flashed an old federal ID. I told him it would be best if he didn't ask any questions, so he didn't."

I thanked him, said Aaron was covering the side exit, and asked him to keep an eye on the front door, describing Cissy and Andrea Satchley in as much detail as necessary, not knowing whether he'd ever met the boss's wife.

"If they come out," I added, "detain them discreetly."

He understood, I suppose, and grunted his assent as he circled the car and stood beside the driver's door, not enthusiastic at having to do police work again.

I walked into the hotel like I belonged there, strolled left to the elevator bank, found one empty and open, stepped inside, and punched the 8. Another guy was moving toward the doors when they closed, and I made no attempt to hold them. The doors slid shut in his disappointed face.

The elevator rose softly, a steady mechanical hum signaling my ascension. It went straight to the eighth floor, and the doors dinged open into a pastel hallway. A short walk past a full-length mirror, a table with a huge flower arrangement, and an old print of fox hunters and dogs assembling in a field. A sign with an arrow pointing left bore room numbers 810 through 835. Eight-thirty-three was apparently just off the corridor.

I unsnapped the holster tab and gripped my pistol as I eased toward the door, not knowing what to expect when I pushed it open. Standing a little to the left of the portal, I took a deep breath, slid the plastic key in the slot as quickly as I could, and when the little green light came on, grabbed the handle, levered it down, and shoved.

I pushed in low, crouching and moving from left to right as quickly as my popping knees would allow, pulling the Glock barrel up, thumbed off the safety. The room was dark, no sound. When my eyes adjusted, I saw that one of the two queen-sized beds was tousled, empty, the other still made up. Bathroom door on my right was slightly ajar.

"Cissy?" I said into the darkness. "Mrs. Satchley?"

Nothing but the hum of an air conditioner.

I slid my free hand up the flocked wallpaper to a flat, toggle-type light switch and rockered it up, leveling the pistol toward the open room. Two lamps flanking the curtained window illuminated the empty room. I stood, cautiously pushed the bathroom door open, and saw a couple of towels on the floor, one hanging on the shower curtain bar. No toiletries on the vanity other than scattered bottles from the hotel-provided assortment. The closet across from the bathroom was empty, a light bulb blinking to life when I pulled the door open, reflecting off a cluster of empty wooden hangers.

I walked into the room, flipped the switch on another lamp beside the first bed, and looked around. The room had obviously been vacated. No luggage of any kind, faint scent of perfume, Black Pearls.

I went back into the bathroom and felt the towels, damp and still a little warm; a touch of fog clung to the bottom edge of the vanity mirror.

I dashed out the door and ran to the stairwell exit to the left, looked through the little wire-laced window, then pushed through. I thought I heard a faint clatter below and started leaping down the stairs, two at a time.

"Cissy!" I shouted. "Mrs. Satchley!" A door opening and closing far below.

I was breathing hard when I got to the first floor landing, glad I hadn't been running up. Pushed open the door, which led into an empty hallway flanked by some high-end souvenir and clothing shops, closed for the evening, a couple of mannequins staring at me from the dark behind the glass. I jogged across the maroon carpet, shouldered through two double doors to the side exit. Aaron was on one side, on his knees, rubbing his head.

"Pushed by me," was all he could say. "That way." Gesturing toward the parking lot beside the hotel. "I'm okay. Go."

I sprinted to the lot, which turned out to be the top level of a concrete parking deck. A rail along some steps leading down, pistol held down in front of me. As I ran toward the stairs I heard a car roar to life below, tires squealing. By the time I reached the bottom, a dark-colored Chevrolet, no lights, Georgia tag, was speeding through a gated exit, splintering the striped wooden arm as it tried to go up.

The car fishtailed on the street, ran a red light; other cars locked brakes, horns blaring. I watched the Chevy grow smaller in the distance, holstered the Glock I'd almost forgotten was in my hand. Damn.

- - -

I loped back to the side door, where Aaron had drawn a group of four people, one of them shining a little light in his eyes as he stood, shaky. A couple of uniformed valets rounded the corner, accompanied by a female security guard, Baynes behind them.

I looked at Baynes; he nodded, guided the valets and guard to one side, pulled his ID wallet out, and started to talk to them.

The man with the little flashlight looked at me as I approached, smiled weakly, explained he was a doctor, and said my friend looked okay, just shaken. I took Aaron by the arm, steered him away from the group.

"Saw 'em coming, running like hell," he said. "Just stood in front of the door and the guy plowed right through me. For some reason, I didn't think he'd do that. A little guy but he hit me just right."

"The women?"

"Right behind him. Didn't get a good look, I'm afraid, but I'm pretty sure one of 'em was Cissy. Don't know if she recognized me before the guy knocked me down. Hit my head on that damn awning pole. I don't know, I might have blacked out for a minute."

"Don't worry about it. They took off from the parking lot like a bat out of hell. You sure you're okay?"

"Yeah, yeah. Sorry I messed up, Houston."

"Forget about it. At least now we know more than when we started. Maybe when you shake it off you'll remember something about the guy."

"Maybe so." Aaron didn't sound very sure.

— - -

The three of us tossed the room. More specifically, me and Baynes; Aaron sitting on the edge of a bed, looking woozy. Except for some candy wrappers and tissue paper in the trash cans, there wasn't much left to toss. A scratch pad beside the phone had been used, the top sheet bearing some faint pen grooves, so I pocketed it and figured I'd look it over back home.

The "Wilsons" had paid cash for the room for a week, so there wasn't anything there we could use. They'd given an address in Greenville, South Carolina, that turned out to be a Wal-Mart. We did learn how they knew we were there. Seems one of the Wilson sisters had told the desk clerk they were expecting a visitor and wanted to be notified if anyone inquired about them, something about a birthday and a surprise. There was no way they would have known we were coming, I don't think, but I had to give the kidnapper or whoever points for being clever enough to dream that one up.

I called Devore and Satchley, gave them a brief rundown on what had happened. They'd gotten no call since we had left, so everything was status quo there.

Baynes was relieved to drop us off at the airport, never once asking for any details about what we were doing and why, and Aaron slept the whole way back after assuring me he'd see a doctor in Charlotte.

The silence gave me plenty of time to think. Now we were back to where we started, maybe worse, since the kidnapper—I assumed Aaron's tackler had been the kidnapper—knew we were able to trace them, which meant that when they went underground again, they'd be harder to find. Probably a lot harder.

That aspect worried me more than a little, since we'd also probably pissed the kidnapper off big-time and he wasn't going to be a happy camper.

Little did we know just how unhappy he'd be.

CHAPTER FIFTEEN

I HUSTLED AARON TO THE Presbyterian Hospital emergency room as soon as we got back to Charlotte. I knew a couple of the ER nurses, who fawned over him like he was the most important person they'd ever met. He was still a little groggy, but X-rays and some kind of computer scan indicated nothing worse than a bad bruise where his head met the awning pole. A little swelling, "but there's always the chance of a hairline fracture," the doctor said.

Just to be safe, I took him home over several protests, and then drove to Devore's house.

Carson met me at the door, and though I'd actually only been gone a few hours, he looked like he hadn't slept in a week. In the kitchen, Satchley looked just as bad. Denny was curled up in an easy chair they'd apparently transported from another room.

"Not a peep since you guys left," Devore said.

"More than likely, we interrupted the cycle. The next call probably won't be pleasant," I told them. "We've scared him, I think, probably made him mad. I doubt seriously that he had any idea we'd be able to trace him.

"The rules could change," I said, trying not to sound as grim as I felt. "I'm going to stick around, get on the phone when he calls.

"I've had some experience in hostage negotiating, so I might be able to keep him from doing anything foolish," I lied. I never took the police department's negotiator course; never thought I'd want to have that job on the force, trying to talk sense into some whacko.

"Define 'foolish,'" Devore said, slightly agitated.

"All I'm saying is that he's probably going to say something to make us think he'll do something rash if we try to track him again. Chances are he won't actually do anything, because hurting the women won't accomplish anything for him and he knows we have the ability to find him," I said, hoping the two husbands would buy it. I really had no idea what the man might do, but encountering him in Atlanta in the flesh did a lot to diminish my belief that this wasn't an actual kidnapping. Though I'll still admit it could all be part of some master plan.

"We're still going to track him," I added. "We'll just take things a step at a time."

"I say we pay him what he asks and get the whole damn thing over with," Devore said. "Reason with him. I don't give a shit where he goes or what he does once I get my wife back, and I know Charles feels the same way."

"I agree," was all Satchley said, and I guessed the two of them had made their decision long before now.

"Ten million dollars is just money. Maybe when we pay him and get the women back, I'll hire you to track the son of a bitch down and dispose of him," Devore said, his jaw set. I'd never quite equate eight figures to "just money," but this was out of my league commercially.

"You're the boss, Carson, and I don't disagree with you," I replied. "Quite frankly, I hope that's the way it plays out. But I've got to be honest with you, people who do this kind of crime rarely leave their victims unharmed, rarely do anything they say they're going to do. We're at his mercy.

"He's calling the shots," I said, not masking my frustration very well.

— ‒ ‒

The call came shortly before three a.m., stirring us all out of a state of almost unbearable weariness. Devore, Satchley, and I each picked up an extension; Denny hit a couple of computer keys and nodded. I noticed for the first time that his phone extension was a little headset, probably something he'd added from his bag of tricks. Thinner, meaner looking than the Primitive Church women's headgear. Lean and mean.

"That was a very, very stupid thing you did," the man said, sounding nearly as weary as we felt.

"It won't happen again, I assure you," Devore said. "Just tell us …"

"You're damn right it won't happen again," the caller interrupted. "And just so you'll understand why, I've got something I want you to hear."

A shuffling noise followed, and then the three of us heard it. A weak moan at first, then something that sounded like a slap, followed by a pained shriek.

"Hear that, boys?" he said, almost cheerfully.

"Now you hear me, you son of a bitch," Devore roared into the phone. "You harm one hair on their heads and not only will you not get your money, but we'll track your goddamn ass down and cut you into chum that even a shark wouldn't want to eat."

Silence.

"Did you hear me?" Devore shouted, ignoring my shaking head.

Another pause; then, "Are you through?"

It was our turn to be quiet.

"Now listen up, Carson, and you too, Charles. The girls want you to listen, too, and listen real closely. I know your detective friend is probably there, too, and I want him to listen more than anyone else. Mr. Cash?"

"Yeah, I'm here."

"Good. Hope your friend's doing well. Now here's how it's going to go from here on out. There will be no more of these surprise visits. One more time and your wives are dead, gentlemen, and I disappear.

"I'm sure you're trying to trace me right now, and it doesn't really matter because you're going to do what I tell you, aren't you?"

Denny gave a thumbs-up sign and pointed to the computer screen, again flashing a number and place. I didn't recognize the name, some kind of hospitality corporation; but saw that it was in Birmingham, Alabama.

"I said, 'aren't you?'"

"No, pal. We're not going to pay you a visit," I said.

"I'm not your pal, Mr. Cash."

"What do you suggest we call you, then?" Getting him to talk more might create a mistake, cause him to lose his technique, give us a clue.

"Oh, I don't know. How about Gabriel? You'd like that, wouldn't you Charles?"

"You're not exactly an angel, my friend," Satchley said.

"No, but you can bet your fundamentalist ass that I'm the one blowing the bugle! Hah! Pretty good joke, huh?"

"Gabriel's fine," I interrupted, not wanting to get into a contest of words. "So what's next, Gabriel?"

"Money, Mr. Cash. Cash money. Hey, I made another joke! I believe I quoted an amount earlier, but because of your transgressions, I've decided I must penalize you. The amount is now fifteen million, Mr. Devore, Charles."

"In small bills, that's a lot of bulk, Gabriel," Devore said. "Won't be easy to carry around, will it?"

"Who said anything about carrying it? Did I say anything about carrying it? Why, for all you know, you're going to ship it FedEx, or maybe even put it in an account somewhere. Who knows? Our little Atlanta meeting has me out of sorts, so I'll call you later and we'll hash things out. Ta-ta."

"Gabriel?" The line was dead. I cradled my phone; the rest followed.

"He's right, you know," Satchley said. "He's definitely in charge."

"For now," I said.

"Houston, he is in charge," Devore said, letting out a sigh. "No matter how you cut it."

"Maybe so, Carson, but I'd like to mull a few things over. Did his demonstration ring a bell with anyone? Did the woman sound like Cissy or Andrea?"

Devore and Satchley looked at each other, then at me. Both shrugged.

"There's no way to tell. You're thinking it was somebody else?" Devore said.

"Maybe. I don't know." To Denny, "You've got the whole thing recorded?"

He nodded.

"Make me a copy. I'm going home. I doubt we'll hear from Gabriel until tomorrow, and I want Aaron to hear it." Dawn, too, I didn't say.

Denny started punching buttons, and in a minute handed me a flash drive.

"Get some sleep," I told the assembly. "We'll take another look at things tomorrow."

Any more conversation at this point was useless, judging by the attitudes and exhaustion that permeated the room.

Devore followed me to the front door.

"How're your finances holding up, Houston?" So frustrated he was crunching numbers. Ever the banker, I guessed.

"Better than your eyelids, Carson. I'm okay. Don't worry about it."

"Look," he said, touching my arm. "I know you're doing everything you think is right, but I meant what I said about paying him and getting this over with. Fifteen million dollars is a lot of money, but I can stand it and I can't stand this waiting anymore." Resignation wore on his face like a billboard.

"We'll come out of this, then we'll maybe regroup and do what you said," I told him, trying to sound reassuring. "You three try to get some sleep in the meantime."

"We will all do what we have to do," he said. "Give Aaron my regards."

"I'm going by his house first. Will do."

I pulled into Aaron's driveway twenty minutes later.

Right behind the ambulance.

CHAPTER SIXTEEN

"GOT A LITTLE DIZZY is all," Aaron said, looking pale as a ghost, small and old in his bed, pillow fluffed up around his head, bedspread pulled up to his chin.

The ambulance attendants had left after telling me somebody ought to stay with him, that nothing appeared wrong but one of them adding "you can never tell with a head injury." I'd called Dawn, asked her to come over, and she almost threw down the phone running out the door.

"You scared the shit out of me, old man," I said, truthfully. "How about you take it easy for a few days?"

"And leave all the good stuff up to you? I don't think so," he said, probably not aware of how weak he sounded.

"Look, Aaron, there's not that much going on right now. I can handle it until you're back up to full strength." Trying to convince myself he would get there, too. I'd never thought of Aaron as an old man until now, and it scared me.

"Houston," he said, reaching from under the covers and gripping my hand. "You're a damn good investigator. One of the best I've ever known. It comes to you naturally, I think, and there aren't many people I'd say that about. But this is a powder keg and I don't know who's going to blow first: you, Carson, or this kidnapper."

"Gabriel."

"Huh?"

"He called. Told us to call him Gabriel," I explained, not wanting to get into details at the moment.

I filled him in on the call, slowly, wondering how much of it he would retain. The paramedics had given him a dose of the painkiller they'd provided at the hospital.

"I've got a copy," I concluded. "Pretty much, it just confirms what I told you."

"So he's slapping one of them around now, making a point?"

"Maybe. Maybe just theatrics, too. Dawn's on her way over, by the way."

"What for?"

"The ambulance guys thought somebody ought to stick around, keep an eye on you."

"I don't need a nursemaid. I didn't call the ambulance, just called that nurse at the hospital. Next thing I know they're knocking on the door. All your friends overreact like that?"

"Guess they just figured with First Southern you've got good insurance, thought they'd pick up some extra money."

"Yeah, well, if you think I'm gonna lie here in bed while …"

"While what, you scalawag?" Dawn said, walking into the bedroom.

"While Magnum here gets all the credit and the babes," Aaron said, grinning weakly. "I was just getting to the babe part and in you walk."

"Bet you didn't know I had some nurse training a few years back," she said, moving around to the side of the bed, fluffing a pillow.

"Long as you keep the thermometer above the neck, I might let you hang around a little," Aaron said. "Just for scenery, you understand."

"How about I work topless?"

"I'll stick around for that. Move over, Aaron," I said, Dawn punching my arm.

"You and me played doctor, Mr. Cash, and you see where that got us," she said, putting the back of a hand on Aaron's forehead. "Let's let the old fart here sleep a little. You'n me can have a cup of tea; talk."

"That better be all it is," Aaron said, eyelids heavy. "Don't be taking advantage of your poor old chaperone."

Dawn tucked him in; I promised to be back, and we walked into the living room, sat on the couch.

"How'd you get out of the house?"

"When it comes to friends in need, Jerry knows better than to ask me why. He's a kind, patient husband, and he knows I love him," she said matter-of-factly, and then pushed it aside. "He can run his office from the house tomorrow if necessary. Call his mother, if push comes to shove. You want to tell me what this is all about?"

I told her about our Atlanta adventure, Aaron's encounter, and the phone call, pulling the tape out of my pocket.

"Aaron got a computer around here?"

We found his laptop in the den, powered it up, and I popped in the flash drive and double-clicked the little icon, watching her face as the dialogue unfolded. She winced at the sound of the slap.

"Guy's playing hardball," she said when it was over. "Doesn't like you much, either. A real short fuse operating there."

"Did that little sound effects episode sound genuine to you?"

"I don't know. Maybe. Maybe not. Whoever that was, she didn't sound too happy. Could have been an act, but I'd bet the slap startled somebody."

"Think it's one of our girls?"

"It would just about have to be, unless you're suddenly dealing with a crowd of conspirators. I suppose it is a little odd he didn't let her say something. That could be because he didn't want any of you to know which one it was."

"Possibly."

"There's something about him choosing that name, too," she said. "Wait a minute."

Dawn got up, walked to Aaron's only bookshelves and plucked out a Bible.

"This thing looks like it hasn't been used in a while," she said offhand as she flipped through the pages. "Here." She started to read.

"'Yea, while I was speaking in prayer, even the man Gabriel, whom I had seen in the vision at the beginning, being caused to fly swiftly, touched me about the time of the evening oblation.' Daniel, chapter nine, verse twenty-one." She looked up, grinning. "Bet you didn't know I was a Bible scholar, either."

She was right. Dawn had always been more religion-minded than me, but I never thought that she might have any working knowledge of the Bible. Never in a million years, actually. I suppose I was gaping.

"Okay, okay. I'll confess. I didn't study to be a nun or anything. Not even Catholic. But when I was a kid, we had to go to Baptist Bible School all the time, and I was particularly fascinated about Daniel. Lion's den and all that, and a few things just stuck. We used one of those hefty King James Bibles with all the cool pictures, and Daniel was, well, a major stud to a twelve-year-old girl. I remembered that the angel Gabriel kinda bailed him out. Listen to this. 'And he informed me, and talked with me, and said, O Daniel, I am now come forth to give thee skill and understanding.'"

"Jesus," I said, not realizing how inappropriate the word might be under the circumstances. "What's 'oblation'?"

"An offering to God, silly boy. Want me to yank out the *Webster's Unabridged*, too?"

"So tie all this together for me."

"Gabriel bailed Daniel out of a bind. Came down out of heaven and talked to him. That reference, I'll bet, was aimed straight at Charles Satchley."

"Wonder if he picked up on it, maybe just didn't say anything."

"Detect any sparks of recognition?"

"The only sparks in that room were from Denny's electronics. They were a bunch of weary puppies."

"It could just be coincidence, but the reference is so obscure I'd have to believe that it was intentional, like it was almost a signal or, at the very least, some kind of clue, or even a plea. Maybe it's time you talked to the reverend again."

- - -

After more than enough assurance from Dawn that Aaron would be well cared for, I headed home, only now conscious of the fact that it was about three a.m. No sense in talking to Satchley until later in the morning, and everything seemed to be catching up with me.

I was so tired I almost forgot to re-chow Bogie's dish, and didn't think to look at the answering machine until I was ready to crawl into bed.

The digital readout showed *4*, and I punched the button.

It took it a full minute to rewind. Brady making sure I got the package; the cable TV company about a late payment; somebody who sounded like Eddie not knowing what to say to the machine; then the long one.

"Cash, this one's especially for you. Here, honey." The sound of a phone being passed. "Mr. Cash?" Cissy's voice, maybe a little stressed. "I'm fine, Andrea is fine. Please just do what he asks and everything will be all right." Phone passed back. "There you go," Gabriel's voice again. "I know you're not stupid enough to bring the cops in on this, so I won't even say anything about that, but my advice to you is to let this thing play out, and we'll all walk away happy. Don't make it personal. Sorry your buddy got in the way, but them's the breaks. If anything happens to him, it's on your head. In fact, if anything happens to anybody, it's on your head. Understand?" Dial tone. Recording tape was beginning to play a major role in the Devore kidnapping case, like somebody didn't care or didn't realize the evidence they were amassing.

I picked up the receiver and punched Devore's number, got Carson's sleepy voice on the second ring.

"Carson?"

"Cash? What's up?" Trying to sound alert, failing miserably.

"Did Gabriel call back after I left?"

"No, we pretty much all hit the hay," he said; then added with some intensity, "Is there something going on?"

"Just a feeling," I said. "Don't worry about it. Go back to sleep. I'll be there in the morning."

No sense in telling him about Aaron or the message at this time of night. I had a feeling Devore and Satchley were primed for a plunge off the deep end, and I wasn't ready to light the fuse.

I hung up, looked in the drawer under the machine for a fresh tape, remembered the one I'd put in was the last in a two-pack, so I advanced it to the end, flipped it over to the other side, popping the little tab to preserve the used portion.

Maybe Gabriel was simply providing himself with a little insurance. I was so tired at this point I didn't know or care.

I set the alarm for eight o'clock and didn't remember my head hitting the pillow.

It occurred to me I'd almost lost all track of time since the day Cissy Devore walked into the office. After checking with Dawn on Aaron's status (okay and getting feistier), I had to double-check the calendar in the kitchen, where I found a couple of eggs and some cheese that hadn't molded yet, whipped up an omelet, and thought about things.

There was more to this case than it appeared; that, most of us knew. The trouble was deciding if it was some kind of setup, one that had maybe gone awry and become a real kidnapping, or if we were all players in an elaborate game.

Gabriel certainly seemed like the real thing. It didn't help that I knew practically nothing about Andrea Satchley, and there were hints that Charles hadn't been completely straightforward with me. I was going to have to do something about that.

I'd never once doubted Devore's sincerity through it all, which surprised me since I have an inherent distrust of rich people. Especially rich people who own banks. I suppose it had something to do with getting turned down for loans so often during my lifetime.

But Satchley; that was another issue. I think he was genuinely devastated by the turn of events, but there were elements that didn't fit. Dawn really got me stirring on the Bible thing, and I hadn't been able to get it out of my mind.

That, plus the adopted son's death, muddied the water a little where the reverend was concerned.

And on top of everything, there was the Joey Trenton situation, which prompted me to call the hospital.

Trenton was still listed in a room, probably with Eddie by his side, so I hung up when the operator switched me. All I'd needed to know was that he was still around. Eddie was something I'd deal with when the time came.

Popping the last bit of omelet in my mouth, I decided the next course of action was to get Satchley alone and ask some questions.

Accomplishing that task was going to be easier than I'd expected.

"Carson's gone to the bank. Said he needed to prepare for the next step and couldn't do it on the phone," Satchley told me at the front door. "Denny and I are standing guard, more or less."

I steered Satchley into the study, told him to have a seat, went to the kitchen, and told Denny he was on point for the moment.

When I went back to the study, Satchley was perched on the edge of the couch, looking a little edgy.

"Couple of things I need to clear up, Charles," I started.

"Whatever I can do, you know that."

"Then tell me about your son."

Satchley looked like he'd been struck by lightning.

"How did you know about Danny?"

"I'm a detective. I detect. My question is, why didn't you say something about it the first time we talked?"

"It wouldn't have had anything to do with what's going on right now. Or it doesn't seem so to me." He sat back on the sofa, trying to relax, failing miserably. "Danny's a chapter in our lives that we've both put behind us. His death was the Lord's will ..."

"Did it have anything to do with your wife's mental state?" I interrupted.

"No. Well, maybe some. Danny was adopted, so it had nothing to do with our sex lives, if that's what you mean."

"Do you mind talking about this?" Not that a negative response would have made any difference.

"It's not an easy part of my life, if that's what you mean, but, no."

"Then tell me what happened."

Raw emotion distorted Charles Satchley's otherwise handsome face as he related the tale.

Daniel was adopted through a Florida agency while his birth mother was still pregnant. The Satchleys got him when he was barely three days old.

"I know it wasn't possible, but he had physical traits that resembled both of us," Satchley said, making no effort to stop the tears. "He was a perfect, beautiful little boy, and we were as proud of him as if he were our own.

"Golden hair, blue eyes, and a smile that only God could have created," he continued. "Danny was actually the reason we formed the Primitive

Church ministry. We'd both decided that missionary work wouldn't be appropriate while trying to raise a child.

"He was six months old when the Lord took him from us," he said, voice lowering. "We had just gotten the house in Palm Springs and went there on vacation; Andrea, me, Danny, and Andrea's brother, Rayford."

"There's something else you didn't tell me about. The brother."

"Not much to tell about Rayford. He's never held a steady job; finally came to work for us at the church, working with youth groups, but he didn't fit well into that, either. Rayford Dowling is gay, almost militantly so, and our elders thought it best if we separated him from the young people," Satchley said. "He was infuriated, actually threatened to sue the church for discrimination, but eventually calmed down about it.

"He loved Danny as much as we did, and kind of became our live-in babysitter. In fact, Rayford was tending to him when the … the accident occurred."

"The accident?"

"Andrea and I had gone to a revival, left Danny at the house with Rayford. When we got home, we found Rayford asleep in front of the television. He'd fallen asleep watching cartoons with Danny, he said, but Danny had managed to crawl out of the house onto the patio.

"We found him floating in the swimming pool." Satchley paused, clearing his throat and wiping his eyes. "The paramedics said he'd probably been there an hour or more. No chance of revival.

"Rayford almost went crazy with grief, cursed God, eventually cursed us. Then, from about the funeral on, hardly ever spoke except when spoken to. Both Andrea and I went out of our way to assure him that we didn't think it was his fault. I don't know that we ever completely forgave him, and I know Andrea didn't.

"I don't think she spoke a dozen words to him privately after that, other than to acknowledge he was around.

"Rayford moved out of our house a year later, never went back to the Palm Springs house again for any reason, and eventually left the church and moved in with some friends in San Francisco.

"Neither of us has talked to him in, oh, probably six, seven years, other than a postcard every now and then. All we knew of him we got from

Andrea's mother secondhand. She died two years ago in Georgia, and Rayford just ceased being a part of our lives entirely."

"So your son's name was Daniel?" I was beginning to get a creepy feeling.

"Yes, Daniel Charles Satchley the Second, named after me. We called him Danny."

"Your first name is Daniel?"

"Yes, but I never use it. My father's name is Wilfred Daniel Satchley, and he's always been called Dan. My mother miscarried what would have been my older brother, who bore my father's name; so I inherited Daniel, and Charles was my grandfather's name on my mother's side."

"I probably shouldn't ask a minister this, but how familiar are you with the Old Testament?"

Satchley blanched again; gripped the edge of the sofa.

"Daniel and Gabriel. So you figured it out?"

"You know who Gabriel is, don't you, Charles?"

"You mean do I think it's Rayford?"

"What do you think I mean?"

"All right. Yes, I believe the kidnapper is my brother-in-law."

CHAPTER SEVENTEEN

"WHY DIDN'T YOU SAY something at the time?" I was trying to control my temper. It gnawed at my chest, but I thought I contained it well.

"I couldn't be sure," Satchley said. "Not, at least, until he gave himself a name. Only Rayford would have made the association with Gabriel. He was something of a Bible scholar. Brilliant, actually. Knows it better than I do."

"Can he harm your sister? Cissy? I mean, pardon my French, pastor, but what the fuck is this guy capable of doing?" Running a scam, with you and Cissy and the Primitive Church gang, I wanted to add but didn't.

"For all intents and purposes, Rayford is a stranger to my family. He's certainly a stranger to the Devores. Besides," he added, rubbing a hand across his face, "what is he capable of doing? I can't say. I haven't seen him in years.

"He was never a violent person. Never," Satchley said, sounding like he was trying to convince himself. "He should have no reason to want to get back at me or his sister. We forgave him."

"But he never forgave himself, and he left. Disappeared," I said. "A lot of things could happen in those years, make him a different person."

"You do believe I would have told you as soon as I was sure myself?"

"Charles, I don't know what to believe at this point. Your brother-in-law has kidnapped your wife and her friend; he's demanding a fifteen million dollar ransom; and, for all we know, he's even been mistreating one of them." I still didn't want to tell him about Cissy's message.

"To be perfectly honest, it was almost a relief to realize who it was," Satchley continued, appearing to ignore my remarks. "No, Rayford doesn't have the capacity to harm someone, I don't think. Anger, maybe, but physically aggressive just isn't in his nature."

"Have you stopped to think that he might have an accomplice?"

The question startled him. "No," he said. "That thought didn't cross my mind."

"What are we going to tell Carson?"

"The truth?"

"I don't want to have to say this, because I don't want to believe it, but this would make someone think you had a part in all this, Charles," I said as straightforwardly as I could.

"I suppose I should be insulted," he said, face sagging. "But you're right. It would look that way."

The look on his face told me it wasn't that way, and I softened.

"This does mean a whole new game plan, though," I said.

"Then let me be a part of it. Maybe I can persuade him ..."

"I don't think that's even remotely possible, but I've got an idea," I said.

And I told him.

- - -

Carson Devore didn't look like a man who'd just had fifteen million dollars assembled in small bills, placed in five large, silver-sided briefcases, and put in the trunk of his Mercedes.

We hauled the cash to a huge safe stuck in the corner of an office above the garage.

"Glad I kept this relic," Devore said, opening the big steel vault. "I couldn't see 'em melting it down. Saved it from the old Charlotte City Bank when they tore it down. Cissy thinks I'm crazy as hell for keeping it."

We stacked the briefcases inside. Money was heavier than I thought it would be. He swung the door shut, turned the big X-shaped handle and twirled the combination dial.

"Now what?"

"We go back to waiting. Or rather, you, Charles, and Denny go back to waiting. I've got some legwork to do that might keep me away for a couple of days."

Devore looked surprised. "A couple of days? What if he calls in the next hour? What are we supposed to do?"

"Give him the answers he wants, negotiate the drop or place, do whatever you need to stall him. I doubt he thinks you've gotten the money this fast, so that will buy you time. I'll check in with you periodically, see what's happening."

"You're the boss," Devore said, waving a hand dismissively. Then he looked me square in the eye and added: "If I think for a minute that delaying will bring any harm to our wives, I'll take this matter in my own hands. Just want you to know where I stand."

"Fair enough," I replied. "But don't do anything stupid. If it comes down to the wire and looks like we'll have to make a delivery, I'll get back here and we'll do it. All I'm asking is for you to buy me some time if you can."

I left in a hurry, mind racing, and drove straight to Aaron's house.

It took me a few minutes to tell him and Dawn about my conversation with Satchley; what I planned to do. Aaron allowed that it was so ridiculous it might work.

"Most heroes are dead, Houston," Dawn said as I headed for the door. She grabbed my arm, spun me around, and kissed me full on the mouth. Startling, to say the least. "Don't be a hero."

I steered the Sebring to the hospital, took the elevator to Trenton's floor, and ran into Eddie in the hall.

"How's the boss?" I asked him.

"A little better, I think," Eddie said, a small hint of relief on his face. "They got good doctors here."

"Good enough that he could spare you for a day, maybe two?"

Eddie looked at me curiously. "Maybe, I suppose." A hint of enthusiasm in his voice, possibly eager to get a chance to get out of the hospital for a little while. Tired of lumbering, frightening nurses maybe.

I pushed Trenton's door open and was surprised to see him sitting up in the bed.

"Cash! Damn. Maybe cheated death one more time. Thought I was gone for sure." Voice still gravelly, a little weak, but light years better than barely a few hours ago.

"Good to see you sitting upright, Joey," I said, not believing I said it. "You being in the pink again, mind if I borrow your boy?"

"Eddie needs a break. Sure. I'll be okay. What's this all about?"

"I'll tell you when we get back. Right now, we've got a lot to do."

A tall, attractive, blonde nurse walked into the room.

"Now I see why you're back from the dead," I said, grinning.

"Get the hell out of here, Cash. Nurse Willis, I got this place in my back …"

I left Trenton to his recuperation. Eddie followed me out of the hospital.

"Mr. Trenton's a tough guy," Eddie marveled.

"Yeah, Eddie, I guess he is."

"You mind tellin' me where we're goin'?" he asked as we walked through hissing hydraulic glass doors into the fresh air.

"Ever been to Alabama?"

CHAPTER EIGHTEEN

"Everybody down here barefoot, pick cotton?" Eddie said as I piloted the rented Buick LaCrosse through the inky darkness down Interstate 20 past the Anniston exit.

Eddie hadn't said much, just a few sporadic, profound declarations like that one. He'd actually surprised me with a wry sense of humor and a better grasp of things literate than I had expected when we took the Delta flight to Atlanta, rented the car, and hit the rolling Southern highway to Birmingham.

"Yeah, and everybody in Charlotte goes to a Baptist church and works in a cotton mill," I said.

"And everybody thinks I eat garlic by the pound, slick my hair with olive oil, and break fingers," Eddie replied, casting a sidelong glance my way. Our eyes met, and I'm pretty sure I detected a flash of indignation, noticed he didn't come across as very "dumbed down" when he dropped his guard.

"They're called stereotypes," I said.

"Whatever. I ain't as dumb as you think, am I?"

"Never thought you were dumb, Eddie; just subservient."

"Whatever that means. I got what Mr. Trenton calls 'street smarts.' You'd do good to remember that, Cash."

"I think you could probably call me Houston." I couldn't believe I was warming to the lug. Without the suit, he looked like a vacationing pensioner. We'd stopped at a mall on the way to the airport. Wasn't easy finding casual clothes for Eddie, but we finally found some jeans, a golf shirt, and a windbreaker at the Sears Big & Tall. He'd topped it off with a Yankees baseball cap, screwing it down on his head with a flourish, even laughed when he looked in the mirror.

"Cash is better. My last name's DiGiorgio, in case you ever write a book."

"Good Southern name."

"Yeah, well, my grandmother lived in Charleston, believe it or not. I grew up in the south Bronx, went to work for Mr. Trenton when I was fourteen. My pop got run over by a truck in a Teamster strike, and Mr. Trenton's looked after me ever since."

"Your mother still around?" I was getting into the history lesson.

"Nah, died last year in Miami Beach, God rest her soul. Mr. Trenton saw to it she had a good funeral. He's a better guy than you think."

Maybe now that he's dying, I thought. Back in the old days the declaration would have been true when pigs flew. "Sorry about your mother. Lost mine before I knew her. Joey talk to you about what he said to me?" Shifting the conversation to the present.

"Said a few things. Look, Cash, I can take care of myself. I try not to make Mr. Trenton think I got much smarts. He's the boss. Calls the shots." A tad defensive.

"Never doubted it for a minute." I didn't tell him that I was shocked to learn a brain lurked inside that massive head.

"Did peg you for a smartass, though. Maybe you ain't," he said. "One thing I learned since we moved south was that all cops ain't smartasses. Ex-cops either, I guess."

"I'll take that as a high compliment."

"Ain't so sure this plan of yours is gonna work, though," Eddie added. Ah, The Plan.

I decided after the most recent turn of events that the best way to nip Rayford Dowling's plot in the bud was to catch him off guard. We'd promised him we would lay back, but that was when we thought we were dealing with an unknown.

Now that I had a pretty good idea where things stood, I figured a stealthy approach was the only real answer. Aaron and I hadn't been sneaky enough in Atlanta, and I'm good at sneaky. Just didn't think we needed it at the time.

With Aaron on the sidelines, Eddie was my only choice for backup under the circumstances. Didn't need to get an Osmond family of co-conspirators going in case all this blew up in our faces. I felt that I could do whatever slipping around was necessary, use Eddie as the muscle for the grab.

I still didn't know whether Rayford was working alone, but I figured we'd deal with that when the time came. From the ten-year-old picture Satchley had given me, it was hard to tell how devious the skinny, smiling kid in the Polaroid might be. In the best-case scenario, Rayford was winging it alone. Worst-case, I doubt he could come up with help the shape and size of Eddie, who'd looked at the snapshot and muttered, "Don't look like a fag, but, hey."

The key right now was to move fast. As fast as possible.

Denny's phone trace turned out to be a Holiday Inn in Birmingham, and it was my guess that Rayford was still using the big Chevy I saw speeding away in Atlanta.

Seemed simple enough. Case the hotel, find the car in the parking lot, and wait. Holiday Inns weren't notorious for perks like room service, so Rayford or whoever would have to come out of the room for any supplies.

Eddie and I would jump him or his henchman in the parking lot, zero in on the room, and nab the girls. Case closed, life goes on, Devore can redeposit the dough.

If Rayford kept the same calling timetable, we should get to the hotel about the time he'd be dialing Devore. If Carson stalled him only for a little while, we should have plenty of time to make our move.

More ifs than I liked, but we were now dealing with a known entity, and I didn't think Rayford was sharp enough to figure out what was going on until it was too late. He'd let us slip up on him in Atlanta. I think that's why he got mad; didn't want to appear sloppy.

"There's the first Birmingham exit," Eddie announced. "We're lookin' for the third, right?"

"According to the map."

"There's two."

The third exit was on us in minutes. I slowed the Buick and we pulled onto a four-lane boulevard; lots of lights, fast-food joints, service stations. The Holiday Inn stood out like a beacon in the darkness. I pulled into the parking lot of a Best Western next door, parked, and we got out, stretched.

"What we don't want to be is obvious," I told Eddie.

He nodded, pulled out his Beretta, racked a round into the chamber, then tucked it in his waistband, pulling the jacket over it.

"We also don't want to shoot the guy if we can help it," I added, reaching around to pat the Glock and straightening my own jacket, a gray London Fog that matched my patterned shirt and black Dockers.

"What, no shoot to kill?" I saw Eddie grin under the ball cap. "It's my favorite sport."

I pulled out my handcuffs, dangled them with one hand. "We get him down, we get these on him, and we talk to him."

"Yeah, well."

"He's never seen you before, so why don't you walk through the parking lot, check it out. Should be a black Chevrolet Caprice, new, Georgia plates, maybe a rental sticker, I don't remember. I'll wait in the car."

Eddie lumbered into the darkness, pushing through a small hedgerow between the two hotels. As he moved toward the Holiday Inn parking lot, I heard a rumble, saw lightning blink in the distance. That's all we needed: a thunderstorm.

I sat behind the wheel of the car, played with the radio until I found a good station hidden deep inside a spectrum of country formats. Turned it down low and leaned back against the headrest. Eddie was gone maybe ten minutes, then appeared at the passenger side door, opened it, got inside.

"Storm's coming," he observed.

"Figuratively or literally?" I had to quit playing word games with him or he was going to get mad.

"I take it back. You are a smartass."

"I deserved that. So what did you see?"

"Only about fifty fuckin' Georgia tags. Anybody from Alabama live here? Three rentals, one a black Chevy, late-model, little sticker in the back window."

"Any people around?"

"Not that I saw. The rooms open up into the parking lot, though, and anybody coulda looked through a curtain. I didn't stop or anything, acted like I was going to a room, then cut back to here."

"See a place where we could sit and watch?"

"Go around to the end of the building, pull into a corner space. It's dark there and I don't think you can see it from the rooms."

I did, and he was right. Good view of the parking lot, too. I reached up, popped the cover off the interior dome light, extracted the bulb, and put it in my pocket. We settled back.

"Remember that night you followed me from the lounge?" I decided it was time to see how much I could tell Eddie.

"Yeah. You live in a nice neighborhood. Didn't mean nothin' by that, just doin' my job."

"I know. You made no secret of it. But something else happened that night."

"Yeah?"

I told him about the shot.

"No shit?"

"I knew it wasn't you, by the way. Aaron saw your piece wasn't threaded for a silencer that night you and Joey came by."

"Wondered why he was so interested," Eddie rolling his eyes, the expression saying "Do I look like I was born yesterday?" He studied for a minute, stroking the stubble on his chin. "Think it was that punk in the Camaro? He was kinda weedy lookin', but I don't know."

"Nah. Tossed his trunk, found a rusty shotgun, not much else. I don't think he was slick enough, either."

"Maybe this Rayford guy?"

"Could be, I suppose. Right now it's the only mystery still hanging out there." I told him about Claude Farnsworth, too. Eddie looking surprised.

"Damn. I suppose you do look sorta like a cop. Wonder why he'd be so hinky, though. They find a gun in the car?"

"Not that I'm aware of." Bouncing possibilities off a mobster's sidekick oddly didn't seem unusual at the moment.

"Maybe a pissed-off husband, somebody freelancin' another case?" Eddie was getting into the game.

"Too much coincidence. Far as I know, I hadn't left anything hanging."

"Some guy you busted when you were a cop?" Eddie was on a roll. "Jealous husband? You fuck around any?"

The only husband I could think of who'd dislike me enough would be Jerry Kline, and I couldn't picture him crouching in some bushes with a silenced pistol. Eddie was giving me some alternatives to think about, though, and it surprised me a little.

"Sounds like it ain't got anything to do with this, you ask me," he said. "Don't fit the pattern."

"Damn, Eddie. You might make a detective after all."

"Now I know you're a smartass. Want a licorice whip?" He pulled a plastic bag from a jacket pocket. "Started on these damn things when I quit smokin', now I'm hooked."

He pulled one out, folded it into his mouth, held the bag toward me. What the hell. I extracted one, popped it in, and started chewing, bringing back memories of my Little League days when we used to gnaw on licorice drops, pretending we were chewing tobacco, spit like the major leaguers. I couldn't suppress a smile.

"What's so funny?"

"Imagine somebody walking up, sees two big guys sitting together in a darkened car eating licorice."

Eddie laughed explosively, black flecks flying, some sticking on the inside of the windshield. I had to chuckle myself.

"Goddam, Cash," he said, catching his breath. "Weird shit go through your head all the time?"

"Just when I'm enjoying licorice whips with a mob goon."

Eddie hooted again, nearly choking. I powered down the window, spat the black, sweet wad onto the parking lot, trying not to laugh.

"This could be an *Oprah* episode," I said. "'Guys who chew licorice on stakeouts and the women who love them.'"

Had Eddie wheezing on that one. I slapped him on the back and he came around.

"You got a woman, Cash?"

"Nah, not really. You?"

"Never had much time. Lookin' after Mr. Trenton's been a full-time job.

There was a girl once, though. Sweet little white-bread chick …" His voice trailed off with the memory.

Things quieted down quickly; Eddie getting contemplative, maybe thinking about what it would be like to have a little woman waiting for him. Try as I might, I couldn't picture it. Soon there was nothing but the sound of Eddie's jaw working on another whip. I scanned the parking lot, trying to stay alert.

"Shit," Eddie said.

"What?"

"Cop car just pulled into the lot. Over there," he gestured toward the far end of the building. "Shinin' the spotlight on the cars."

Somebody could have called us in, I thought. More than likely just a patrol check. It looked like an umarked unit.

"Crank your seat back, that little lever on the side," I said, reclining mine. Our heads dropped below the windows seconds before the spotlight swept through the interior.

We listened as the car, a Crown Victoria, rumbled by. After a couple of minutes, I eased up, saw it leaving the lot.

"Private company," I said. "Probably hotel security making a routine sweep. Occupational hazard. I doubt he'll be back for a while."

"Apparently our boy watches for him, too," Eddie said, pointing toward the middle of the building where a door opened, someone stuck his head outside. "That him?"

The man, slight build and wearing what looked like a jogging suit, eased onto the walkway, letting the door close behind him. From here he looked like the guy in Atlanta, but fifty million people looked like the guy in Atlanta. Couldn't tell if he matched the photo.

"Maybe, maybe not. Let's see where he goes," I said.

Four eyes tracked the man as he walked into the parking lot, casual but looking around. He stopped beside a black Caprice, fumbled with a key, opened the door.

"That's the car. We follow him or take him out here?" Eddie ready, tense.

"If we jump now, he could possibly get inside, take off. Then we'd be screwed. Let's wait a minute."

The man got inside the car, leaned across the seat and appeared to be getting something from the glove compartment. He sat upright, looking down in his lap, fiddling with something, then turned to get out, an object in his hand. A gun maybe? It was hard to tell.

"We need to get him before he gets back to the room," I said, gently opening the door. "If that's a gun, do what you gotta do but try not to kill him."

Eddie grunted, opened his door, and we both rounded the hood of the Buick, slow at first, closing the distance. The guy was facing away from us, then froze, maybe hearing our footsteps.

Without looking around, he started sprinting for the door, maybe twenty feet away. Eddie blew past me, moving remarkably fast for a man his size. The man stopped, wheeled around. I heard what sounded like a cat spitting; Eddie feinted right, then barreled forward. He nailed the man not ten feet from the door, hitting him at the knees and knocking him on his back, Eddie crawling on top. They had gone down in a heap and I heard the spit again as I ran up. Eddie grunted.

The man worked an arm free; something in his hand. My heel came down on his wrist and he shrieked, loosing his grip. A pistol clattered across the sidewalk, heavy with a silencer.

Eddie clubbed him in the back of the head with his Beretta. The guy's head lolled, then rested on the concrete, quiet. I pulled out my handcuffs, ratcheted one against the man's free hand, and twisted. He started to groan, and Eddie slapped a paw across his mouth. I worked his other arm free from Eddie's bulk and closed the other cuff tight, dragging him partially free of Eddie by the chain, making sure the guy was out. He was.

Remarkably, no curtains opened, nobody came running out.

"You okay?" I noticed Eddie wasn't getting up.

"Yeah. Missed me. Mighta twisted my knee," he said to the sidewalk. "Go for the door."

I fished through the man's pockets, found a key, and walked to the door, pressing my ear against it first. No sound inside, but a light was on.

For the second time in what seemed like only a few hours, I braced to open a hotel room door not knowing what was on the other side.

I twisted the key and pushed, pistol in my free hand.

CHAPTER NINETEEN

I WAS LYING FLAT ON my back, staring up at a stippled ceiling. Somewhere a television was tuned in to what sounded like an old sitcom. People were laughing sporadically. I blinked against the harsh glare of a light coming from somewhere.

I raised my head to look around. It felt like somebody had driven a spike through the top of my scalp and I quickly lowered my head back on what felt like a carpeted floor, left it there for a minute and raised up again, this time looking around.

It took me a minute to realize I was on the floor of a hotel room, half in, half out the door. Raining outside, hard. Blink of lightning, crack of thunder.

Slowly and not without pain, I raised up on an elbow, then knees, then on my feet, swaying a little. I grabbed the open door for support. Holiday Inn, Birmingham, my brain was signaling through the fog, synapses firing slowly. Room. Guy with gun. Eddie. Eddie? I plodded outside, stiff-legged, looking both ways.

Two figures, lying in a heap on the walkway. Someone talking in the distance, couldn't tell where. I reached up to my forehead, brought my hand back; blood. Damn, the pain. Throbbing. My foot struck something and I looked down, saw my pistol at my feet; bent over, woozy, picked it up. Clip still in. I put it back in the holster and lumbered, unsteady, to the figures on the walk, eyes trying to focus.

Shit. Eddie and that guy. Eddie still on top, face down. I nudged him between the shoulder blades.

In a flash, he rolled over, right arm flailing. I blocked it. "Whoa, boy. It's me. Cash," I said.

Eddie looked up at me, eyes glassy. "What the hell happened?"

"From the looks of it, I'd say we were both cold-cocked." I looked around, and about five feet south of Eddie's feet was some kind of metal pipe. I walked over, looked. A chromed shower curtain rod, best I could tell. Dented about halfway, maybe a few flecks of blood. Picked it up. Heavy. A cheap chrome rod with steel rebar inside, probably bulked up by the hotel people so it wouldn't bend from towels and clothing being hung on it. I glanced at the row of parked cars. The Chevrolet was gone.

Eddie sat up, touching the back of his head, mumbling something.

"You went through the door, I heard a noise, somebody comin' toward me," he said. "Before I could get up, wham. Right in the back of the head. Saw stars, I think. Footsteps haulin' ass."

"Could you see who it was?"

"Nah. Too quick. More'n one, I'm pretty sure."

"Male or female?"

"Beats the shit out of me."

The other figure stirred and I rolled him over. Rayford Dowling, without a doubt. Eyes closed, not quite back with us.

"You steady enough to help me transport ol' Ray here inside?"

"Yeah, but I'm gonna need a bottle of fuckin' aspirin soon."

We carried the semi-conscious Dowling into the hotel room, tossed him on the bed. Eddie, limping a little, disappeared out the door; came back holding the silenced pistol by the trigger guard, laid it on the dresser to the right of the room.

"Looks like we solved your riddle," he said, gesturing toward the gun.

"Go get some ice. We need to wake up our guest, have a little chat."

To my amazement, all the activity didn't seem to have stirred a soul at the Holiday Inn, or at least kept everyone behind their secure curtained windows and double-locked doors. Could have been the hour, I supposed, looking at my watch. A little after midnight. The humming air conditioners probably masked the noise we'd made. It wasn't exactly a no-tell motel, but I could see where a Holiday Inn in Alabama might draw a don't-get-involved crowd.

I glanced around the room. Overnight bag on the dresser, unzipped with a few things inside. Some clothes scattered around. That faint perfume smell competing with an antiseptic odor.

Eddie came back with a little plastic bucket brimming with cubes, shut the door.

"Lemme see your head," I told him, wetting a towel. I dabbed at the base of his skull, turning the towel a sickly pink. "I think you'll live."

"Looks like you got the worst of it. Turn around," he said, taking the towel. I winced when he touched the top of my head. "Got a knot comin' up."

We found no holes in either of us, so Rayford's shots apparently went wide.

I took the ice bucket and dumped its contents on Rayford's face. He spluttered, blinked, squinted against the glare of the room lights.

"What? Where am I?" He raised his arms, saw the cuffs, let them fall to his chest. "Oh, yeah."

"Rayford Dowling, I presume?" I said, Eddie moving around to the other side to loom.

Dowling squinted, turned his head to look at both of us. "Bobbsey twins," he rasped.

Not harboring much patience at the moment, I took his jaw in one hand, twisted his face toward me. "You feel like talking? Good," I said, not waiting for an answer. "How's about we start with your roommates."

"Which one of you is Cash?"

"Figured you'd know that already." Squeezing his jaw a little for emphasis.

"If you don't mind moving your hand." He reached up. Eddie grabbed the cuff chain and jerked his arms back down with his left hand, brought the Beretta around with his right, and pressed it between Dowling's eyes.

"We ain't in the mood for bein' nice," Eddie said. Dowling looking startled.

"Okay, okay. Tell your gorilla to remove the gun, Cash." Eddie responded reluctantly. "Could I have some water?" I nodded at Eddie, who retrieved a plastic cup from the bathroom sink, handed it to me. I tipped it to Dowling's mouth, he swallowed, coughed. "Thanks."

"Now, where were we?" I said.

"Where are the girls?"

"Thought you'd be able to tell us that."

He looked at us again, squinting, faking a daze now, I think. "You mean to tell me they overpowered you two goons?" He started to laugh, more like a shrill chuckle. "Son of a bitch."

"Somebody decided to make like Sammy Sosa with a curtain rod," I explained. "Took us by surprise."

"Andrea used to play softball in the church league. Guess she hasn't lost her touch," he said.

"Want to tell us why a kidnap victim would use her rescuers for batting practice?"

"Haven't you figured this out yet, Cash? This never was a kidnapping. Not really, anyway. Andrea engineered the whole thing."

I think Eddie was the only surprised one in the room. For me, the pieces of this puzzle were beginning to fit at last, but somehow I didn't feel redeemed. I'd actually wanted to believe Cissy was in distress.

"Now that we've got you, that kinda screws things up, doesn't it?"

"Hardly." He was smiling and I didn't like it. A sneer, actually, obviously amused.

"Want to explain that?"

"Devore's already made the drop. I'd guess right now your victims are on the way to pick it up, and when they get it, it's goodbye fifteen million, farewell the misses Devore and Satchley forever. They're gonna disappear like …"

Before he could finish I was grabbing the phone, punching Devore's number. Carson answered.

"Good news, Houston," he said, sounding cheerful. "We've paid the money and the girls are on the way home. We've been trying to find you but didn't know how to call. Figured you'd check in.

"Sorry I had to act on my own, but, well, it seemed like an opportunity …" Devore feeling good about himself, decisive.

"How long ago, Carson? Where?" I interrupted.

"Let's see, it's been a good three hours. I left the money in the trunk of Cissy's car in the airport parking lot."

"Is anybody watching it?"

"Gabriel said if he saw anyone around, it'd be over. No, I didn't want to take that chance. Cissy's supposed to call when the swap is made, then Charles and I will pick them up."

"Not to put too fine a point on it, Carson, but you've been had."

Silence on the other end.

"Get somebody to the airport fast," I told him. "Go yourself if it would be quicker. I'll explain later. Eddie and I have got Gabriel. It's a setup."

"But the girls …"

"Go. I'll try to explain later. There may still be time."

I gave him the room number and he hung up. I started pacing, calculating some times in my head. It would be close.

"There's no way he'll get there in time," Dowling said, watching me. "We'd already booked the flight to Charlotte earlier today. Private charter. It was a member of Charles's church, as a matter of fact. Real helpful, particularly after Andrea told him it was urgent. What time is it?"

"Pushing one a.m.," I told him.

"They should be unlocking the car right about now," Dowling said with a crooked grin. "Tough titties, Cash.

"Might as well undo these things," he continued, raising the cuffs. "I've played my role. I'm not going anywhere."

"Not until you do some explaining," I said, unable to mask the frustration in my voice.

"At least let me sit up," he said, casting a sidelong glance at Eddie, who stepped back. Dowling fluffed the pillows, leaned back on the headboard. "Okay, ask away."

— — —

"First," I said, picking up the silenced pistol, "Where'd you get this?"

"Friend in San Francisco sells guns, made me the silencer."

"You do a little target practice at my house?"

"Yeah. Just a warning was all Andrea wanted, so there was never any intent to shoot you, just scare you a little. Saw the opportunity when you bent over. Bet I wasn't fifty feet away. Aimed high, by the way."

"Why?"

"Andrea was a little pissed when she learned that Cissy had hired you. She figured most PIs are just husband-chasers, so she thought a little message would inspire you to drop the case. Guess she was wrong."

I watched him talk, trying to decide if it was an act. He seemed relaxed enough; telling the truth, I guess. "Why the kidnap scenario? I mean, why go to so much trouble? Why didn't she just leave?"

"You've got to know Andrea. First, she wanted money and lots of it, which she wouldn't get from Charles. Plus she wanted to scare Charles; hurt him.

"It all goes back to Danny," he said, his face darkening. "Thought she blamed me, but all these years she's apparently been focusing her hate on Charles, particularly since he refused to adopt again.

"So, anyway, out of the blue a few weeks ago, Andrea calls me, asks me if I could help her with something," he continued. "I was unemployed, she said she could provide me with some 'serious money,' as she put it.

"Said she had this friend whose husband was rich as Croesus and who she had wrapped around her little finger. Andrea's good at that. She's done it to me for most of our lives. Everybody wants to please Andrea and I can't really say why, because she's spiteful."

"But why get Farnsworth involved? Why did Cissy hire all these people to follow her around?"

"Farnsworth was going to be her henchman, she thought, until she began to realize he really had 'found the Lord,' as Charles likes to put it," Dowling said. "She was going to get rid of him—figuratively, by the way—until he conveniently did it for her.

"As for Cissy," he said, "I can't tell you much. I was keeping an eye on her for Andrea, making sure—and these are Andrea's words—that she didn't 'stray.'

"Then I saw all these people popping up; then you, and Andrea got nervous, told me she wasn't worried about anyone but you. She didn't like the idea of a professional getting involved. That's when she asked me to scare you off and, well, you know the rest," Dowling said, beginning to sound weary.

Now the important part, at least to me. "What was Cissy's role in all this?"

"She didn't have a role," Dowling said. "In fact, I doubt she's too clear on the whole kidnapping thing. At least she wasn't at first. That was Andrea's baby.

"We kept Cissy in the dark. The whole slapping and groaning thing, that was Andrea's idea. She did a pretty good job, didn't she?" He half-grinned. "My whole pissed-off routine was an act, Cash. I mean, I was acting for a few million bucks, and I'd done some theater in San Francisco. Convinced you, too, didn't I?"

I frowned. "There's been a touch of phoniness to this whole thing, right from the beginning. I just can't understand Cissy conning her husband."

"Oh, she didn't know about that, I'm pretty sure." Dowling said, surprised. "Cissy thinks the money's coming from Charles and that she'll be able to call her husband and explain everything when it dies down. She doesn't have a clue as to the amount Andrea wanted. 'Back alimony' is how I think Andrea referred to it. It has been almost like a game to Cissy, really. As smart as I thought she was when I first met her, in a lot of ways she's like a little girl that has to be led along. By now, she's more than likely wising up, though.

"Like I said, Andrea had it all put together in that devious little brain of hers. It was her idea to tack on the extra five mil, trying to see how far she could push it."

"But what about Cissy's calls to me?"

"First one we didn't know about. She was, I suppose, going to tell you about her and Andrea running away. Andrea caught her on the phone, pulled the cord out of the wall, chewed her out. Told her it was her way or the highway. You should have seen the look on Cissy's face, like a scolded puppy," Dowling explained. "The second call we staged, told her it was to keep you off the trail because things were getting too hot, what with the Atlanta surprise. She was eager to do it, like she was making up for the first call to you.

"That whole second line was taped, which is why we didn't give you a chance to talk to her," he said.

"Damn," was all I could say. "What happens when they get the money and Cissy wants to talk to Carson?"

"Andrea hasn't figured that one out yet."

I just looked at him with a blank expression.

"Want my opinion?" Dowling asked.

"Sure. Why not."

"When Andrea gets her hands on that dough, her next master plan will be how to get rid of Cissy Devore."

CHAPTER TWENTY

WE DISPATCHED EDDIE TO get us something to eat. While he was gone, the phone rang and a nervous front desk clerk asked if anything was wrong. Somebody must have called after all. I told him there'd been a small domestic dispute that was resolved; thanked him for his concern.

I uncuffed Dowling, obviously no longer a threat, and he took a shower, changed into a clean track suit from the overnight bag.

"Out of curiosity, where'd you get the gorilla?" Dowling asked, amused.

"A friend of a friend. Aaron, as you know, was out of commission," I said.

"Sorry about that. I just meant to push him out of the way. I'm not exactly the thug type," Dowling said.

"I'll be sure to tell him that," I said flatly.

"No, I mean it. I told Andrea early on I didn't want to get involved in any rough stuff."

"What do you call shooting at somebody, that anger crap on the phone?"

"If I'd wanted to hit you, I could have," he said. "Four years of military school, expert marksman and all that.

"The gun was another of Andrea's ideas and it was easy for me to get, but I told her up front no fireworks, that it would be for show. The warning shot was as far as I said I would go, and it seemed appropriate at the time."

"Yeah, well. The two shots in the parking lot …"

"Self-defense. Honest to God, I didn't know it was you guys. Actually thought I was being mugged." He waved a hand dismissively. "Somebody trying to roll the queer."

"Queers don't wear signs," I said, argumentative.

"Past experience," Dowling said, looking me square in the eyes, then tried to affect a heavy Southern accent. "Alabama boys don't like no quares.

"As for all the phone stuff, that was acting," he concluded with a Jon Lovitz flourish. "Putting on a show for Andrea, pulling one over on Charles. In truth, it was fun."

And convincing, I didn't say.

We watched *Headline News* until Eddie returned, carrying a large bag stuffed with cheeseburgers and fries, another bag with three large Cokes.

The three of us made quick work of the burgers, which Eddie chased with a handful of aspirin, all the time eyeing Dowling warily. I popped a couple of ibuprofen gelcaps, and the throbbing began to subside.

"What I can't figure," Eddie said, commenting for the first time, "is why go to all this trouble? I mean, couldn't the woman have just stolen the money from the church, made a clean split? Her husband woulda covered for her."

"I guess it's just Andrea's way," Dowling said. "Do everything dramatically, make it unforgettable. She had it all figured out. She was sure nobody'd raise a stink because of the people involved, never once thought you'd call the police. 'Fear of impropriety,' she called it. It was a gamble, I suppose, but Andrea gets excited when there's risk involved."

"Gamble, huh? Think that's what she'll do with the money?" Eddie curious; familiar with gamblers, no doubt.

"Wouldn't be surprised. Andrea likes chance. Went wild once in Vegas, nearly cost Charles his ministry."

"Goes wild with shower curtain rods, too," Eddie said, rubbing his head. "Wonder how Miss Devore took that."

"Probably scared the shit out of her, especially when she saw who it was," Dowling mused.

The phone interrupted our conversation and I picked it up. Devore, sounding like a kid who'd just lost his bicycle to the neighborhood bully.

"The car's gone," he said. "The girls weren't there, either."

"Sit tight," I told him. "We'll be there in the morning. Time to make new plans."

"What the hell's going on, Houston? Will we ever see our wives again?" he asked, dejected.

"If you mean are they in danger, the answer's no. I'll explain when we get back. Think you can send the company jet to Birmingham?" I gave him the number of the airport from the phone book.

"It'll be there in two hours or less," Devore said. "Tell me something, Houston?"

"Got a whole lot to tell you and Charles. Get some sleep and don't worry. Houston Cash is still on the case, for what it's worth," I said, trying to sound reassuring, more energetic than I felt.

I hung up the phone and turned to Dowling. "You still hoping for that money?"

"It would be nice, but I think I'd rather just become one of the good guys, put my short criminal career behind me."

"Don't mind going up against your sister?"

"At this point in my life, I'd consider it a privilege. I'll even work for minimum wage."

"Then let's check out of this place," I said, standing. "We've got some work to do."

CHAPTER TWENTY-ONE

Trying to convince Carson Devore his wife had initially escaped him willingly was like trying to make the pope believe Mother Teresa sold crack.

"I'm sorry, Houston, but there's just no fucking way, if you'll pardon my French," an irritated Devore said, red-faced. "I don't know what this guy has told you," he said, motioning toward Dowling, "But Cissy wouldn't be a part of something like this. She just wouldn't."

Our reunion had started explosively, particularly when the sparks flew between Satchley and his brother-in-law when Dowling followed me into the Devore house. We'd dropped Eddie off at the hospital, where he planned to get his noggin looked at after checking on Trenton. He tried to convince me to get an X-ray, too, but I'd had worse headaches, and declined.

Satchley also couldn't fathom betrayal by his wife, though he ultimately admitted that she "might still harbor some bad feelings about the past, but I can't believe she would go to this extreme." Knowing as he said it that his wife was probably fully capable of what she was doing, maybe hoping for the best.

"You're going to have to believe it, Charles, because it's true," Dowling said, not masking the scorn in his voice. "I don't know, maybe she's gone around the bend, but you know and I know that she's capable of it."

To Devore, Dowling was a little gentler. "Mr. Devore, I couldn't honestly say that your wife wasn't a willing participant at first, but I don't think even Andrea could hide what's going on at this point.

"I'll admit," he said, becoming introspective, "when I first got into this deal, it looked like fun. I wanted to see you squirm, Charles, and the idea that we could get this kind of money, well, you can't imagine it unless you've spent a large part of your life with no money at all.

"Andrea convinced me it was just a drop in the Devore bucket; made me believe that, once the smoke had cleared, everybody would resolve their separate problems and things would be hunky-dory, happy ending, case closed, and I'd have enough money to disappear for good," he continued. "Now I know that's so much bullshit, and now I want to help make things right."

Neither of the husbands looked like they were buying Dowling's sudden conversion, but on the trip back to Charlotte I'd become convinced that Rayford really didn't care anymore. The fun was gone. It was like a junkie emerging from the other side of a bad trip. He was exhausted and ready to play whatever game we came up with, ready to even the score with his sister for dragging him into the web.

Devore stood up and started pacing. "So now we've got a kidnapper we can't turn over to the police, our wives are still at large and have enough money to disappear forever if they want, I may find that I owe a favor to a thug …"

"Neither Eddie nor Trenton want anything out of this," I interrupted, wanting to shift the conversation away from what-ifs and toward what we needed to do now. Nor did I want to get into my Joey Trenton "inheritance," where Eddie was concerned. That part of this story had shifted away rather dramatically from the Devore-Satchley case.

"So you say," Devore said.

"What we've got to deal with now, Carson, is finding the women, maybe getting your money back …"

"I don't give a rat's ass about the money," he shot back.

"Okay, the women are the priority, of course. Agreed?"

Everyone nodded. Even Dowling, but I let the irony pass.

"Rayford here says Andrea likes games of chance. Any truth to that, Charles?"

Satchley fired a narrow-eyed glance at his brother-in-law, then nodded. "She had a problem with gambling once, it's true."

"Problem? Come on, Charles," Dowling started.

"No more arguments!" I was surprised to hear myself shouting, which I didn't do often. Startled looks all around. "Personal disputes, doubts, whatever. All that's out of the picture until Cissy and Andrea are brought home, safe and sound."

"Here, here," Aaron said, walking into the room. "Now somebody want to tell me what the hell's going on? Who's this guy?" He gestured toward Dowling.

"I'm the kidnapper," Dowling said cheerfully, extending a hand Aaron instinctively took, then dropped. "Glad to meet you. Rather, glad to see you on your feet."

"Atlanta," was all Aaron could say, looking at me with widening eyes.

"You and me have got some talking to do," I told Aaron as I took him by the arm and steered him down the hall. "Gentlemen," I said over my shoulder, "you're at ease for a while."

-    -   -

It took me a good thirty minutes to bring Aaron up to speed and for him to assure me he'd recovered well enough to get back into the hunt.

"Son of a bitch," he finally said, a touch of awe in his voice. "Mrs. Satchley turns out to be the wild card."

"Funny you should put it that way. Feel up to a trip to Las Vegas?"

-    -   -

Both Devore and Satchley insisted on being a part of what we were now calling "Phase Two" of the investigation, and nothing would change their minds.

"We've got more at stake in this than anybody, and if you want to argue about it you can just resign and we'll do it on our own," Devore told me as the two of us weighed the situation in the study while Charles had a word of prayer in the kitchen with Rayford, and Aaron briefed Denny on what would be the home base operation.

I knew it would be useless to spar with the ex-marine, but I informed him that the preacher might be a little out of place where we were going.

"Which is?" Devore asked.

"The obvious choices are Atlantic City and Las Vegas, based on what Dowling's told us," I said. "There are other casinos, but if you had a yen for gambling and a trunkful of cash, where else would you go?" I didn't tell him I knew Andrea had been to Vegas and, in my way of thinking, would probably go back there. It might come up in conversation with Satchley later, but by then, I hoped, we would be wrapping this up.

"I know my way around Atlantic City," Devore offered. "I'll keep Charles out of the spotlight. Maybe a disguise or something."

"Okay, then, you and Charles can go to New Jersey; me, Aaron, and Rayford will fly out to Vegas, if that suits you," I said, trying to picture the television evangelist wearing glasses, a big nose, and a mustache. "We're leaving Denny here on the off chance Cissy or somebody calls."

"If they're driving, we should get there ahead of them. Got any ground troops you can trust up there?"

"We merged with a Jersey bank last year, and some of my security people are in place. I could probably muster a few of them," he said.

"You're going to need to blanket the casinos, share some current pictures with your people and, while you're at it, make a couple dozen for me. I worked on a case with the Las Vegas police department a few years ago and can probably get a little help for our contingent."

"What're we going to tell these people, Houston?"

"Use your imagination. Hell, tell 'em you've got a runaway wife with an accomplice. At this point, it doesn't really matter. Just stay away from the police and don't let anyone do any grabbing but you and, for God's sake, grab Andrea first if you can."

"So you don't think Cissy's running?"

"I don't think she is now, but we won't know until we find them, will we?"

"I guess not," Devore said, a touch of dejection in his voice.

"There's something you've got to understand, Carson. Cissy had to be in some kind of state of mind to embark on this adventure and she might not be the same woman you thought you were married to. I don't know and you don't know, but be prepared to deal with her not wanting to come back."

"I suppose you're right."

"What I'm trying to say is that she may not leap into your arms. This isn't a 'kiss and make up' scenario. For all we know, they'll run like hell as soon as they see you."

"I love her, Houston," Devore said, eyes welling. "All I want to do is see her. If she doesn't want to come back, then maybe at least she'll be willing to talk. And if you're the one who finds her and she doesn't want to come back, well, don't force her."

"I won't."

"One more thing," he said, touching my arm as we turned to leave the room. "Tell her I love her and all I want is for her to be happy, even if being happy means being away from me."

I stood there for a minute looking at this diminutive, scrappy man who'd built one of the country's largest banks. The expression on his face told me he'd give it all up for his wife, and it was a picture I swore silently I'd share with Cissy Devore, regardless of the outcome.

CHAPTER TWENTY-TWO

GARTH BROOKS HAS FRIENDS in low places. I do, too, but some of my friends aren't so low on the totem pole that I can't occasionally climb up to their perches and ask a favor or two.

Lieutenant Pick Sanders of the Las Vegas Police Department was one of those people. I'd helped him chase down a suspect in a six-state burglary ring back in the good old days, and Pick, short for Pickford, had never forgotten, especially when I showed up in Vegas to testify and helped him put the suspects away for fifty years or so.

Getting him to have his squad cars watch for a green Mercedes convertible with North Carolina tags in his bailiwick wasn't a problem. He asked no questions when I told him I only wanted to know where it was, "nothing actionable," I said, still trying to sound like a cop.

Pick knew I'd gone private and, better still, knew why. Ex-cops with bones to pick in the upper echelon probably make up the largest of the badge-toting fraternities.

"Lemme know when you get out here," he said on the phone, a strong Brooklyn twang still in his voice after twenty-five years in the desert. "We'll go get a steak, talk about old times. Bring that sorry-ass Drake with ya, too."

I'd relayed the message to Aaron after we had deployed our troops. A call to Eddie brought the surprising news that Trenton was being allowed to go home. Eddie was eager to help nurse his boss back to health.

On the plane west, I shared my observations about Eddie with Aaron. Devore had booked us first class on US Airways, but as a concession to Satchley he'd put Rayford in coach, swearing they were the only available seats. Once we got to the airport Rayford took it calmly, particularly when he saw the guy he was sitting beside.

"You're saying Eddie's not the pug you thought he was?" Aaron sounding doubtful.

"Appears slow rivers run deep, even when it comes to hoodlums, as Carson calls them," I said, grinning. "Make no mistake. They've been the bad guys for a long time, but I guess Eddie's as on the up and up as he can be."

"Damn. Next thing you'll be telling me is you and Frank Malone have buried the hatchet."

"Oh, didn't I tell you about that? We're going into business together. Asshole & Son. Guess which one's the asshole?"

Aaron spit his bourbon and Coke on that one, dabbed himself with the little napkin.

"You think Dowling's on the up and up, I mean helping us and all?" Aaron asked, changing the subject.

"I believe he'd like to put his sister in her place, but, no, I won't trust him completely until all this is over. I think maybe he's got his eyes on the big prize."

"Yeah, that kinda money thins blood. You think Carson and Charles know you've sent them on a wild goose chase?"

"You never know," I replied, straight-faced. "Andrea might fool us all; head north."

"You know as well as I do that Vegas is the flame for that moth. She'll want to go back there, strut around where she lost before, prove to them or herself she's got enough juice to break the bank now. It's a gambler's addiction. Go back to the scene of the crime, so to speak."

"But she's also smart enough to weigh whether Charles would expect her to go there."

"Personally, my money would be on the theory that she won't think about Charles for a second, much less that he'd follow her. Or even care, for that matter. Cissy, on the other hand, is her big problem now," Aaron mused. "How's Satchley taking all this time off from the church, by the way?"

"Says they'd just taped a month's worth of shows and were getting ready for a vacation, that he won't be missed for a while. They do it a couple of times each year, head out to Palm Springs."

"Must be nice to be a TV man of the cloth."

"I don't know. Satchley's surprised me. I almost think he'd rather be on that prison ministry and out of the spotlight."

"You gonna become his organ player?"

"I see that knock on the head didn't affect your sense of humor. You haven't explained, incidentally, how you're so full of P&V this quickly."

"That ex-girlfriend of yours was drivin' me crazy. Had to get out of the house. I'm okay, really. Even got her to look after your damn cat while we're gone," he said, patting my arm. "You won't believe me, but I sure as hell wouldn't be doing this if I didn't feel up to it."

"I know. Old fart stuff. You're not getting any younger, all that." I didn't want him to know how I really felt; how pale he looked. How old, all of a sudden.

"Yeah, well, this old fart can still kick your rookie ass," he said, gripping my wrist for emphasis. It was a line he'd used often in our police days, and always elicited a grin from me.

"We'll put on an Indian wrestling exhibition for Pick when we get there. Take bets. It is Las Vegas, after all."

"Hey, that's not a bad idea. We'll book Caesar's Palace. It's still there, isn't it?"

"Beats me. I haven't been out here in, what, ten years, twelve? It isn't just the strip anymore, I'm pretty sure. Hell, they're blowing up hotels they built less than twenty years ago."

Aaron settled back in the seat, eyelids drooping a little. I was beginning to feel the effects of the past few days, too, fading a little.

"Maybe we'll skim a few grand off Andrea, spend a couple of days, hit the tables. I could use the time off," he almost whispered.

Before I could say anything, Aaron was nodding. Found myself fading, too.

The next thing we knew, the flight attendants were telling us to store tables and raise seats.

— — —

"This may work out better than I thought," Dowling chirped as we walked up the concourse. "Got a name and number."

Aaron looked at him oddly and I couldn't help but grin.

"Keep your mind on your work," I said.

"You're the guys got to sit in first class. I had to make do," Dowling said, confusing Aaron even more. Aaron Drake wasn't quite up to the twenty-first century yet and I figured I'd have to explain later.

A figure emerged from the crowd.

"Suppose anybody could find a half-assed cop around here?" Pick Sanders growled as we followed the herd to the baggage claim area.

"Best I can see, there's nothing but half-assed cops around here," Aaron said, extending a hand. Sanders almost pulled our shoulders out of the sockets pumping a beefy right arm, ignoring Dowling, who looked a little nonplussed until I introduced him as our "assistant," followed by another wrenching handshake from the burly Vegas detective lieutenant.

"Grip's a little limp there, fella," Sanders said.

"He's not a cop," I offered quickly.

"Yeah, well, still could use some time in the gym. How're you boys doin'?"

"Fine, Pick. How's the wife?" Pick Sanders had lucked up early in his career, married a Las Vegas showgirl who was either nearsighted or loved uniforms, then set about loving Pick, a union that produced four kids.

"Sandra's swell. Just wish I could get her to eat better. 'Specially after she said everything she ate went to her tits," he said, punctuating the remark with a burst of laughter. "You tell her I said that and I'll have the both of you sweeping sidewalks at the Golden Nugget in orange jumpsuits."

He grabbed Aaron's overnight bag while Dowling and I shouldered ours and followed him through the glass doors to a "No Parking" curb where he'd tucked his unmarked black Impala.

"Damn," Aaron said, sliding into the sleek car. "Vegas cops got it made."

"Won this one in a keno game," Sanders chuckled. "Where you staying? Or should I say you-all to youse guys from the Grits Belt?"

"MGM Grand, driver, and step on it," I said, trying to affect a dignified tone. "And that's the Country Ham Belt to you Joizy gize."

"MGM Grand? Shee-it, Corn Pone, you musta sold all the crops this year." Sanders produced a cigar, bit off the stub, lit it, and never missed a beat in the conversation as he steered through airport traffic like Mario Andretti piloting a New York cab. Dowling sat beside me in the backseat and held onto the armrest for dear life, looking a little green around the gills.

"Got a banker picking up the tab," I told him, then launched into the Cissy Devore–Andrea Satchley search mission, hitting the high spots and leaving out the Rayford Dowling/Gabriel the Kidnapper episodes, much to Dowling's relief. Basically, I just said the women had absconded with some of the banker's money and that Mrs. Satchley had a thing for the craps tables and such.

"Probably right about her wanting to return to the scene of the crime," Sanders said. "I've seen it happen a million times." What he didn't see was the cab driver flipping us the finger as he zoomed around him on the expressway. "I put a BOLO out with the squads, called it a special out-of-town investigation. Nothing's turned up yet, but I expect you two have a game plan," he said.

"More or less," I said. "Might need a hand along the way."

"I got comp time comin', so's all you got to do is call. You know that," Sanders said, chewing on the cigar, piloting the Chevy at around seventy with a pinkie. "You better come by the house, too, or Sandra'll be pissed."

"Wouldn't miss it for the world. How're the kids?"

"Pick Junior's goin' to UNLV in the fall; Deborah made all-state on the basketball team; Freddie's havin' a little trouble in math; and Pam, well, she's kinda gotten into the alternate scene a little, wants to pierce everything. Kids."

He whipped into the porte cochere of the massive MGM Grand Hotel, skidded to a stop beside a stretch Hummer that must have been eighty feet long, and popped his "Las Vegas Police Department OFFICIAL BUSINESS" card on the dash as a valet approached, spotted the sign, looked inside the car, and spun around, headed back to the Land of Big Tippers.

We walked to the front desk amid glitter and expensive clothing, and a clerk eyed us warily. "Cash, party of three," I said. He punched a computer keyboard, glancing occasionally at the four of us like we were from the planet Venus.

"Ah, here it is." He did a double take. "The Gable Suite, uh, Mr. Cash. May we assist you with your luggage?"

"Nah," I said, trying to be cool. Devore undoubtedly set us up in style, maybe tugged a few high finance strings. "We'll manage. Any messages?"

The clerk's fingers played across the keys. "Yes, one. Would you like it sent to your room or …"

"I'll take it now if you've got it."

He turned around, examined a section of narrow slots that looked like the backside of a post office tier, pulled out a slip of paper, and handed it to me.

"'In Atlantic City, having a wonderful time, wish you were here.'" Carson trying to be flippant. The message line followed by a phone number. I tucked the slip into a pocket of my Sears sport coat, the clerk spotting the label, turning up his nose ever so slightly.

A skinny bellhop who looked like one of the original Las Vegas settlers guided us to the suite, opened the door, walked inside, touching and adjusting things, turning on lamps. Bellhops always looked like they were doing something; figuring, I suppose, to justify the tip. I slipped a fiver into his hand when he gave me the keys on his way out. He glanced at it without expression.

"You need anything, sir, you let us know. Have a nice stay at the MGM Grand," he said curtly. Five bucks likely meant a piker in this place. I hoped the doorknob didn't hit him in the ass on his way out.

"Nice digs," Sanders said, ambling over to a monster fruit basket and extracting a handful of grapes. "You guys hungry?"

I tapped the room service number, ordered some steaks for me, Aaron, and Pike, a fruit plate for Rayford. No comment.

We made small talk until the food arrived, and all of us ate like it was our last meal. I told Pick about the tailor I was to see; he made a note.

"You three might as well relax until morning, unless you want to look around the hotel," Sanders said, stabbing the last piece of asparagus on his plate. "You look like you could use it. My guys are watching the roads. Anything shakes loose, we'll give you a call. I get off at eleven but they're supposed to call me if they see anything."

Sanders left, his departure followed within minutes by a knock on the door. A hotel employee handed me a valet claim check. Devore had had the car delivered to the hotel. A Hertz Cadillac. I was liking the man more and more.

"So what do you two want to do?" I asked my traveling companions as Aaron walked toward the master bedroom, looked inside.

"I see what I'm going to do. Pike's right. Won't be able to accomplish much tonight. If the women are driving they wouldn't be here before tomorrow for sure, maybe not until the day after," Aaron said. "If they ditched the car and flew, they're going to be checked in under phony names, probably, and may not come out until tomorrow.

"I'm gonna hit the sack," he said. "Two beds in here, one in the other. You snore, Dowling?"

"I can't tell. I'm always asleep. I'll take the small bedroom, though, so you guys will feel safe," he said, winking at me.

"Whatever," Aaron said, disappearing into the bedroom, then his voice from inside. "Damn. Thing's got two bathrooms. What a hotel." Another door shutting.

"I think I'll try to get some sleep, too," I told Dowling. "Might as well be on our toes tomorrow."

"I'll go down and scout the casino. I slept pretty good on the plane, need to work off the jet lag," he said. "This is the nicest hotel in town, so it might be the place Andrea would choose.

"If I see anything, I'll buzz you," he added, then slipped quietly out the door, a vision flashing briefly across my mind that he might not come back at all, then it disappeared. We had to trust him now, I suppose.

I heard the shower sputter to life in the master bathroom, took my duffel into the smaller one and stripped down, climbing into the glass-doored shower stall and twisting the knobs until a fine, steamy spray pounded my skin.

I toweled off and slipped into an MGM robe, walked into the big bedroom, and saw Aaron already face-down under the spread of one of the queen-sized beds.

I was asleep in minutes, thoughts of what lay ahead fading quickly from the fatigue.

CHAPTER TWENTY-THREE

THEY SAY THERE ARE at least a thousand light bulbs for every man, woman, and child in America in Las Vegas. I didn't feel like counting, and not a single one of them was going off in my head as I groped for a strategy to illuminate the whereabouts of Cissy Devore and Andrea Satchley.

Aaron and I had ordered up breakfast. Dowling, still sleeping after an apparent late night of exploration, didn't budge while we were showering and dressing, so I didn't bother him, happy he had come back. We were going to have to keep him out of sight anyway, because the minute Andrea spotted him I was sure they'd run like hell.

Dowling would be the home-base coordinator, staying in the room and manning the two phone lines until something happened. Once we had the women located, I knew I wouldn't be able to keep him away from the chase, confrontation, or whatever evolved; "locating them" being the key phrase here.

I wasn't feeling optimistic.

"Fifteen million dollars can buy you a lot of privacy, if privacy's what you want," Aaron mused, poking at his scrambled eggs. Hash browns were the closest the hotel could come to grits, so our acquired taste in the salty, pulverized hominy would go wanting on this trip. "Hell, it could buy you your own private casino."

"I think that's the key," I said. "Andrea's going to be wary, and there's a whole back room mentality in this town for the highest of high rollers. We're not going to walk into the Golden Nugget and find her pulling on slot machines. I'm hoping Pick'll get us through those back doors."

"Wouldn't doubt there are plenty of people in Vegas who owe Pick a favor, but there's probably as many more who don't," Aaron said.

"If he can get us a list, we can hit the *dos* first, then wing it with the *don't*s." I was saying "we" but knew it would be me. I wasn't completely convinced that Aaron was up to a full head of steam yet, so I'd pretty much already decided that he could do the soft legwork, hitting the public places. He'd probably argue, but it seemed to me one could work the high-rolling halls easier, not draw so much attention.

"Want to tell me how you plan to pull that off?"

"I'll let you in on a little secret. Carson is bankrolling me on paper. Said he would assure me a line of credit at any casino here; I've just got to call somebody at a bank here. Even told me I could spend some of it if I had to."

"That Carson. What a kidder." Aaron looked amused at the prospect of his protégé walking around Glitter City like some backwoods James Bond. "You gonna knock 'em dead in your Sears sport coat? Or is it J. C. Penney this trip?"

"Hey, I do the best I can," I protested, smiling. "Besides, Devore gave me an address. Said the tailor would have me outfitted first class by lunchtime. He's even lining up a limo and driver."

"You can't just look like a millionaire, you've got to act like one," Dowling said, walking stiff-legged into the room, hair mussed and eyes slightly bloodshot.

"And I suppose you're the one to give me lessons?"

"Damn straight. I was brought up to be the classy one in my family. Just never managed to get the bucks to back it," Dowling said with a grin. "It's easy, really. All you've got to do is act like everyone else is lower class than you. Here. Let me show you. Shake my hand."

I extended my right hand, gripping Dowling's firmly.

"Now, see, that's all wrong. You take my hand …" he demonstrated, "then let it go like I've got smallpox." He released it like it was on fire.

I laughed. "I don't see why a millionaire can't be a normal person."

"A billionaire can be a normal person, however eccentric. Sam Walton wore Wal-Mart clothes and carried his lunch in a paper bag," he said. "Thing is, you're going to be newly rich and taking it to the extreme. Proud of it. Showing off. That's the only way you're going to fool these people. Yes, you'll be a bumpkin with a lot of dough and they'll see you as a mark," he said. Then, darkly, "But the second they take you to be a cop, private or otherwise, you're out the door and the word spreads like wildfire. You've got to remember, you're going to be dealing with people who the feds try to infiltrate on a regular basis, so they've made it an art form to detect phonies."

He had a point. A cop in Armani is a cop, but if I worked at playing out the rube angle, I should be safe.

"These can be mean people," Dowling continued. "Really mean. But if you curry their favor, they'll treat you like a sultan. That's why I think Andrea's here. They treated her like the Queen of Egypt and I believe it got to her, made her want to come back as a real queen."

"Fifteen million is pretty damn close to royalty where I come from," I agreed.

"Tell you what, you go to that tailor and get everything set up," Dowling said, plucking a croissant out of the bread basket and pulling off a corner. "I'll school your pal here on the geography of Vegas." He tottered back into the bedroom, returning with a fistful of what looked like brochures.

"I cleaned out the concierge's supply last night," he said. "Real friendly guy. Mr. Drake and I will know Las Vegas inside out by the time you're back."

Aaron couldn't help but grin, maybe softening a little from his first encounter with Andrea Satchley's brother. "You're not as dumb as you look, kid. And the name's Aaron."

"Very well, Uncle Aaron. Go get one of those fancy pens and notepads and get ready to learn about the flashy side of life," Dowling said, a look of relief on his face.

I dressed and headed for the address on Carson's note, Aaron and Dowling heavy into streets and boulevards as the door shut behind me.

This was going to be an interesting visit.

-   -   -

The tailor was a slight, thin, balding man who called his business

"Pierre Fuget" but admitted to me he was born Lennie Dershowitz in the south Bronx eighty-two years ago.

"When I told my business partner thirty years ago I was moving to the desert to set up shop in Las Vegas, he said 'Why don't you call yourself Pierre? Fuck it,' so I just took him at his word," he said with a wheezy laugh, the *word* sounding more like *woid*. "Carson told me he wanted me to make a silk purse from a sow's butt," he wheezed. "I t'ink he likes you."

Lenny stretched his measuring tape at all kinds of angles, put what looked like a half-made, inside-out jacket on me, drew chalk marks all over a pair of pants, fitted my size twelves in some pretty fancy, shiny tassel loafers ("They're all the rage these days") he said cost more than his first house in Brooklyn, then told me to come back at noon.

The shop was located in what passes for downtown Las Vegas, though I couldn't really tell where one set of lights ended and another began. Disney World for grownups, more recently catering to families, with explosive, special-effects entertainment that didn't do much to mask the real reason the city existed, which was to deprive as many people of as many dollars in as short a period of time as possible.

I wandered around looking at the people; every size, shape, and income level imaginable. A stooped old woman with frizzy white hair pushed past me, clutching a cloth bag like it contained her entire life, which it probably did. A panhandler leaning against a wall and staring bleakly at everyone who went by, glancing at me, and hustling away. Dowling was right about looking like a cop, and I knew I'd have to work on it.

On an impulse, I pushed through the door of a shop with a sign as subtle as they can get in Vegas that read "Unisex Makeovers by Felicia," with some kind of dual-sided profile picture. Inside, it looked like a barbershop, with three empty chairs in front of a long mirror, lots of towels, bottles with different-colored liquids, that odor of something pungent you hated when it was slopped on your hair.

In a meager attempt to make the room a little splashy, the proprietor had hung a few plants, stuck some god-awful artwork on the wall on either side of a pink beaded curtain in a doorway that led to another area I wasn't up to looking at. I was trying to figure out one of the paintings when the beads clicked and a seven-foot black woman appeared in a blonde wig and way too much makeup.

"May I help you, sir?" The woman said in a Darth Vader voice, obviating the fact that she was a he and didn't much care who knew it. On the police force in the old days, we called 'em "shims."

"I just needed a haircut, but I'm not sure I'm in the right place," I said, surprised at how sheepish it came out.

"Sweetie, you in the right place," he said, following it with a hearty, rumbling laugh. "You want a new look, I fix you right up. You want to keep that old look, which by the way look like shee-it, I do that, too. You fixin' to go undercover or somethin'?" He winked and flashed the biggest set of teeth I had ever seen.

"Oh, I'm not a policeman, if that's what you mean," I stammered, suddenly intimidated by this towering person.

"Honey, you maybe ain't no po-leese-man now, but you was at one time in your life or my name ain't Dee Dee." Another laugh, like that guy in the old Seven-Up commercials.

"Okay, you've got me on that one. Used to be."

"And you ain't from Kansas, Dorothy. That North Carolina I hear in that hush puppy voice?"

"Damn, you're good," I said, smiling in spite of myself. "Charlotte."

"Well, hush my mouth, baby doll," he said, gripping my arms and guiding me gently backward. "Sit your grits-eatin', hog-sloppin' and, might I say, tight ass right here in ol' Dee Dee's chair and he fix you right up."

I plopped in the middle chair, half dazed, while Dee Dee whipped a pink chiffon coverup over me and racked the chair back, my neck resting against a plastic sink indentation. I knew about a thousand people who would have given everything they owned to see me right now, and he must have read it on my face.

"Don't worry, sergeant, I ain't gonna eat you. As a matter of fact," he said, abruptly shifting vocal gears and affecting a British accent, "I believe I shall convert you into, oh, I don't know, perhaps Tom Selleck without the mustache or, now what was that guy's name, played Spenser on television … Urich! Robert Urich! Damned if you don't look almost just like him!"

He produced a nozzled little hose from somewhere and started dousing my head with warm, pleasant-feeling water, squirted something from a bottle, and started massaging my scalp. It actually felt pretty good.

"Why do I get the impression you're not who you seem to be?" I said.

Dee Dee reached under the chiffon and gripped my right hand with his. "Delbert DeLeon Stancil from Fayetteville, North Carolina, formerly first sergeant, Eighty-Second Airborne, deployed to Special Forces, 2002, retired, came out west and changed his life, sir!" he replied in a military staccato, then switched back to his African-American patois. "But don't you let that bother you none, now, heah?"

I laughed out loud, closed my eyes to avoid the spray. "Well, Delbert, you sure as hell changed your life."

"That's the way here in Las Vegas, darlin'. Ain't nothing what it seems. You want to change your hair color? I can make it temporary, only last maybe a couple of weeks."

"What makes you think I want to look different?"

"Honey, you walk in this shop lookin' like Dick Tracy, you not here for a trim."

"You've found me out, Delbert," I said, grinning. "What would you suggest?"

"It's Del, and I'd say somethin' subtle. Blonde or redhead and you'd stand out like a swingin' dick at a leather bar, you so tall. Your hair's brown, so I'd say let's make it darker, near black. You be surprised how different you look when I'm done. I throw a little on the eyebrows, too." He continued working, his huge hands amazingly deft and gentle. "Don't let this getup confuse you, neither. Del likes his women. This just a gimmick. You don't do shit in Vegas you ain't got a gimmick."

"Del, you're the biggest goddam gimmick I've ever seen in my life." That thunderous laugh again.

"Six-ten in my bare feet and can't play basketball worth a shit," he said, working away. "I answer that question before you ask it. Do with everybody."

I felt like I was in Floyd's Barbershop in the old *Andy Griffith Show*, only this Mayberry was somewhere on the other side of Oz. Casual conversation with Del came naturally, but anybody listening and watching would think they were having a bad methamphetamine trip.

"What you here for, anyways, Mr. Used to Be a Cop?" Del asked casually.

"Name's Cash. Houston Cash. I'm a private investigator now, working on a little case," I said, comfortable with the admission.

"It ain't no little case, you doin' this much, I don't think."

"I suppose not. It wouldn't make any headlines in the paper," I lied a little, "but I don't need to be recognized by the person I'm looking for." No point in going into detail on why I really wanted the change, which was simply not to look like a cop.

"Sugar, when Del through with your ass, your momma won't pick you out of a lineup," he said with another Seven-Up laugh.

Forty-five minutes later, Del spun the chair around and I looked, stunned at the reflection.

"Damn," was all I could say. The man staring back at me sort of resembled Houston Cash, but in a much bigger, Tom Cruise kind of way. Kind of a Hollywood hairstyle, conservative but not too much. Del grinning as he stood behind me.

"I told you I do it right," he said, handing me a bottle. "This conditioner after you shampoo makes it easier to put it back like it is. Don't need nothin' special."

The price was a hundred dollars; I gave him an extra fifty, and he smiled. On the way out, I looked around, then had to ask. "Who's Felicia?"

"My wife," Del said, showing me those amazing, incredibly white teeth again. "Assistant prosecutor for the state of Nevada, felony appeals division."

"Your wife know what you do for a living?"

"Shit, she my best customer."

His laugh echoed off the walls as I walked out the door.

Welcome to Las Vegas.

- - -

"Uncle Aaron, there's a stranger at the door," Dowling said, wide-eyed, as I walked into the room. He whistled. "You ever change your preference, sweetie, you give me a call."

Aaron was flabbergasted. "You got that from a tailor?"

I grinned. "Nope." The hotel room rocked with laughter as I told them about Dee Dee Stancil, ending with a warning to Aaron that if he told anybody back home about this episode, I would personally serve his balls to the carp that populate Freedom Park Lake.

"They'd put me in a home," Aaron said. "I will have to re-introduce you to Pick, though. He's on his way over, by the way."

"They find anything?" My pulse quickened, but not for long.

"Nah, but he's bringing that back-door list for you. Said he'd set you up where he could, but there were a few where you'd be on your own. He's probably gonna ask you to take notes for the department's future reference, too," Aaron said, staring at me like he was seeing me for the first time. "Son of a bitch. It's amazing how different you look. Might check ol' Dee Dee out myself when we're done." Hard to imagine Aaron in Stancil's chair. Hell, it was hard trying to imagine me there.

He and Dowling had pretty well mapped out Las Vegas, even to the point of setting up certain perimeters that, once checked by Aaron, would be called in and cleared off a precisely-gridded sheet Aaron said Dowling had laid out, then taped on a wall. I couldn't help but notice that Aaron had apparently already delegated himself to check the brightly-lit side of the search, maybe with a little help from Dowling, and I didn't correct him, glad I wouldn't have to argue any points about him being my sidekick.

We ordered some sandwiches from room service and the two of them, actually acting like partners, told me the system they'd worked out. Dowling had obviously warmed to Aaron, and vice versa. Aaron had that effect on people, and the retired detective treated the Satchley in-law like a son who'd misbehaved and then been redeemed.

When they wrapped up their plan and we'd polished off the sandwiches, Dowling went back downstairs to make sure he'd copped all the brochures he needed (and probably to get another look at the concierge). Aaron stared at me, still amused. "That's a good look on you. Keep it and you might win Dawn back."

"She's a married woman with three kids. I could look like Clark Gable and she'd still be faithful," I said.

"You wouldn't know it to hear her talk when she was looking after me," Aaron said. "She might be living with another man and bearing his children, but she's still definitely carrying a torch for you, bucko."

"That's ancient history and you know it. Like your plan, by the way," I said, changing the subject, but pondering the possibilities.

"Rayford's a pretty sharp cookie, in spite of himself," Aaron said. "All that military school training didn't go to waste. I'm startin' on the first grid right after lunch or whenever."

"Not worried about Cissy spotting you?"

"Nah. I'm nondescript enough, I'll melt into a crowd. You, on the other hand, kinda stick out. Lotta short people in Vegas. Besides," he said, "I don't think Cissy would run. Rayford said the Satchley woman didn't see me in Atlanta before he bopped me." Aaron casual about the Atlanta clash, obviously forgiven and forgotten.

"I want to feel that way, too. To tell you the truth, I'm not so sure Cissy'll be with her. Out here it's Andrea Satchley's game. She might tuck Cissy away for safekeeping."

"Either that or she'll have her on a leash, keep a close eye on her."

"That, too. Guess we won't know until the game starts."

"I hope it's just a game. I don't like dealing with an unknown, and the Satchley woman's a big unknown. Rayford couldn't tell me much more about her other than she's aggressive, sometimes a little crazy, and can be meaner'n a snake. Didn't sound like many preacher's wives I've known."

"Yeah, Charles didn't provide many details about her either, except her instability after their child died. What he said jives with the aggressive part, but he didn't say anything about mean."

We stopped talking when Dowling came through the door toting a few more brochures. "I heard the 'mean' part," he said. "You must have been talking about my dear sister."

"Mainly, we were saying how little we know about her," I said.

"To tell you the truth, I probably know less about the grown-up Andrea than you do," Dowling said, plopping on the sofa. "She was a pretty cool little girl, protective of me, but when she grew up she started what I call her 'quest for greatness.' Told me many a time she was going to marry a rich man and live a life of leisure. Dad would laugh and say nobody deserved it more. Mama would just tell her to find a good man," Dowling said, staring at the travel folders in his lap. "When she married Charles, they thought she'd found both because, as Mama said, Charles had 'promise.'"

"I thought you said you were brought up to be the classy one," I said.

"I was supposed to be one, she was supposed to marry one. That's the difference. Charles went to Duke on a basketball scholarship, Andrea got there from church grants. My parents weren't poor, but sending me to a military school pretty well drained the family college fund. When Charles graduated and did his prison gig, it disappointed the hell out of my father, who thought he'd be the minister at some fancy Presbyterian Church, but Mama told him Charles's time would come."

"Why didn't Andrea graduate?"

"I don't know; getting a head start on feathering the nest, maybe. She had problems with college, couldn't adjust real well," Dowling said, dismissively.

"Anyway, both of my parents died before Charles founded the Primitive Church," Dowling continued, a reflective, sad expression on his face. "Cancer, within six months of each other. It wasn't a good time in my life. At the funeral home, Andrea declared she would fulfill our parents' dream or die trying. I guess with fifteen million she's gotten pretty close."

"Or will die trying," I said.

CHAPTER TWENTY-FOUR

LENNIE HAD THREE SUITS, a tuxedo, a dinner jacket, two sport coats, four extra pairs of pants, and six different pairs of shoes, along with all the necessary accessories, waiting when I got back to Pierre Fuget. He paid no attention to my new look, which I suppose was good. The Rolls Royce limo outside was assigned to me, too, he said, along with the driver, an off-duty deputy sheriff named Earl.

"Got any exploding pens or rocket launchers?" I asked, smiling. Lennie didn't get the James Bond joke, just said he was doing what Mr. Devore wanted, which included not asking questions, "like what the fuck did you do with your hair, but it's none of my business." I didn't ask to see the bill, but I was pretty sure just one of the Armani suits cost four or five thousand dollars by itself.

I loaded the clothes into the trunk of the vintage '56 Rolls Silver Shadow, and Earl opened the back door for me. Earl, it turned out, was provided by Pick; the Rolls came from a car-collecting buddy of Devore's who ran a local bank.

"I'm trying not to attract attention, so they put me in this?" I said to Earl as we pulled away from the shop.

"You obviously don't pay much attention to the cars in Las Vegas," Earl said. "This one is tame compared to most of 'em. A heap, almost."

On the short trip back to the MGM Grand, Earl told me he'd worked some special interdepartmental assignments with Pick but actually did do some private driving on the side. His role as a chauffeur started as an undercover assignment; he found out what they made, and took it up to send his oldest boy to college. He regaled me with a few stories of the mob types and movie stars he'd driven for; I told him a little about the case, and by the time we pulled into the hotel driveway I was ready to head up to the room.

"Should I keep the engine running?" Earl asked.

"I'll be a little bit. Go grab a beer or something, pick me up in about an hour."

An overeager attendant helped me carry the clothes and bags up to the room, and I slipped him a ten after we unloaded. Dowling went nuts when he saw the wardrobe, insisted on helping me match everything up, each item preceded by "Do you have any idea what this costs?"

In short order, I was decked out in a black number with tiny gray pinstripes, red and blue silk regiment tie, matching handkerchief in the pocket, glossy wingtip shoes. I looked at myself in the mirror and couldn't believe what I saw.

"Cash. Houston Cash," I said, trying my level best to imitate Sean Connery's accent.

"You look good enough to eat," Dowling declared. Aaron blushed and I laughed.

Pick's timing was perfect. He made his entrance after pounding on the door, looked at me, and busted out laughing. "What in God's name have we got here?"

"I'd do my James Bond imitation again, but nobody seems to think it's very funny."

"No, I like the look. Class. Las Vegas class. Don't look like a cop any more, that's for damn sure. What'd those shoes cost? A month's pay?"

"Near about. You got the list?"

Pick reached in his pocket and produced two sheets of paper, flattening them out on the coffee table. "A dozen casinos cater privately to the highest rollers; several more have private rooms but let in just about anybody with a hundred grand to spend, usually groups on junkets," he said. "At one time or another, we've had people inside all twelve of the big ones, still have a few good contacts in place.

"I've written the contacts' names, but you're gonna have to memorize them 'cause having their names on any list would cost them their covers," Pick continued. "I say all this to you to let you know that if you get in any kind of trouble, there's somebody you can count on for backup, maybe."

"Maybe?"

"Depends on what kind of trouble it is," he explained. "Short of a threat to your life, you're probably on your own. Also, there's maybe four casinos where I got bupkus. We'll worry about those if and when the time comes."

"Fair enough. What about hardware?" I asked, producing the Glock, which fit surprisingly well in the small of my back under the Armani. The possibility of gunplay never actually occurred to me after the Birmingham fiasco. Precautions never hurt.

"Most of the higher rollers bring bodyguards along who don't hide what they carry. Could be metal detectors in this one, this one, and this one," Pick said, pointing to casinos on the list. "Might ought to save them for last. In the others, the owners have enough of their own firepower around; they're not likely to check a guy acts like a high roller."

"Devore gave me a guy's name at a bank here in Vegas, said to call him to establish a credit line at whatever casinos I needed," I said, producing a card Carson had pressed in my hand before we left. "Okay for me to share the list with him? Not that he knows anything about anything, which he doesn't, but I just want to make sure I'm not ringing some kind of bell here."

"Yeah. It's pretty much public knowledge that these places have special facilities. They've got regular fronts, too. Since you're new to the game, what'll probably happen is the casino will establish your credit line, somebody will notice the amount and let the backroom boys know," Pick said. "More'n likely, somebody will meet you at the door and take you to the private lounge.

"Wouldn't hurt for you to call them or get pretty boy here to do it as your assistant. Let 'em know you require special handling, if you know what I mean."

"I'll call myself Mr. Floyd," Dowling deadpanned. If anything in the past day or so, I'd learned Rayford was impervious to insults, implied or otherwise, and I didn't really think that's what Pick had done.

We made the calls, first me to the banker, who'd been waiting to hear from me. He didn't know who or what I was, only that Carson Devore had requested establishment of a five million dollar credit at any casino I selected. I almost swallowed the phone.

"Five mil! Jesus!" Pick said. "Now I know I'm going private."

"It's not for me to spend," I hastened to point out. "Just get me in the door."

"Speakin' of gettin' in the door, you know much about our games of chance, Houston?"

"I dabbled in a few things when I was out here before; know blackjack and poker, a little about craps. I'll stay away from the sophisticated stuff, baccarat and all that. I'm supposed to be new at the game, after all," I said. "My cover will be that I'm a successful developer. That's a vague enough occupation, Carson and I agreed. All you have to talk about is property values, that kind of thing. I should be able to wing it."

"Sounds like you got your bases covered," Pick said. "Anything else I can do?"

"Earl was a nice touch. Good to know I've got a cop outside the door," I told him.

"Made the switch easy enough. I dropped by the shop, spotted the car, talked to the driver, who I happened to know. He won't say anything about bein' replaced, by the way, should anybody bother to ask."

"You want to help these guys, you're welcome to sign aboard," I said.

"Me help the great Aaron Drake? Why, I'd be honored," Pick said with a deep bow. "Learn at the feet of the master. God, I feel like a rookie."

"Wise ass," Aaron said. "Okay, okay, I'll let you carry my bags maybe."

"I'll check back when I get off," Pick said, looking at his watch. "In about two hours."

"We'll need some sort of signal," I said. "I'll call the room, ask for Mr. Drake. That means I've got something. Then I'll find a private phone, give the details. If I haven't called back in, say, thirty minutes, then you guys'll need to move toward wherever I am. No news, no call, other than just checking in."

Dowling nodded. "I'll be on the phone, and we've got this nifty cellular provided by the hotel in case you call us en route," he said, producing a small pocket phone with one of those touch-screen features. Much as I hated high tech, I had to admit it was neat looking. I wrote down the number on the back of the banker's card and stuck it in a pocket.

"So Frick and Frack here will chase the grid, you're at the nerve center, and I'll be the back-door man. Damn, what a setup. Just like in *The Sting*," I said.

"All this to get a coupla dames to go back to their husbands," Pick mused. "Life's a bitch, ain't it, Frack?" He patted Aaron on the shoulder. "No sign of the Mercedes, by the way. My money says they ditched it or parked it outa town, came here in something else."

"Came here in style, no doubt," Dowling said.

"Gentlemen," I said, brushing some lint off the suit. "Let's go play."

CHAPTER TWENTY-FIVE

Never in a million years would I have thought I'd be riding in the backseat of a Rolls limousine through the glittering streets of Las Vegas, but here I was. Never mind that it was a job and that none of the trappings were really mine. It was a moment to savor. If I'd thought, I would have gotten my picture taken. I looked out the window, watched people walking by, expensive cars passing, lights that burned day and night.

"What's the first stop?" Earl asked over his shoulder.

I pulled out Pick's list and looked at the name on top. "The Platinum Palace."

"Nice place," was all Earl said. Before going to the casino, we stopped at a branch of the bank Devore had linked me to, I walked inside and was set upon by a nervous vice president after announcing my name in the teller line. He took me aside, told me he would personally handle my request, then seemed disappointed when I only asked for "a few hundred dollars," figuring I'd need some pocket money. I signed a slip of paper and exited, to his disappointment, with two thousand in tens, twenties, and fifties.

In a few minutes, Earl and I were pulling into another driveway. I couldn't help but notice how most of them looked alike. A doorman scurried up and opened my door as Earl got out. Not sure of the protocol, I waited for Earl to come around the Rolls and walk with me to the gaudy entrance.

We strolled inside and Earl whispered from the corner of his mouth, "Stand here. Leave this part to me." I stopped and he walked to what appeared to be a concierge's desk, said something to the uniformed man standing behind it.

The concierge looked at me, smiled and nodded, picked up a phone and said something, then signaled a woman in a similar color scheme who walked up to the desk, exchanged some words, then hustled over to where I was standing, beginning to feel a little self-conscious.

"Mr. Cash," she extended a hand. "We understand you prefer a degree of privacy, so if I may, could I escort you?" Early on, we'd decided I should use my own name, not expecting to run into any old clients out here, and the guys I'd helped Pick salt away were gone for at least another decade. It made things less complicated.

I shook the young woman's hand, then followed her through a hallway to the left, serenaded on the trip by noises coming from inside the casino. Bells clanging, voices, whirring machines; the sound effects of people losing thousands of dollars a minute, I suppose.

We walked down the hallway, modestly decorated compared to the entrance. Subtle prints on the wall, muted lighting, an occasional plant. At the end of the hall, two large, brass-trimmed doors with a keyboard lock in the middle. The woman punched a few numbers, then pushed one of the doors open and graciously motioned me inside, stepping to the right politely.

I was struck at once by the simplicity of the large, open room. Not much in the way of decoration: huge crystal chandeliers in a grid pattern casting light on two rows of slot machines, which I thought odd in a den of high rollers.

"Some of our guests like to play the machines or use them as a distraction for friends or children," she said, noticing my eyes traveling to the slots. I didn't see any children. Two elderly men in tuxedos were pulling arms, feeding coins. Young, giggly things on their arms, cooing occasionally if a bell rang or coins clinked in trays.

We walked past the machines, most of them idle at this time of day apparently, and into the main chamber, where maybe a hundred men and women gathered around craps tables, blackjack stands, poker tables, and other assorted casino fixtures. I paused, looking around the room. In one corner, what I guessed to be a baccarat table was active; to the right some other intense gaming at a table involving cards and a spiffily-dressed dealer. In the corners of the room, surrounded by tall potted palms, were what looked like lifeguard chairs, maybe six feet off the floor, on which sat men in dark suits who looked across the room with bored expressions. I could have sworn one of them had an assault rifle in his lap, but I didn't dwell, not wanting to look hinky.

Women in skimpy, extremely low-cut attire moved through the crowd carrying trays with cigarettes, mixed drinks, and other treats for the gamblers, most of whom would reach and grab something without looking. I expected a few grabbed the girls from time to time, and from the expressions on their faces, it was accepted as part of the job. The lifeguards' eyes followed the women around the room, maybe using them as target reticles for their armament, I didn't know.

What caught my attention more than anything else were the women among the clientele. Fifty or so Cissy Devores and Andrea Satchleys, trophy wives or girlfriends, a number of them "friends" for the day, I had no doubt, all expensively attired and blonde, brunette, auburn-tressed, some of them possibly showgirls all dressed up, others doubtlessly regular companions. Most of them posing; there to be seen, admired. Only a few of them looking like they, not the men around them, were the actual "guests." A couple of them had studl- looking model types in their wake. Equal opportunity.

For whatever reason, inexperience, I suppose, I hadn't expected there to be so many of them, and it dawned on me that the task of isolating Cissy and/or Andrea was going to be a much more daunting task than I'd first believed.

"Mr. Cash?" My escort stirred me out of my reverie. "Do you have a preference?" For a split second, I didn't know what she meant; then it dawned on me.

"Blackjack, I suppose," I said, trying to sound like I'd said it before, meagerly attempting a tone of boredom, the rich guy not sure what he wanted to do with all his money. "At least that's where I'll start."

Armed with that instruction, the woman first led me to a cashier's window, where I signed a slip of paper and was handed a tray of chips, silver and gold, worth, I was told, five hundred for silver, a thousand for gold. I must have been holding twenty, thirty grand minimum. Then I saw a small demarcation on the tray that said, simply and spelled out, "Fifty Thousand." I hoped she didn't hear me gulp.

"Will you be joined by anyone later, anyone we should watch for, perhaps?" my escort said, maybe not used to lone wolves, as she steered me to the blackjack section.

"No, unless you're not busy for the next little while," I offered. Cavalier, I thought. Goofy, it probably sounded.

She smiled demurely and I extended a free hand concealing a folded fifty, which she seemed taken aback to receive. It occurred to me in a flash that she might think I was offering to buy her time, and I blushed.

"Forgive me," I said, "but this is my first trip to Las Vegas in a while, and I honestly don't know what the tipping protocol is these days."

"Oh, we don't expect or accept tips in the reserved section," she said, relieved, holding the bill out.

"I insist," I said, blocking the return with a touch. "You've given me a lesson and I simply have to pay for it."

"Well, thank you, but ..."

"It's just between us. Honest."

"Very well. If there's anything else I can do for you ..."

"I'll put my lips together and blow," I said, watching her reaction.

"Bogart and Bacall. You're a very nice man, Mr. Cash," she replied, grinning. "If you need any assistance, just ask for Callie." With that, she disappeared toward the front door.

I found an empty seat at a blackjack table not yet dealt, sidling in between a flushed, well-dressed man in his sixties and a gorgeous, tall blonde who appeared not to have let the drink bearers pass her too many times.

"Another knight joins the battle," the woman said, slurring her words just a little. "Maybe he'll give you some luck, Phil."

The flushed man, apparently Phil, mumbled something and placed three silver chips in a row on the green felt table. I deposited two, the woman pushed one gold chip from a stack, and the dealer flipped cards face-down in front of each chip, then in front of himself, followed by face-up cards. I got a ten of hearts and an ace of diamonds; Phil got a six of clubs, a two of spades and a jack of diamonds; the woman a queen of hearts. The dealer gave himself an eight of hearts. I wasn't paying too much attention to the table; probably should have.

I glanced around the room as casually as I could, trying to focus on every woman's face. None of the ones I saw even faintly resembled Cissy, but the backs of blonde heads made it difficult to determine if Andrea was about. My scan distracted me from the game and apparently distracted my sloshed playing partner.

"Nervous?" she said to me.

"No, just not used to this. I'm new at the game," I told her, trying to focus on the business at hand.

"Well, Mr. New at the Game, you just picked up a quick thousand dollars," she said, smiling under somewhat glazed eyes. "Dealer pays nineteen and higher and Phil won two out of three, so you must be lucky." She slipped her hand under my arm. Phil didn't seem to notice. "Stick around."

I stayed at the table for a dozen passes, then pried her loose from my arm and said I needed to circulate. I'd netted twenty-five-hundred bucks, told her I wanted to quit while I was ahead, which drew a surprised, perplexed stare. Phil, she said, was about thirty grand in the hole, didn't know the meaning of the word "quit," and did I want to accompany her to the dice table. I declined, and elbowed my way unceremoniously into the crowd.

It wasn't easy trying to see and not be seen in a group this size, but I was fairly comfortable with the fact that Cissy wasn't here and Andrea didn't know what I looked like, as far as anyone knew. I tried to introduce myself by encounter to every woman in the room; none of them was named Andrea. None of the blondes, anyway, and it occurred to me that Andrea could have changed her looks as easily as I did mine.

After two hours, the Platinum Palace was a wash and I made my way to the front door, up three thousand from what I'd started with. Lucky at gambling, unlucky at detecting, it appeared.

Earl brought the Rolls around and we headed to the next stop, the Nevada Star, where the setup was basically the same as the Platinum, only a few more people. A bit gaudier than the Platinum; a Tex-Mex scheme with longhorns on the wall and lifeguards wearing gaucho jackets and sombreros, looking sillier than they probably realized or cared.

By the third casino I was wondering where all these people got all this money to blow. Earl and I stopped at an International House of Pancakes, where I checked in with Dowling.

"Aaron and Pick have gone through two grids with no luck," he told me. "Devore checked in a couple of hours ago, said they were still up and running, no luck. Didn't ask him if he meant the tables. I'm trying to imagine Charles playing the high roller. He was uncomfortable as hell when he and Andrea came here before. Hates the glamour." A surprising trait for a television evangelist, I thought.

"I'm striking out regularly," I said. "I'll hit a couple more, then call it a day. We can regroup and compare notes. Any chance," I added, "Andrea would try to change her appearance?"

"Not in this lifetime," Dowling said. "Andrea's too vain to be anybody but Andrea, no matter what the circumstances. You're looking for a blue-eyed blonde, through and through."

"I guess that's some consolation."

"See ya when you get here," he said, and hung up.

"Three down and nine to go," I told Earl, sliding into the booth.

"Lemme see the list," he said between forkfuls of pancake. "I might be able to knock off a couple real quick. This woman sounds like somebody who'd go straight to the top. All these places are fairly classy, but some are the classiest, if you know what I mean."

Earl studied the list, made a couple of marks, rounded the choices down to three: The Oasis, Desert Gold Inn, and Sahara Shamrock.

Being the superstitious guy I am, the Sahara Shamrock sounded like a logical choice. I told Earl about Billy's place back home and he shrugged. "What the hell. You never know. Let's try it."

－　－　－

I had a creepy feeling when we pulled into the Sahara Shamrock driveway. Except for different faces and color schemes, the layout was much the same as the others, only it appeared the owners of this place did their level best to hire Irish-looking employees. My escort to the private lounge was a rosy-cheeked redhead with a slight lilt to her voice.

I was beginning to feel the pressure of the day and the Glock seemed to weigh a ton in my back, but I'd gotten over any latent nervousness about being checked. So far so good.

"Let me guess," I said as we walked down the green-carpeted hallway. "You're from Ireland."

"Dublin, to be precise," she said with a brilliant smile. "There's actually quite a few of us here. The owner is of Irish descent, too. Many of us here for scholarships. The casino sends a great deal of money to universities in Ireland."

I noticed she didn't give the owner's name and I didn't press the issue. "A large Irish contingent comes here?" Small talk she'd probably heard a million times.

"Indeed, they do. A touch of home in America, as you'll see in the decorations," she said, opening a large oak door. We moved through without any alarms going off, and my gun felt a little lighter.

The room looked like what you'd expect an Irish pub to look like, only a thousand times larger. Tables of heavy wood, flocked wallpaper, with a small clover pattern. The population had a fresh-scrubbed, if wealthy, look, pale faces not used to the desert sun, dozens of Kennedyesque mannequins, many of them likely named O'Something. The drink and smoke bearers were still scantily clad, but with a "Top o' the mornin'" sheen. I felt like a guest at an Irish Society ball, mingling with the cream of the Celtic crop.

And someone who looked a lot like Andrea Satchley concentrating mightily in the middle of a group around a long dice table.

I almost panicked, left my escort quickly, and blended into a queue near the blackjack section, hoping it wasn't obvious. I was a head taller than most of them, and directed my gaze toward the familiar-looking blonde, trying to focus in the somewhat subdued light, not sure. I let my gaze shift to either side of her and saw no one who looked like Cissy Devore, just a couple of big, dark-suited guys who acted like they were supposed to be nearby.

Risking the loss of my anonymity, I knew I had to get closer. I moved as casually as possible to a cashier's window, ordered some chips. Green and gold, fives and tens (times a hundred, of course).

Hoping my movements were as un-overt as possible, I stopped at an empty chair at the first blackjack dealer I encountered, sat down and played a couple of hands, glancing up toward the craps table, now about thirty feet away. The woman who looked like Andrea never raised her head, staring intently at the table.

I got up after losing my last hand, strolled to the poker section, now fifteen feet from the craps table, and sat down again, placing a small pile of chips in front of me. The dealer, dressed in a green and white outfit with an old-timey green eyeshade, announced the hand and started playing out cards. It was hard paying attention, but I managed to lose two thousand dollars before looking up again.

The woman was gone.

In a panic, I excused myself from the table and started walking around the perimeter of the room, eyes darting to every face aimed my way. No Andrea Satchley—or her look-alike—anywhere to be seen, only two blondes with their backs to me. I worked my way around to angle toward their faces. No dice.

Had she seen me and fled? Was it Andrea, or did I just want it to be Andrea? I decided it might be time to call in the troops. No use taking any chances. We'd come too far for me to discount even a whim.

I moved toward the door, and a hostess intercepted me.

"Can I help you, sir?"

"I need to find a phone, if it's possible."

"Follow me," she said, leading me through the door and to a chamber off the hall, where a row of telephones was sectioned off like open booths. I thanked her, and she walked away. I punched the hotel room's direct number, and Dowling answered on the first ring.

"I think I might have seen her, Rayford."

"Where are you?"

I told him, he said he'd summon Aaron and Pick. "Crank up your cell phone and wait," he advised.

I walked as casually as possible to the casino entrance and asked a valet directions to the parking area, explaining that I didn't want to leave just yet, only needed to talk to my driver. After some verbal jousting when he offered to run the errand for me, he reluctantly pointed to an area west of the driveway, and I saw Earl leaning against the Rolls. I hustled over, told him the situation. He opened the back door and I climbed inside.

Within a few minutes, the cell chirped. I looked at the display and punched the appropriate picture. It was Aaron.

"What's the score, chief?" he said.

I explained what I'd seen, adding that I wasn't sure but it could be, and she could have seen me, could be running.

"Pick and I'll be there in a few minutes. Sit tight. We'll come straight to you, then go from there."

I told Earl to position the car so we could see the entrance. He pulled the Rolls into an angled parking slot in what must have been the valet holding area; nobody approached us, and we sat and watched.

"May be a back door," Earl said.

"We'll just have to take our chances until the rest of the guys get here."

"Or I can mosey around," he said, cop gears grinding.

"If it was her, I don't think she'd be obvious. She may be watching us right now, waiting to see what we're going to do." I leaned to the window, looked up. Not many rooms open to the front. Just a few hundred. "I don't know if she might have recognized me or just got antsy, maybe felt me looking. I can't imagine that she knew me, but I just don't know. She's possibly seen me a couple of times. Figured we wouldn't take any chances, and things seem a little stale right now anyway." I felt like I was babbling, nervous energy playing through my mouth; Earl watching me, nodding.

"Suit yourself, but if it was me, I'd …"

Before he finished the sentence, Pick's black Impala rumbled in beside us, him and Aaron in the front seat, Dowling in the back. Couldn't have been too far away. They got out of the car and into mine.

"Nice wheels," Dowling observed. "In case you're wondering, got the hotel phone on call forwarding," he added, patting the cellular clipped to his belt. "I just love modern technology."

"What I'm worried about is Andrea spotting you," I said, a little irritated.

"If it's Andrea you saw, by the time she'd see me it shouldn't make any difference. As Uncle Aaron would say, 'The smoke would already be risin' off the doo-doo.'"

"I know the managers here," Pick interrupted. "I'll go in, tell them we're working something, get 'em out of the way. Or at least get 'em prepared."

He got out of the car and ambled inside; returned in a few minutes.

"No problems from them. Discreet's my middle name. We have to run after somebody, no employee's gonna get in our way."

"Earl and I'll go around to the back, start moving forward," Aaron said. To me: "You and Rayford go in the front way like before."

"Pick, you set up at the desk, in case a certain good-looking blonde tries to make an exit," Aaron instructed, taking charge like the Aaron Drake I'd known so many years ago on the force.

"Looks like we've got our assignments," I said as cheerfully as possible. "Gentlemen, start your engines, as the good ol' boys would say."

CHAPTER TWENTY-SIX

It DIDN'T STRIKE ME until we were through the private salon door that Dowling was unarmed, and I said something to him about it.

"I don't think we need cannons," he replied with a laugh. "Andrea's not likely to try to shoot her way out."

"I suppose you're right, but this cat-and-mouse game could still get messy. You should have stayed at the hotel."

"And miss this? I don't think so. Besides, I'll bet I can run faster than you, and it wouldn't be the first time I've hit my sister with a flying tackle," he said. "If she spots me, the jig is up and she'll know it. I think she'll just go quietly."

"Maybe so. You go right, I'll go left."

"And I'll be in Ireland afore ye." Dowling disappeared into the crowd.

No one looked nervous. Oblivious, I suppose, to what was going on. No reason to think the customers would have a clue. But inside I was tense, adrenaline pumping with the anticipation that this whole mess might be over soon. I looked over heads, watching Dowling work the room, both of us simultaneously scanning faces. It was hard to believe that only a couple of days ago he'd been our adversary; now he was getting into the job with more zeal than any of the group.

Figuring there was no way to be subtle, I walked up to every blonde within sight and looked her straight in the face, evoking smiles from a few, curious frowns from others. Dowling was doing the same thing, grinning sheepishly every time one turned around.

It didn't take us long to scour the whole audience, and we met back at the front doors.

"No Andrea, but some really nice-looking people," Dowling observed. "The interior decorating could use some work, though. Can you say 'Too frigging green'?"

"No Cissy, either. Maybe I was just chasing a ghost. Let's go check on the guys."

We strolled back up the hallway, meeting Aaron and Earl at the front door. They'd seen nothing, either. Aaron motioned for Pick to join us, telling me he'd checked the register.

"No way to know how or whether she'd even check in," he said, looking around the huge lobby. "No Satchley listed, and it'd take us half the damn day to check 'em all. She may have just dropped in, be staying somewhere else."

"Or maybe I didn't see what I thought I saw," I admitted.

"That, too," he said.

"Or maybe not," Dowling said suddenly. "Andrea and some goon just stepped off the elevator."

Before any of us could say anything, Dowling took off at a trot. Our eyes followed his trajectory and there stood Andrea Satchley, wide-eyed as her brother sprinted toward her.

Then things started happening.

The "goon," as Dowling called him, shoved Andrea into the arms of another big man, who put his arms around her like a Secret Service agent protecting the president, hustled her in the opposite direction, disappearing in the crowd. The man reached under his jacket, and I knew what was going to happen next.

"Get down!" I shouted to no one in particular, pulled my Glock in what felt like slow-motion, and dropped onto one knee. "Rayford! Hit the floor!"

People were diving everywhere. Casino employees, looking startled, stepped back, a couple of them producing walkie-talkies from nowhere.

The goon had something in his hand he was raising at Dowling. I centered my pistol on his chest and pulled the trigger; both our weapons discharging simultaneously. Dowling's forward motion carried him a few more feet before he splayed, face first, onto the emerald green carpet and lay motionless. The force of my ten-millimeter jacketed hollow-point slammed the shooter against the wall beside the elevator door; he slumped and slid to the floor, dropping his gun, a crimson stain spreading in the center of his chest, one leg jerking spasmodically. No vest, obviously.

I sprinted to Dowling; Earl took off after Andrea and the other man, Aaron close behind, guns drawn and held high, as Pick pulled out his LVPD shield and ordered the spectators to stay where they were, a few of them beating a hasty retreat anyway in the pandemonium. Screams came from everywhere, people hitting the floor or running. I think a couple of women may have fainted.

I knelt beside Dowling, turned him over gently. Blank eyes stared, a half-smile on his face, almost an expression of amused surprise. The bullet had caught him square in the heart, stopped it instantly, hardly any blood at all. Tidy. The way Rayford would have liked it. He probably never knew what hit him.

Shit.

Shit, shit, shit.

- - -

"I'm gonna need your piece for ballistics. Here, take mine," Pick said, shoving his Sig Saeur in my hand, wrenching me back to reality. "Earl's on the phone. They're behind 'em. Take my car."

"But I don't know anything about this city," I said. A ridiculous protest, considering the circumstances, but I wasn't thinking straight.

"Earl'll guide you on the phone. Here," he said, thrusting the cellular into my empty hand. "Use the blue light, break the speed limit, I don't much give a shit. If anybody asks, Earl deputized you and you were in continuous pursuit of a fleeing felon. I think there's a state law'll cover that if we get in a pissin' contest with an ADA. I'll take care of things here. Now get your ass out there pronto."

I pressed the phone to my ear and shoved Pick's gun into my holster as I half-ran, half-stumbled out the casino doors and plunged into the black Impala. I twisted the key, still in the ignition, and shoved it into drive, sliding sideways into the street before I knew which direction I was heading.

"Talk to me, Earl," I shouted, juggling the phone and the steering wheel.

"You come out left or right in front of the casino?" His voice clear as a bell. You had to love modern technology.

"Left."

"Go down to the end of the street and hang a right at the light."

I did as instructed, nearly losing the Chevy in a skid as I rounded the corner, pedestrians scattering, cars screeching to a halt, horns honking.

"Okay, I'm on it," I told Earl.

"Now just haul ass straight away. You're maybe five, ten miles behind us, but we're headed like a shot to Sloan. Little burg outside the city. Got a feeling that's our destination. Lot of big, fancy canyon houses there. Just keep comin' 'til you see us," his voice getting a little staticky.

"You might be fading on me, Earl," I shouted, not realizing I was shouting. "I think the battery light's flashing on this thing, too." I held it away from my ear momentarily, saw the *battery low* indicator blinking.

"Hang it up. Press the *power* button. If I need to call …." The sentence disappeared briefly in a shower of static. " …know Earl's car number, otherwise you'll see us, probably. Any change, I'll call you …" The phone died.

I tossed it on the seat and glanced around, finding the police car's installed phone, then turning on the police radio under the dash. Heard cars checking out at the casino. I still couldn't accept the fact that Dowling had been shot. Quick and clean, almost as if it didn't even happen. Why the hell did he take off like that? I knew the answer before I'd asked it, though. To him, it had always been a game, probably from the very beginning when he'd been summoned by his sister. By the time he had become a part of our unofficial posse, I believe he was actually having a lot of fun. Big brother chasing little sister because she'd been bad. Never thinking for a minute that Andrea was apparently playing for keeps.

I cursed myself; cursed all of us for not thinking that security might be one of the first things Andrea Satchley would buy with her ill-gotten wealth. Security that obviously meant business, maybe more so than she'd expected, though I really didn't know. "Mean," Dowling had said. I don't think she saw her brother killed but I couldn't be sure; couldn't be sure, either, if she gave a damn.

I was passing one car after another, weaving back and forth across the four-lane blacktop, almost oblivious to my surroundings. The old cop instinct kicking in. I hadn't realized that when I turned on the police radio, I also apparently thumbed the blue light switch and set off alternating headlights, strobes in the grill. Cars were bailing out of the way left and right. When it hit me what I was doing, I toggled the light switch off, looked in the rearview mirror, and a Nevada state trooper's car was growing in the distance, apparently in hot pursuit.

He'd have to follow me all the way. I pushed my right foot to the floor and the Impala roared, bucked, and climbed to about a hundred and twenty as I broke into open road, buildings and utility poles flashing by like a black picket fence in the desert. The patrol car stopped gaining but stayed with me.

I saw a speck a few miles ahead, and in what seemed like only a minute I was slowing, pulling onto the shoulder behind the Rolls, Earl and Aaron standing on the gravel beside it, watching me.

"They went up this road," Earl said as I walked up to them. "It's a driveway into a ranch just behind those hills." He pointed to where the gravel narrowed in the distance. "I know the house. Used to be owned by Liberace, believe it or not.

"It's a rental, and I expect that's where our friends are holed up."

"It never fucking occurred to me she'd buy firepower," I said to no one in particular, still shaken, still fuming.

"Don't beat yourself up, Houston. We all shoulda thought about it," Aaron said. "How's Rayford?"

My look spoke volumes, and Aaron's face sagged.

"Damn," he said. "I was actually getting to like the little fart. Son of a bitch. His own goddam sister."

The Nevada state car came sliding up behind the Impala, an officious-looking trooper getting out of the driver's side, Pick jumping out of the other.

"I left a buddy in charge of the shooting scene," he told me as he walked up. "Trooper Whisnant here offered the ride."

The highway patrolman, all spit and polish and experience, nodded in my direction. Marine brush cut, sunburned, freckled face, a few creases belying his years on the force, no doubt. "Chuck Whisnant," he said, shaking hands all around. "Glad to help. Pick here said I could stick around, maybe help out if it's all right with y'all.

"Us North Carolina boys got to stick together," he said with an exaggerated drawl, grinning broadly, then with a stern look: "and it might be a 'situation,' as the captain calls it, so you might need a little state authority."

I nodded, too frustrated to protest. Everyone else seemed to agree.

Earl explained the layout and where he thought Andrea and the remaining bodyguard had gone. Pick nodded.

"Think she has any idea her brother's dead?" Pick asked.

"I honestly don't know. I kind of doubt it," I said.

"I suppose we oughta call in some troops," Pick offered, looking at me, knowing better.

"I'd rather you didn't just yet."

"The shooting at the casino makes it a local homicide, but Sloan's outa my jurisdiction," Pick mused. "Suppose we could wait a little before calling in the locals or the state boys, couldn't we, Chuck?"

The trooper nodded, a look of understanding spreading across his face. Semper fidelis of the badge set.

"Here's the deal," I said. "We haven't seen Cissy yet, so we don't know if she's at the house or where she might be. Andrea's got at least one hired gun, maybe more at the house. Without Rayford here to give us a read, we don't know what to expect from her.

"I think I ought to go up there by myself," I concluded.

"The hell you say," Aaron interjected. "Getting your ass shot off, too, won't help matters. Maybe we ought to let the locals handle it."

"In the meantime, Cissy might become a hostage, we'd have a standoff, and God knows what else," I argued. "Except for the casino incident, which kind of resolved itself, this is still more or less a civil matter and it'd be nice to spare these guys the paperwork. Let's at least try it my way. If there's too much heat, I'll come back out and we'll go by the book, call in the FBI, the Fifth Fucking Cavalry for all I care." My relatively calm veneer was wearing very, very thin at the moment.

"I don't like it either, Aaron, but Houston might be right," Pick offered. "Those folks in there haven't done anything but run away, so there's not a crime here …yet.

"Hell, without prosecution, there's no crime on the money part, either, and from what Houston says about the husbands I doubt there'll be too fine a point put on anything criminal. That woman's going to have to live with her brother getting killed and it might be punishment enough."

I looked at my long-time friend, Aaron now wearing an expression that spoke volumes only to me. I could hear him thinking, "Yeah, well, how right has Houston been up to this point?" Our eyes met, him taking in my expression; then a sigh. No second guesses.

"You got a rifle in that car, trooper?" Aaron asked. Whisnant nodded, walked back to the cruiser, and returned with a scoped .30-06 sniper rifle and a box of shells. "On the Special Response Team," he explained as Pick walked away, popped the trunk on the Chevrolet, and came back with a pair of wire-cutting pliers, binoculars, a flak jacket, and a couple of ammunition clips for the Sig. Cops keep everything in their trunks. Never know when you might stumble on a siege.

"Put this on." He extended the jacket to me.

"I don't see where …"

"Put it on or we're all going up there like the goddam cavalry, guns blasting, fuck the consequences."

I shrugged my jacket off and buttoned up the bulletproof vest, already sweating before I fastened the last clip. I looked past the cars, watched the sun slip toward the horizon, shadows lengthening; the desert air was starting to cool.

"Pick, I'll take your car to the edge of the rise, walk the rest of the way. You guys can set up there. Got a spare radio?"

Pick unclipped a walkie-talkie from beneath the Chevrolet dash and handed it to me.

"It's tuned in to a private police channel we can monitor at the car. Doesn't even go through central dispatch. You see anything, you let us know. I'll radio headquarters, tell them we're doing some checking around, call off the dogs for now. I'll send 'em on a wild goose chase to a coupla hotels, buy some time. The sergeant I left in charge'll wait to hear from me anyway after he sorts things out at the casino."

"What's the range on this thing?" I asked Whisnant, examining the rifle.

"Effective in the crosshairs at maybe a six, eight hundred yards, then it drops a little. Pumped-up shells."

"The house is maybe five hundred yards from the ridge drop-off," Earl said. "You'll go up the driveway; there's a gate, some low scrub cover on both sides of the fence, then open ground for maybe three hundred feet to the house. Plenty close enough.

"Best as I can remember—I've only been there a couple of times— there's no electronic security other than a camera at the gate. Whole thing's fenced with six-foot chain link, barbed wire on top, like most big ranches around these parts. Keep the four-legged varmints out. Lotta glass on the house, no curtains to speak of."

"Varmints?" I asked, thinking of things that slithered.

"Occasional snake, maybe a coyote, though there aren't many of those left around here. Unless the woman or her hired help brought dogs, shouldn't be any," he said. "It's gettin' dark, so I wouldn't worry about what I couldn't see."

"They know you were chasing 'em?"

"Shouldn't. We just kept them in sight. They were in a hurry, but not running from us, I don't think. Wouldn't hardly expect a police pursuit in a Rolls."

"So there's a chance they don't know their buddy is dead," I said. "Might be sitting tight, waiting to hear from him."

"Could be," Aaron said. "But if the second guy's like the first, I doubt they'll be expecting much. Might at least expect him to be questioned by the police, sitting in jail."

"Okay, here's what I think. Cissy's got to be here. I can't imagine that they'd have her at a separate location. Too scattered, too hard to consolidate. The question is whether she's here because she wants to be or she's being held. I'll use the scope and binoculars to see if I can locate her, then the others."

"Whatever you find, you let us know," Aaron said.

"I'm not trying to be a hero. Don't worry."

We took the cars to the edge of the ridge; I gathered up my equipment and set out on foot.

What I hoped would be the last chapter of this case had begun.

CHAPTER TWENTY-SEVEN

CRAWLING THROUGH THE UNDERBRUSH brought back a swirl of memories from my childhood, like when I tried to be a Boy Scout, as much to escape my old man and his drinking as anything else. Me and two dozen eleven-year-olds at Camp Steere on Lake Wylie, learning to make fires, poach eggs in orange peels, that kind of thing. Nothing much about desert survival, though.

The Army Reserve taught me a few things about stealthy approach, and my cop training was mostly "hide your ass and don't get shot." Basic instincts, in other words.

If there ever was a seat-of-the-pants detective, it was Houston Cash, but I'd survived to this point. It was that survival instinct that told me walking up a driveway, rifle slung over one shoulder, binoculars in hand, was no way to sneak up on anybody, so I got off the gravel and started making my way through the stiff underbrush, most of it barely five feet high so I crouched a little, my back telling me this was not a normal way to walk.

As I made my way toward the top of the hill, I wondered about Andrea Satchley and what kind of woman it took to mastermind what she'd done so far. Ruthless, maybe. Scheming, no doubt. And now she was a cornered animal, or would be one as soon as things started hitting the fan, I figured.

She knew we were here, so she had to know the jig was almost up. Since she'd plotted this extravagant maneuver from the beginning, there was no telling what might be going on in that mind right now, maybe even giving it all up, cutting her losses. Somehow I doubted it. Running away isn't surrendering; it's gathering your thoughts and planning your next move.

It was that move I was worried about.

It took me about fifteen minutes to get within sight of the fence. I stopped maybe five yards away and looked around. Nothing to indicate there were motion detectors or any other booby trap. I moved to the fence and gingerly touched it. Cold steel as the day rapidly moved to night; no electricity. Thermal shifts in the desert were always abrupt, or so I had been told, hot to cold, little in between.

The coil of barbed wire was old, rusty, wound around Y-shaped brackets at the poles. It almost crumbled as I snipped the strands with Pick's cutters, first thinking I'd go over, then thinking better of it and snipping a hole in the chain-link fabric. What the hell.

I slid through, snagged my shirt coming out the other side. I looked at the tear and wondered if you could repair three-hundred-dollar shirts as simply as the single-needle button-downs from Sears.

The scrubby bushes—you couldn't really call them trees—seemed a little thicker on this side of the fence, and I tried my best not to make any of them move as I worked my way ahead, not paying attention that the fast-arriving dusk was shifting to complete and utter darkness; God's blackout.

Desert nights are like no other. Pitch black but for the starlight, and a new moon meant I wouldn't get any help from the sky. Had to feel my way along, for the most part, until abruptly I broke into a clearing.

The yard seemed to slope at about a twenty-degree angle. At least I guess it was the yard. Mostly rock and sand, some dry grass crackling under my feet. My own private Afghanistan scenario, sans Al-Qaeda, I hoped. I moved on slowly, then suddenly the ground dropped away at a much steeper angle and the house rose into view, a black mass reaching toward the starlit heavens.

It was a huge, modern structure, lots of peaks and arches stabbing the starlight, harsh glares blasting through full-length windows before being eaten by the darkness fifty or so feet from the looming, black house. I lay down on the ground at the ridge line, prone, and pulled out the binoculars, unslung the rifle, and placed it beside me. Feeling a little guilty, I shucked the Kevlar vest, too. It was hot and cumbersome and if I was going to get shot, it probably wouldn't do me all that much good. I raised the binoculars to my eyes.

The interior of the house was bright, lots of wood paneling, modern furniture. I moved the glasses from window to window and detected a movement to the far right. A man walking through the room. A very big man, hard to make out his face but he could have been the one who'd hustled Andrea out of the casino.

Another figure met him in the middle of what looked like a huge den; they embraced, kissed. Her long, blonde hair fell across her back as she tilted her head up, then looked toward the window. Andrea Satchley, not acting like a fleeing felon, best I could see from this vantage point.

"Charles wouldn't want to be seeing this," I said, aloud I think. Andrea not acting like a woman married to a preacher, either. Not like a woman being married to anybody, actually.

She sat on a black upholstered sofa and continued looking up at him, smiling. They were talking but I never was very good at reading lips. He took off his jacket, revealing a shoulder holster harness, tossed the coat on a chair, walked out of the room.

"I'll get back to you," I muttered to myself, continuing my scan of the house. It was multi-leveled and some of the rooms were obviously bedrooms, others kind of like sitting rooms or studies; a kitchen, where the guard reappeared, getting something out of the refrigerator. A beer. Two.

I looked into all the windows where there was light, couldn't tell whether the dark spots had windows or were just walls, then one suddenly winked on at an upper level, a little dimmer than the ones below, and I watched as a woman crawled out of a bed. Cissy, I was pretty sure. I thumbed the focus dial.

She stood up, dressed in jeans and what looked like a man's shirt, wiped her eyes, walked stiff-legged to a door, opened it, and disappeared. A bathroom, I supposed.

I kept the glasses trained on the room and in a couple of minutes Cissy reappeared, walked to the door of the bedroom, and stopped. It looked like she was knocking on it. Then pounding, arms flailing.

I shifted my gaze down and saw the guard get up from a chair and walk farther back into the house, then Cissy's bedroom door opened. She said something to him, he went out, closed the door, she walked back to the bed and kind of collapsed on the side, head in hands, not a happy camper.

They were obviously keeping her locked up and that didn't look good from a rescue perspective, but it validated what Dowling had said and what I'd been feeling almost from the beginning: Cissy Devore was not, at least at this point in the game, a willing co-conspirator in this operation.

I backed up into the scrub and unclipped the walkie-talkie from my belt, keyed the button.

"Checkin' in, guys," I said.

"It's about time." Aaron's voice, frustrated.

"I'm at the house. All I've seen are Andrea, the bodyguard, and Cissy," I whispered into the speaker. "Guard's got a gun, Andrea seems to be having a grand old time, and Cissy's locked in a bedroom."

"Ready for us?"

"Not yet. I'll come back to you guys and we'll talk. Doesn't look like anybody's going anywhere anytime soon up here. I'll take one more look around, should be back to you in a few minutes or so."

"Make it snappy."

"Hey, Aaron, it's dark. Gimme a break."

"See ya when ya get here."

I turned the radio off, twisted around to pick up the rifle, saw a silhouette in the darkness; before I could react, cold steel pressed behind my right ear.

"Who the hell are you?" came a flat voice.

"You see a Boy Scout troop around here anywhere?" Probably not a good time to be glib.

Something caught me on the side of my head. Pain. Seeing stars that I don't think were in the sky.

"I take it you haven't." Jesus, that hurt.

"What is it?" Another voice, sounding a lot like this one.

"We got a visitor."

The second shape materialized, something in his hand, then some kind of cloth bag slipped over my head.

"You know where to take 'im. I'll get this stuff."

I doubted I was going on an amusement park ride.

CHAPTER TWENTY-EIGHT

I CLOSED MY EYES, PAIN shooting through my head. Best I could tell, they'd walked me through the house, down some stairs. I was a little confused. Hadn't lost consciousness from the little love tap, but it hurt like hell. There was a head-conking continuity in this case, it would appear. One more might be the last, I thought, the effort not without pain. I tried to touch the left side of my face where the pain seemed to originate, realized I couldn't raise my arm, felt something cut into my wrists behind my back. Tied up. For some reason, I couldn't remember that happening. Maybe he'd hit me harder than I thought. Things didn't look good. I grunted with the effort and heard a rustling nearby.

"Mr. Cash?" A voice I vaguely recognized. "Mr. Cash, are you okay?"

"Cissy?" Cobwebs clearing. I remembered being in the yard of the Nevada ranch house, recalled talking to Aaron on the walkie-talkie, then not much else. Wondering why it was so difficult to think, sure I hadn't lost consciousness.

"Mr. Cash, I'm so very, very sorry." A rustling noise, a body pressing against mine. "I wish I could …"

"Where are we?"

"In a basement or something, I'm not sure."

"You tied up, too?"

"Yes. Tape, I think. That silvery stuff."

"Duct tape." I strained against my bindings. Hands and feet. When the hell did they do this? Maybe the hit on the head, combined with the last one, did something to my train of thought. Not a fun thing to ponder.

"Mr. Cash, you've got to believe me when I tell you I have no idea what's going on." Her voice pleading.

"I'm not sure what I believe," I replied, trying to sit upright, not exactly remembering the sitting down part. I scooted backward until my back hit a wall, ran my hand along it. Concrete block, I think.

"I didn't think it would go this far," she said, starting to sob.

"Can you work around to me, maybe get this thing off my head?"

"I'll try." I felt her press against me, squirm around a little. "I can't get my hands up high enough. Lie down."

I rocked over on my side. The floor had an odor, gritty but not damp. Probably not much mildew in the desert. "Try it now."

Some more shuffling noise, then I felt her hands on the fabric, clutching and pulling. The hood slid off and I blinked. So dark I still couldn't see much, but I could make out Cissy's shape in the darkness.

"Where are we?"

"Like I said, in a basement, I think."

"No, I mean where? Is this part of the Las Vegas house?"

"Yes. They brought me downstairs after they put this thing on my head. I think it's some kind of pillowcase."

"Let me get it off. Turn around." With some effort, not helped the pain in my head, I worked my arms around my legs and got them in front of me, thankful for long arms, reached over, and pulled the cloth bag off Cissy's head. Her hair came tumbling out, less of it than the first time I saw her. I couldn't see her face in the pitch-black darkness, but my hand brushed her cheek; it was wet with tears.

"Who's they?"

"Those men Andrea hired."

"How many?" Head throbbing with every word, but thinking a little more clearly with the effort.

"Three."

Down to two now, I supposed. The one with Andrea and one I didn't count on. "Do you know them?" A stupid question, I guess.

"I never saw them until we got to Las Vegas. They met us at the airport." Apparently some advance preparation on Andrea's part.

"So you flew in."

"We drove to South Carolina, then left the car in Greenville and flew here in a private plane. Andrea told me I could leave whenever I wanted, but asked me to come here with her first. She acted pretty scared, but I know now it was just an act. Before you say it, I will. I've been stupid. Completely stupid." Sobs again. "I can't believe all this is happening. I really can't. God help me. God help us."

"We're going to have to talk sometime about your relationship with Andrea Satchley, but now's not the time," I said, trying to calm her down, struggling with the headache. "All I know right now is that I've been whacked on the head twice trying to get to you …"

"Twice?"

"Alabama."

"That was you?" Genuine shock, I think. "Andrea told me it had something to do with her brother. Wouldn't let me look. I couldn't have looked anyway; wouldn't have, I guess, I don't think, but …"

"Her late brother."

"What do you mean?"

"Rayford Dowling's dead." No way but the direct way at this point in the game. Shock value.

"Oh, dear God. Oh, God."

"He's been the second one to die so far, Cissy. Actually, the third, if you count …"

"I didn't know," she sobbed. "You've got to believe me, I did not know. Oh, Jesus. Who else?"

"Starting with a guy by the name of Claude Farnsworth. Ring a bell?"

"Mr. Farnsworth? Andrea's bodyguard? Back in Charlotte?" Cissy getting near hysteria, so I figured it was time to stop the revelations for the moment, before she fell completely apart.

"I'll try to explain at some point, but right now we've got to figure a way out of here. Aaron and some friends are on the outside, probably wondering where the hell I am. By the way, where the hell am I?"

"Andrea said this place used to be owned by a racketeer. She said she liked it because it had 'special places,' I think was how she described it," a bitterness emerging in her voice, anger taking over. Good. "This must be one of them."

"Do you have any idea how long we've been here?" Maybe I did go out for a while; hard to tell.

"I don't know. I really don't. You were here when they brought me down."

"How long after you woke up?" I was straining to establish a time of reference; not an easy task under the circumstances.

"Woke up? Oh, you mean … how did you know about me taking a nap?"

"Let's just say I was watching right before this happened. Planned to swoop in, pluck you out, and sort this mess." Some swoop. I felt like I'd been butting heads with a freight train, losing big time.

"Let's see," she said, her voice getting stronger I think, coming back down to earth, focusing a little. "That wasn't very long ago. Maybe half an hour, forty-five minutes. Not much more."

"Good. Then Aaron and the guys should be wondering what's happened to me. May be moving in as we speak." Appropriate time for a little optimism, given the circumstances.

"I don't think they'll find us, Mr. Cash."

"Houston, Cissy. And why not?"

"I think I've figured out that this 'special place' is underground. A hidden passageway behind a bookcase. Andrea showed me the entrance but we didn't explore. If that's where we are, then Andrea's …"

"Andrea's what, sweetie?" Light flooded the room, I blinked against the harsh glare, then focused on Andrea Satchley in a form-fitting beige jumpsuit, properly made up in all her blonde, blue-eyed beauty, an obvious mad cast to those eyes, I noticed right away. "What, Priscilla?"

"I was just going to say that Andrea should be here soon," Cissy said, a touch of anger. Looking at her close up under the lights, I noticed her face was drawn, circles under the eyes. Not the woman who'd walked into my office what seemed like a hundred years ago. Maybe her mother.

"How perceptive of you." Andrea walked over to Cissy, leaned down, kissed her on the mouth, then backhanded her abruptly, knocking her flat on the floor, the sound of the slap ringing in the cinderblock room. The woman reeked of Black Diamonds perfume. Two very large men appeared in the doorway behind her in dark suits over white crew-neck shirts; one glanced at me, the other touched Andrea's arm gently, maybe trying to call off the dog, get on with the program.

"Get your fucking hands off me, Matthew," Andrea said, jerking the arm away. The guy looked startled, maybe a little pissed, but took a couple of steps back, hands free by his side, probably wanting to slap her but controlling the urge.

"Passageway's secure, Miss Satchley," the other one rasped in a cigarette-ravaged voice.

"Thank you, Mark," Andrea said, composing herself, then turning to me. "We have a problem here, Mr. Cash, and I've got to decide what to do about it. I presume you have reinforcements outside."

"You presume correctly." No sense in hedging. "They're more than likely right on your heels this very minute." Trying to exude confidence.

"I doubt that," she said, a crooked smile distorting her features. This was one whacked-out woman. "If they're up there, they're looking through an empty house.

"You see, Mr. Cash, this fine abode was built in the 1950s by a man of Italian descent who was afraid of two things: nuclear war and federal authorities. Not only do we have this lovely underground shelter," she said with a wave of her hand, "but we have a very convenient passageway that surfaces in the middle of the desert a good half-mile from here. An ingenious layout, wouldn't you say?

"And the wonderful thing about it," she continued, "is that nobody knows this but us, and I wouldn't have known it but for the skills of my friends Matthew, Mark, and Luke." She gestured to the two men who forced smiles, enduring the loony tune for a price, no doubt. And for Mark, from what I'd seen before, maybe a tad more than money. "Matthew, Mark, and Luke. Good Biblical names. I expect Charles would appreciate the irony."

"'Yea, though I walk through the valley of the shadow of death …'" I started.

Andrea stepped toward me and unleashed another backhand, the large diamond on her left ring finger cutting a groove in my cheek. Her husband's token of love now a weapon. Seemed appropriate.

"No need to get pious on me, Mr. Cash. No need at all. I've spent a life enduring piety and I don't want it …"

"Maybe we oughta be going, Miss Satchley," the one called Matthew said hesitantly, fidgeting a little.

So here it goes, I thought. Matthew or Mark will dispatch Cissy and me, then they'll find our bones maybe fifty years from now when they finally excavate this hole.

"So what would you like to be, Mr. Cash? Part of our insurance, or should we go ahead and take care of loose ends right now?"

"Never liked being a loose end, Miz Satchley." The best thing I could do at the moment was buy time, clear my head, work out some kind of countermeasure; though the prospects didn't look so good.

"That's what I like to hear, though I'm really not sure of your value. What do you think, boys?" She looked at the men; both shrugged.

"Don't need no murder raps if we can help it," Mark offered. "'Less you want us to, that is."

"Afraid you're a little late for that, fellas," I said, hoping to play the only trump card I had. "Of course, right now you're all just accessories."

Andrea and her partners looked at me, puzzled.

"Oh, you don't know, do you?" Getting bolder. What the hell. If I was signing my death warrant, might as well do it with pizzazz.

"Know what, Mr. Cash? We really don't have time for riddles." Andrea getting impatient.

"I guess there's no good way to tell you, Andrea, but you're a lonely orphan now."

For a split second Andrea Satchley looked dismayed; then a cold wave swept across her face. "Ray," was all she said, then seemed to brighten, madness kicking in again. "I suppose it was inevitable, since he's obviously the reason you people came here. Too bad. I'll say a prayer for him tonight.

"Cut 'em loose," she said to her sidekicks, then turned back to me, face tight. "I know you won't give us any trouble, will you, Mr. Cash?"

"I was raised to respect women," I said.

"Good. Then we'll wait a few more minutes for Luke and ..."

"Not much sense in that. Luke's not coming either," I said. Lowering the last boom, not wanting to spend any more time in this bunker than necessary.

Andrea looked at me again in that peculiar, slightly twisted way. Then the freeze came back.

"Whatever. Let's get this show on the road, gentlemen. More money for you two, right?"

Matthew produced a switchblade and sawed through the duct tape bindings on Cissy's ankles and wrists, and then mine. I got up slowly.

"Anybody got an aspirin?"

Andrea walked up, looked at my head. "You'll live." She gave me a push toward one of the walls. "Hit the button, Matthew." A section of the wall we faced seemed to retract, then slide to one side. Somewhere machinery groaned. "Still works like a champ," Andrea said, flecks of spittle forming on the corners of what probably was, under normal circumstances, a pretty nice mouth.

The portal opened into a long, narrow corridor, also lined with concrete blocks, intermittent lightbulbs recessed in the ceiling, diminishing into the distance like the throat of a dragon.

"They had real craftsmen in the fifties," Andrea said, rubbing a hand against one of the walls, then finding another switch that closed the door behind us. "Sharp. Really sharp. I hate to leave this place. Found it almost a year ago, thanks to Matthew and his friends."

A year? Andrea's plot was a lot thicker than I would have thought.

She prodded me forward, Cissy walking stiffly ahead, appearing downcast and dazed. Maybe "overwhelmed" was a better word.

"Sounds like you've been working on this thing for a while," I said as we moved through the tunnel.

"You don't know the half of it," Andrea said, proud of her accomplishment. "Ever since I met Priscilla, I've been waiting for this time in my life. Finally getting what my daddy always said I deserved."

Cissy remained silent.

"Priscilla, darling, don't get me wrong. I did love you, honey. It's just that a woman needs a few things in life, and I wasn't getting them from my husband. Or you from yours, for that matter." Andrea getting chattier than I'd expected.

Cissy whirled around, eyes glowing. "Don't talk about Carson in that way, Andrea. You know I love him."

"But you weren't getting what you wanted, were you, now, darling?"

Andrea baiting her as she moved us ahead. "You needed a friend and I was the best friend you could find. Now isn't that right?"

"I thought you were my friend," Cissy said sullenly, turning and marching on. "I thought we were more than friends."

"You'll have to forgive her, Cash. Disillusioned young woman married to an older man; empty life. The classic story."

"What were you going to do if this all worked out?" A question I had to ask.

"Silly man. It is working out," Andrea said indignantly. "Just a few complications, but I'll figure something out."

"I can't help but notice you're not carrying the money." Goading her for no particular reason; maybe a little risky, but I was working my way through this a step at a time, grasping for whatever I could shake loose.

"I took care of that right away," she said, smiling. "Put it away for a rainy day. But I won't bore you with the particulars."

"Bore me."

"Now if I told you, you'd know too much and that might become a problem, Mr. Cash. Some things are better left unsaid."

"But why did you go public at the casino? Why not just disappear?" I had the feeling this would be my only chance to fill some gaps, prodding Andrea while she was on a roll.

"To be perfectly honest, I never thought you'd come here. I guess I counted on dear old Ray to keep his mouth shut, wait for his money. Looks like he didn't trust his big sister." Calculated and crazy as she was, Andrea sounded perfectly calm while she talked. "Looks like he paid the price, too." Nary a trace of regret now, it seemed.

"Do you really think you can get away with this?"

"Dear boy, I am getting away with it, as you put it. We're just going from point A to point B. You and your friend are going to love point B."

I didn't want to ask. Andrea didn't wait for a reply.

"Once we've got you safe and sound, Carson and Charles will get another phone call, only this time we'll drop all the bullshit and acting, since everybody seems to know all the silly little details. They leave us alone," she said, matter-of-factly, "they'll eventually get you back. Or at least Priscilla. I'm not sure about you yet. No dollar value beside your name that I'm aware of, except maybe your name itself. Ha! I made a little joke!"

"Disposing of me might cause you more problems than you'd need," I said, trying to sound ominous.

"You already told us we've got two dead, so one more wouldn't likely make any difference."

"Three, actually." I couldn't believe I was saying it. Getting into the rhythm of the conversation, I suppose. It didn't actually seem to matter. "There's Farnsworth."

"Claude was an accident. Can't pin that one on us. True, I'd had higher hopes for him. He just screwed up," she said, sounding like she was talking about a bank account balance. "His mistake was listening to Charles instead of me."

"You know, of course, if you give this up now you're just an accessory. Might even have a pretty good defense since you weren't directly involved. Hell, call it quits now and there might not even be any prosecution."

"Give up! That's a laugh. They'd put old Andrea in a nuthouse, and what kind of life would that be?" She had a point. "I want to live, Mr. Cash. And since your friends haven't brought the authorities in up to this point, they're not likely to from here on.

"I'd say things are going pretty well."

"How about the M&M boys?" I asked, turning to look at our silent escorts, who didn't return the gaze, staring straight ahead.

"Matthew and Mark know which side of the bread their butter's coming from," Andrea said, an analogy that didn't make much sense but I wasn't prone to correct an insane woman. "They're perfectly happy to live out their lives in luxury, aren't you, boys?"

A grunt from Matthew was the only response.

"It's truly amazing what you can get people to do when you wave millions of dollars in their faces, Cash. I'll bet even you could be bought if the price was right."

"I'm already employed," I deadpanned.

Cissy stopped, and we all almost collided.

"This is a dead end, Andrea," she said dully, standing in front of the wall.

"Not for long, sweetie." Our captor felt along the concrete blocks again, found what she was looking for, and a hiss preceded the barricade swinging outward. We stepped through into what appeared to be a shallow cave carved roughly enough out of the rock to look genuine, then into the cool night air. A breeze assaulted us, the air smelling sweet after the dank tunnel.

A black Chrysler minivan was backed into a trough of low desert scrub. Matthew walked to it, got inside, started it up, and pulled it out onto the gravel apron. Mark slid open the side door.

"Your carriage awaits," Andrea said with a flourish, curtsying cutely. "Boys, the hoods."

The cloth felt cold against my face.

"Can't have you watching where we go, so I would suggest you leave them on," Andrea said.

Cissy and I were helped aboard, placed beside each other on a bench seat. I reached over and squeezed her arm. She felt stiff and unresponsive. The van started moving.

"It's going to be a little while." Andrea's voice. "Anybody know any good campfire songs?"

- - -

I fought the drowsiness that was no doubt a side effect of the head injury, tried to stay alert enough to calculate the mileage, listen for traffic and other noises. I couldn't hear any other vehicles for a long time; then we sped up, got on what must have been an interstate. After that, it was hard to keep track, and I eventually succumbed to the weariness.

How long it was before I stirred back to consciousness I couldn't say, but Cissy's head was resting on my shoulder. Through the weave of the hood it appeared to be brightening outside and the traffic seemed heavy, horns honking, vehicles passing nearby. The van was silent except for the sound of its engine, so more than likely everyone but the driver, Matthew as best as I could remember, had dozed off. I was tempted to raise the bottom of the hood but fought the urge, figuring the first thing I'd see was Matthew or Mark aiming something that shoots in my general direction. Somebody stirred; then Andrea's voice, sleepy.

"Home again, home again, jiggity jig," she said, yawning. Somebody poked my arm. "You two up?"

"Bright-eyed and bushy-tailed," I responded flatly. Cissy seemed to continue to sleep, unmoving.

"Much as I'd like to get another look at those baby blues, I'm afraid we'll have to keep you covered a little longer," Andrea said. "Not much, though."

I heard her mumble something to someone, then felt the van swing, probably exiting off a ramp. Lots of traffic noise still, stops and starts, probably at intersections, then open road once more. After maybe thirty minutes of silence, the van bumped across something, stopped briefly, pulled ahead for a few minutes, slowed, then stopped, engine off. The noise of a garage door lowering.

"Rise and shine, sweetheart." Andrea again; Cissy stirring.

The van doors opened and we were helped out. My head didn't seem to be throbbing as badly, but I still felt pretty rotten. A hand on my arm guided me up some steps, through a door, along a carpeted hallway, then down two flights and through another door before we stopped.

"Wakey, wakey," Andrea said. The hood was lifted, and I blinked against the bright light. We were in a large, comfortably-furnished room, like a den. No television, but attractive tan leather furniture, wooden tables, peach-colored walls. No windows, either. A bathroom off to one side. I looked at Cissy, sleepy-eyed but stunning. Andrea and Matthew watching us, Mark missing.

"You two get comfortable," Andrea said. "Plenty of towels in the bathroom, so take a shower if you'd like. Together, if you want." She grinned. "Matthew'll bring you something to eat at some point."

They left the room and I heard a deadbolt slide home in the heavy, solid wood door. No hollow-core construction here.

"Place familiar to you?" I asked Cissy, who walked to the long sofa and flopped down with a sigh.

"No."

"Feel like cleaning up?" She looked at me, eyes searching. "Alone, by the way," I added quickly.

"You can go first if you want to," she said.

"Doesn't matter to me."

"Before you do anything, though, let's have a look at that head." She got up, nudged me into the bathroom; a large, bright affair with green fixtures, garden tub, separate, glassed shower stall. Mirrors everywhere. A couple of hotel-style terrycloth robes hanging beside a chromed rack of towels. Cissy turned me toward the mirrored wall behind a double vanity. I looked like hell; dried blood; puffy, dark circles under my eyes. Hardly fighting form.

"You look like you've been run over by a truck," Cissy said, dampening a towel and dabbing my face. "I like the new you, by the way."

"It was originally intended to be a deception. Like your hairstyle, too. Really accentuates your face," I said, wincing when she touched the quickly-staining towel to my temple, dabbing the residue. "Ouch."

"Sorry. I'm really sorry about all this."

"We'll talk about it when we're fresher."

"This doesn't look as bad as I was afraid it would be," she said, leaning closer, breath on my cheek. Having unclean thoughts about the boss's wife. "Still probably wouldn't hurt to get a doctor to look at it."

"I doubt Matthew or Mark have their licenses," I said.

"What are we going to do, Mr. Cash?"

"Houston. We're going to get out of this, Cissy."

"Andrea's obviously crazy as a loon. I don't know why I didn't see it sooner. I mean long before this got started."

"Crazy, yes, but I don't think crazy enough to do us any harm. And you'd have had no way of knowing, really."

"Matthew and Mark, on the other hand, appear quite capable of doing some damage, don't you think?"

"They're a couple of tough guys, but when I told them about Luke and Rayford, they didn't react like killers." I had no idea how killers would react; just trying to allay her fears, maybe mine, too.

"Two people dead sounds like killers to me. Three if you count Mr. Farnsworth, though that was before the bodyguards."

"But our escorts weren't constructively involved in any of them. Luke might have been the bad guy of the bunch, or what he did may just have been a reaction. No, I think we're safe for now."

"'For now'?"

"As cool as Andrea is, I think everything about her grand plan has been screwed up, and in that mixed-up mind of hers, who knows? I won't sugar-coat anything." I looked her in those gray eyes. "She's got plenty of dough, could hire somebody to take care of things."

"I'll shower first," she said, shrugging, and, I could see, finally getting her act together. She pushed me gently out the door and closed it. In no time I heard the water running in the shower.

I walked around the room. Good-sized, maybe twenty by thirty feet. At least Andrea didn't have us in a closet. Could have been a lot worse. On one side was an empty place where a television might have been, a TV cable stub protruding from the wall. I found a phone jack behind an end table. I scanned the corners, every nook and cranny a camera or listening device could have been hidden. Clean, as far as I could tell. The absence of a television and phone told me Andrea had planned to use the room for a holding cell, probably for Cissy. No lamps, either. Nothing, in fact, with a cord. She probably hadn't thought about the robe sashes, maybe a twisted-up towel as a handy homemade garrote. Had to think of any and all possibilities for subduing whomever.

I sat in one of the two large, beige chairs. For the first time in my career, I was a prisoner. I didn't like it. I patted my pockets, now empty of everything. I noticed for the first time they'd even taken my belt. Two-hundred-dollar Gucci number. The watch, too. A Rolex. Bet one of the M&M's was wearing it now. My once-shiny shoes were now badly scuffed; I slipped them off, pulled out the insole, and found the Swiss Army knife I'd carefully installed there when dressing at the MGM Grand.

I still remembered a few things from my Boy Scout days. Especially the "be prepared" part.

CHAPTER TWENTY-NINE

CISSY EMERGED FROM THE bathroom wrapped in one of the robes. Nothing else, it looked like. She smiled one of those weary, what-the-hell smiles. Perking up a little. Actually perking up a lot.

"It's amazing what a good, hot shower can do for the soul," she said. "Your turn."

I brushed by her, the sweet smell of soapy clean. Some of the smell natural, more than likely. Carson was a lucky man.

"I can't wear perfume," she said, apparently noticing my reaction to her scent. "Allergies. Andrea, on the other hand, bathes in the stuff."

And it apparently rubs off, I thought, remembering my early encounters with Cissy and the faint aroma of Black Pearls.

The shower felt as good as I expected, stinging a little where I'd been cold-cocked. There was a small shampoo bottle, another hotel-like touch, but I knew we weren't in any hotel. I soaped up, let the stinging spray beat me all over, twisted the control nozzle, and toweled dry. Nice big, fluffy hotel towels. A pattern emerging here. Maybe Andrea stole them. Would have been in keeping with her demeanor to date. Found a comb, ran it through my hair, took the towel and wiped the steam off the mirror, taking a good look. Better than a few minutes ago, still not used to the makeover, feeling almost like I was looking at someone else. A less grungy someone else, thankfully.

I ran some water in the tub and hand-scrubbed the shirt, getting as much of the dirt and grime out as I could, draped it on the shower stall to dry, the tear from the fence not too noticeable. Put on my Calvin Kleins, then the pants; shrugged on the remaining robe, the sides of which barely met in front, thinking these robes always seemed to be manufactured with Munchkins in mind.

When I walked back into the room, Cissy was stretched out on the sofa looking up at the ceiling.

"What if this were our last day on earth?" she mused dreamily as I took one of the chairs and flopped.

"You're supposed to be thinking 'This is the first day of the rest of my life' or some homily like that," I said, looking at the form of her lithe body under that terrycloth, amazing hills, mysterious valleys, all laid out nicely. Bad thoughts I was having a hard time suppressing; Carson's face difficult to conjure at the moment.

"No, I mean it," she said, earnest if a little embarrassed, eyes locked on mine. She untied the sash, letting the robe fall open to reveal that amazing body, no tan lines, perfect, seamless naked female.

What came next is what comes naturally, I suppose. Two people, a man and a woman, facing not-too-happy prospects of the future, forgetting for a moment about husbands, lost happiness, all that stuff that vanishes when you know it shouldn't. She rolled off the couch onto her hands and knees, crawled over to me and untied my robe, pushing it off my shoulders, then working at the fastener on the slacks. My temperature and other things were rising. In seconds, we were both naked on the carpeted floor, stroking, hands and mouths moving, touching places. My head might still have been hurting, but I didn't know it.

I violated every personal rule I'd ever had at that moment, losing any resistance in the passion Cissy had pulled from me. Except for the early days with Dawn, I can't remember making love more passionately.

When it was over we robed again, maybe both a little embarrassed, but shame wasn't an emotion I could detect, inside or out.

Cissy got back on the couch, I sat in the chair, and we looked at each other; no talking at first, just looking.

"I love my husband," she said softly, long lashes unblinking, gray eyes staring holes into and through me.

"I don't doubt it for a minute."

The door opened before anything else could be said. We both remained quiet as Matthew walked in with a tray, put it on a table against one wall, and walked out without a word, never looking at either of us. The deadbolt slid home.

The food was just a couple of thawed-out frozen dinners and glasses of water, but we both descended on it greedily, shoveling with the plastic spoons our captors had provided. I couldn't remember a meal ever tasting better. We finished in no time, looked at each other and laughed, me wiping the corner of Cissy's mouth, she mine. Intimacy I knew only fit the moment, fleeting but nice. Then she sat on the couch, I walked into the bathroom, put on the nearly dry shirt, came back, flopped into a chair.

"I don't know what that was, but damn, it was good," I said, stifling a burp. "The food, I mean," I added hastily. "Not that the other ..." Stammering. Gotta forget that moment, file it away as a brief, weak interval.

"I pretended it was filet mignon," Cissy said, grinning, seeming to ignore my momentary discomfort.

"Now that we're well-fed, maybe we ought to think about getting out of here, maybe leave Matthew a tip on the table."

"Can we? I mean, really?"

"We can sure as hell try, but not before I get a little history lesson. You up to it?" Hoping.

"Where do you want me to start?"

"How about at the beginning."

Cissy took a deep breath and launched into her association with Andrea Satchley.

-    -   -

The two of them met the first time about a year ago at what Cissy described as a "social function" without elaborating.

"I was drawn to her. She's really got a very magnetic personality, and the only person in my life was Carson. I didn't have the warmest family in the world. Carson's wonderful, don't get me wrong, but I had always felt there was something missing in my life," she said. Don't I know it.

Andrea started calling her often; they would meet, go out together, things like that, according to Cissy. The relationship became "a sisterly thing at first, telling each other secrets, a lot of touching, laughing," she said. "Then the touching became, well, more intimate, and I was swept up in it all. Blindly, I guess. I'd never been so close to a woman and, at the time, it seemed, well, natural."

"She took you to bed," I said, not a question.

Cissy blushed and lowered her head, then looked at me. "Yes, to bed. I was so naïve. It was like a new adventure, something I'd been taught most of my life was wrong." Like what we just did, perhaps. "I don't want you to think …"

"I don't think anything, Cissy. Really. She saw you were vulnerable and took advantage of it. Working your weaknesses. No more, no less." Not after what we'd done, at any rate. Me beginning to think I'd done the same thing, maybe feeling guilty, but it was a passing thought. I didn't dwell.

"Anyway, we sort of became even more intimate, and she started to ask me a lot of questions about my life, Carson, our lifestyle, personal and private things that I didn't mind sharing at the time. She ate it all up, said it was like listening to someone telling you a fairy tale. I had complete confidence in her. You'd have to have been there to understand. I mean she really, really had me fooled.

"Then she asked me, maybe a month or so ago, if I'd like to take a little vacation. An adventure, she called it, and it intrigued me. I had no idea what she was planning at the time." Tears beginning to squeeze out of those eyes. "I swear to God I didn't know anything about the kidnapping, the money, any of that. Not even when it was going on, until it was too late for me to do anything about it.

"'We'll take our little trip, then you can square everything with Carson and we'll all laugh about it,' she said," Cissy continued. "She said it would be like a game, two kids running away from home. Thelma and Louise." Long pause. "The first time I realized it didn't appear to be a game was when I called your house.

"They—she and Rayford—caught me on the phone and disconnected it. That was when I first saw the real Andrea, the one you've seen in the last day. From that point on, I felt like a prisoner; felt like I had to do everything they asked me to or … or I don't know what would have happened."

I watched her face as she talked. Clear, fresh, and, most importantly, honest, I think. "What about Atlanta? Birmingham?"

"I didn't know who we had run into in Atlanta. All of a sudden Andrea and Ray told me to throw everything in a bag, we had to get out of the room. In Birmingham, Andrea told me some of Ray's old acquaintances were after us, chasing a debt or something like that. I suppose I should have known better, but I was so tired and frustrated by then, so afraid, I just did whatever she told me to do.

"When Ray didn't come back into the room right before we left, Andrea told me to hide in the bathroom. That was when she hit you and the other man, I guess." A pained expression. "I didn't get a look at your faces. All I saw were three knocked-out men on the ground, one of them Ray. Andrea didn't stop, dragging me along, said things would be straightened out eventually, not to worry.

"We drove to an airport, took the plane to Charlotte, found my car in the parking lot, and drove to Greenville, Andrea telling me along the way that things had gotten out of hand but that she'd straighten it all out.

"Those men met us in Las Vegas, and from that point I was treated like a prisoner. The game was over." She sighed, wiping a cheek. "I didn't know, Houston. I just didn't know. I only found out about the money when we got to Nevada. Andrea and Ray never said anything in front of me about it. But when I asked her what was in those silver cases we loaded into the van, she said it was a 'present' from home, didn't elaborate."

"What about all the preliminary stuff, getting me and those other people to follow you around?" Trying not to sound like an inquisitor, but needing the questions answered, knowing this might be my only chance.

"Andrea had made me paranoid. She told me she'd hired a bodyguard and that I ought to do the same. Completely convinced me I was being stalked by someone. Suddenly everybody around me became somebody after me, now that I look back on it. I didn't even stop to think how she might have known such a thing. Like I said, I was naive. Maybe 'pliable' is a better word. I asked Mr. Trenton first, just on a whim; then I hired Debbie's brother, not taking it too seriously at the time."

"Did you tell her about them?"

"Yes, but she didn't seem satisfied with the ones I'd asked, told me I should get a professional. That's when I asked Aaron, and came to you." She paused, looking down, talking toward the floor. "I didn't want to say anything to you about her, so I wasn't completely up front with you those times in your office. I know now that I was wrong, but it seemed appropriate at the time. I didn't realize until it was too late that one was associated with the other. Then it all came apart, didn't it?"

"I suppose that's a good way to describe it. Coming apart. My guess is that Andrea was setting the stage to make it look like a real kidnapping. I'm a little surprised she suggested a 'professional,' as you put it, since being a professional helped me zero in on what was happening." I looked at her for a long time; then stood up, looked around the room. "Wonder what time it is?" Time to change from talking about the past to the present, at least.

"I sort of tried to figure it out in my head, but I don't know how long we slept. I'd guess at least mid-afternoon, hungry as I was." She wiped her face with the sleeve of the robe.

"Aaron and the troops are probably going nuts right about now," I said, trying to picture them tossing the Nevada ranch, wondering what the hell happened to me.

"Troops?"

"We recruited some local help. It looked like we were about to wrap things up. I was supposed to be headed back to them when, I guess it was Mark, bopped me in the yard. One thing I'm sure of is that we're not in Las Vegas any more, Dorothy. From the length of the drive, I'd say somewhere in or near Los Angeles, since any other direction would have been mostly sand and sagebrush."

"The Satchleys have a place at the coast. Think this could be it?" She stood up, too, starting to pace.

"I doubt it seriously. I would think Andrea wouldn't go anywhere she thought Charles could find her. She'd also go somewhere she wouldn't be recognized. LA is a big city, easy to be anonymous, so my money's on LA."

"What do we do now?"

"We start doing something about getting out of here." I produced the knife. "This is all I've got, but I think I can make the most of it."

"That little thing?" She eyed the Swiss Army knife, looking tiny in my hand. "You're going to try to dig our way out of here?"

"Nope," I replied, grinning. "I'm just going to create a surprise or two."

CHAPTER THIRTY

MATTHEW HAD BROUGHT THE food in without preamble or warning, but I figured it was only because we weren't listening at the time. We decided to take shifts at the door, ears pressed against the water cups pressed against the door. Another old Boy Scout trick I remembered, the cup amplifying noise outside. Amazing how much I retained from so little time as a scout, wondering briefly how much of a superman I'd be if I'd stayed with it.

If, as I hoped, we could hear them coming down a hall or steps or hear doors shut, Cissy could go into the bathroom, close the door, run the shower. I'd brace myself against the wall beside the door, waylay the messenger, disarm him if possible, and we'd be one step up on the game.

"If it sounds like more than one coming, we won't do anything," I cautioned Cissy after explaining my plan as succinctly as I could. "I feel a lot better, but I don't think I could handle both of the guys at once.

"Now that Matthew's been in here and we haven't tried anything, I believe we can catch 'em by surprise," I said. "They're going to assume we're passive, and they certainly don't know I've got the knife."

"You might think you feel better, but don't you think I ought to help? Even with one? I've had a few self-defense courses," she offered.

"I think I'll be okay, especially with the element of surprise. Don't want him grabbing you. Me, either, for that matter. It might screw things up. One on one is the best way, and I probably should be that one."

"It's just that I feel like I ought to be doing something more," she said, dejected. "I mean, just running and hiding …"

"You're playing a critical part," I said. "You're the distraction. Once we've got him we'll play it by ear. You might have to use your skills on Andrea," I said reassuringly. "Listen, the whole idea is that we've got to establish some kind of advantage. We've got to get out of this alive."

Cissy insisted on taking the first listening shift. Without benefit of a timepiece (she was watchless, too), we just decided we would each do it until we got tired, then swap. We didn't have to wait long.

"Footsteps," Cissy said after only a few minutes next to the door. "More than one set, I'm sure."

She darted to the couch, I slouched in a chair. Within a few seconds the deadbolt slid and the door opened. Andrea and Mark walked in, looking around like a couple of plantation owners checking the slave quarters.

"Just thought I'd tell you we've just about got everything in place," she said, expressionless.

"Everything as in …" I pressed.

"Details, Cash. Just details. No need to bother you with it." She seemed concerned, brow knitting over that crazy glint.

"Talked with anybody?" Trying to get her to drop at least a little information, wondering for a split second if we could take them both, deciding pretty quickly it probably wasn't a good idea.

"Not yet. I'll be sure to inform you when the time comes. Not," Andrea said with no small touch of cynicism.

"Don't suppose we've been on the afternoon news." Fishing for a time frame.

"You know better than that, Cash. No way these people are going to go to the police at this point in our little contest of wills." Andrea, getting angry. "There wasn't even anything in the *Times* about the Las Vegas shooting." Mark shot her a look that Andrea didn't pick up on, unaware she'd just given us a clue to where we were. I kept a flat expression, like it didn't sink in. I don't know whether he bought it or not.

"Anyway, we'll be keeping you two here for a while, but you'll be well taken care of, well fed, as long as you don't present any problems," Andrea continued. "If you do, then there's a much nastier place you'll have to be kept." She didn't elaborate and I didn't want to ask. "Do you understand?"

"Sure," I said. "A dungeon, no doubt."

"Worse," she said, a crooked smile distorting her lovely features. "Much worse. Now," switching mood, businesslike. "I've got a few things I have to do, so Matthew and Mark will be taking care of you while I'm gone."

Mark walked over to Cissy, took her by the arm.

"I don't think it would be such a good idea to keep you two together, so Cissy is coming with us to our other place." To Cissy, who was looking at me like a deer in headlights, "Not the dungeon, sweetie; just another room." Back to me, a smile. "No sense in having our guests plotting against us, now, is there?"

Before I could say anything, Mark was pushing Cissy out the door, Andrea behind them, looking over her shoulder at me, maybe trying to gauge a response, see if she'd thwarted anything.

"You be good, now, and Cissy will be just fine," she said, closing the door.

The deadbolt did its work, and my job just got a lot more complicated.

-     -   -

I don't know if my lack of expression had fooled Mark, but I did know that we were in Los Angeles, or at least somewhere nearby. I doubted that Andrea was talking about the *New York Times*.

But now that they had Cissy somewhere else in this place, wherever it was, I began to doubt my previously-devised plan would work. I might be able to waylay one of the bodyguards, but if they set up some kind of system, I could be putting Cissy in jeopardy. Think, think, think, Houston.

I figured I'd have to take the chance.

-     -   -

I was beginning to nod against the cup when I heard faint footsteps outside the door. One person, from the sound of things. I darted into the bathroom, turned on the shower, ran back out, closed the door, and took my place only seconds before the door swung wide in my face. I couldn't tell which one it was from behind. Both of them had greasy black hair, both about my size. He was carrying a tray and, upon hearing the shower, strolled casually toward the table.

I held my breath and jumped.

Matthew swung halfway around and I caught him on the jaw with a hard right, sending him sprawling and the tray clattering against the opposite wall. He brought a left elbow into my solar plexus. The pain felt like a hot poker, but I got my right arm around his neck and held on. He was trying to work his hands free under him, probably going for his gun or a stiletto, when I brought the knife around and pressed it to his neck.

"This is fuckin' stupid, Cash," he growled. "You won't get away with it." He opened his mouth as if to shout.

"Say one word and you'll be writing it in blood on the floor, asshole." I poked his neck with the knife, a drop of blood emerging.

He froze.

"Now lie flat like a good boy," I said, working my way on top of him and pressing my knee into the back of his neck.

"Can't breathe," he rasped.

"That'll be the least of your problems if you don't lie still," I said, probing around his back and sides with my free hand until I found the bulge of the pistol, pulled his jacket up, and drew it out. A little more probing and I found the switchblade tucked into a sock. I pocketed the knife, pressed the barrel of the Beretta to the back of his head, and stuck the Swiss Army knife in front of his eyes. "Ever been a Boy Scout, Matthew?"

He just glowered. I grabbed the back of his jacket collar, gun still pressed against the base of his skull, and pulled. "Get up."

Adrenaline still pumping, I had a coppery taste in my mouth. Time to throw down the gloves.

"Where's Cissy?" I asked, dragging him into the bathroom and cutting the shower off.

"Another place, away from here," he lied. I cocked the Beretta next to his ear. Very slowly for emphasis.

"I have absolutely no patience and no time to fuck around, Matt."

"Upstairs," he said. "A bedroom."

"Mark and Andrea?"

"She's gone somewhere. Shoppin', she said. He's in the room with the woman."

"When's she coming back?"

"How the hell should I know?"

"Tell you what, Matthew. I'm going to assume you're telling the truth, but if we go out of this room and I hear anything move, anybody say anything, a mouse fart, whatever, I'm going to pull this trigger and examine your brains to see if they tell me something. You know, like tea leaves."

"I'm tellin' the truth," he said.

"How about you lead me to Cissy's room, then, and we'll get the gang together." I tapped the side of his face with the pistol. "Move."

Matthew half-stumbled out the door into a hallway, up two short flights of stairs and into a large, open room, lavishly furnished, one wall all glass. It was dark outside; I could hear the crash of surf on rocks.

"Malibu," I said. "Figures. Which way?"

"Up there," Matthew said, gesturing toward a flight of stairs against the far wall that ended in an open, railed landing overlooking the den.

"Okay, we're going to walk up to the door, you're going to knock, tell Mark you need to talk to him. If you've got some kind of signal you'd better use it, because if the door doesn't open, you know what will be decorating it."

"Yeah, yeah."

We got to the door and Matthew knocked twice, waited, then once more.

"It's me," he said.

"What's up?" Mark answered, unlocking, then opening the door wide, totally unprepared.

I shoved Matthew through, knocking Mark down with his friend on top of him, climbed on top of both with a knee in each back and the Beretta stuck between their faces.

"Avon calling," I deadpanned, probing Mark's jacket until I came up with another Beretta and yet another switchblade. "You greaseballs all use the same gun, have the same stocking stuffers?" I stood up, kneeing their backs with a little extra thrust. "Get up. Slow, with hands where I can see 'em."

The two men stood, and I noticed Cissy for the first time, standing in the bathroom doorway looking stunned. One side of her face looked puffy and red; she clutched the robe tightly around her, protective.

"Getting a little frisky, Mark?"

"I …it doesn't matter," she said, rushing to my side, looking fearfully at Mark. His eyes followed her, mouth tight. I backhanded him with the Beretta in my right hand, keeping the one in my left trained on Matthew's face. Mark went down like a sack of potatoes.

"Hey, what the fuck?"

"Here's the deal, Tweedledee," I said, hands trembling with anger. "You touch this woman again, you're dead. No warning, no smart words. I just pull the trigger and you don't have a face anymore. You got that?"

Mark mumbled something.

"What? What's that you said? Hell, I might just pistol-whip the both of you, make up for Las Vegas."

"Yeah. Okay." If looks could kill.

To Cissy: "You recognize this place now that you've seen it?"

"Yes, I think so. Andrea told me she'd rented a beach house and that we'd go there someday. She told me all about it. This is it, I'm pretty sure."

"Go see if you can find some tape or cord or something so we can make our friends here comfortable."

Cissy disappeared out the door, and I waved the two men over to the bed. Covers rumpled, probably from Mark's attempts at Cissy. "Have a seat, guys. In fact, why don't you just lie down?"

The two of them stretched out side by side, never taking their eyes off me, trying the cold stare treatment.

"Fold your hands on your chests, fingers entwined, if you know what that means," I said. They complied. "I see any of those hands move, even an inch, and this'll be the picture they put in the papers, only I'll make sure you're holding each other, naked, face up so they can see the holes."

Cissy came back with a large roll of duct tape. Something every house in the world seems to have.

"Found this in the kitchen pantry," she said.

We bound Matthew and Mark at the wrists, ankles; then strapped them together, then to the bed, and still had enough tape to turn them into chrome mummies if we'd wanted. I considered it for a minute.

"Now before we finish the job, let's have a little chat," I said. "Cissy, I don't know about you, but I could use a stiff drink."

"I think there's a wet bar in the den."

"Scotch, if there's any to be had. Neat. You see anything going on outside, you get up here fast."

After she left I zeroed in on the boys again, both looking like amateurs at a bondage festival in their silvery spider web.

"How much you two getting paid?"

"None of your fuckin' business," Matthew said.

I walked over, tapped him on the forehead with the butt one of the pistols. Maybe a little too hard, I don't know.

"How much, Mark?" I said, raising the other gun, butt-first, over his face.

"Five hundred grand apiece," he said, eyes looking at me with so much hate they watered. "Ten percent of Miz Satchley's take, she said."

I laughed. "You two don't have even the remotest idea what her take was, do you? You've both been screwed royally."

They looked at each other.

"How's fifteen million dollars sound?"

"Fuckin' bitch," Matthew muttered. "Don't matter anyway ..." he started, Mark butting him with a shoulder.

"Let me guess. Once me and Cissy were gone, you were gonna roll Andrea for the balance?" Their looks told me the thought had crossed their pea-brained minds. "Let me try another one. Luke was the brains of the operation?"

Their silence answered the question.

"What makes you think your boss-lady's even going to come back?" I asked. Their expressions said the thought hadn't even crossed their minds. "I mean, what's to keep her from just going on, hiring a new escort, getting the hell out of Dodge, leaving all four of us here to rot in paradise?"

"The money's in the basement," Mark said, loosening up a little. Maybe the reality of the situation settling in. "She ain't gonna leave that."

"If she's been carrying the cash around, how come neither of you decided to pop her, take it, and forget the whole thing?"

"We don't kill, Cash. Not part of the deal. Don't matter how much money you got if you got a murder rap followin' you around," Mark said.

"Too bad Luke didn't have that principle," I said.

"Luke was stupid," was all Mark would say.

"How'd Andrea get up with you guys?" Curiosity getting the best of me.

"We all three worked security at a casino when she and her old man came a while back," Mark said, Matthew rolling his eyes. "She came up to us, asked us if we did any free-lance work."

"Let me guess. Matthew, Mark, and Luke aren't your real names. I'd put money on your real names ending in vowels."

"Fuck you." From Mark.

Cissy came into the room with a drink in each hand, extended one to me, took a tentative sip from the other.

"You know how to work one of these?" I asked her, holding up a pistol.

"I've never touched one in my life."

I showed her how to operate the gun, handed it to her. It looked like a cannon in her hands. Took both hands just to hold it up.

"I don't think you'll need it, but if either of these guys acts like he's going to do anything, you just point it in their general direction and pull that trigger there. I've got to make a phone call."

I walked over to the bedridden tough guys. "One more question," I said. "What's the name of the road this house is on?" They told me; I racked off a couple of strips of duct tape and spread the pieces across their mouths.

"You boys be quiet. Try to get some sleep if you can."

I strolled through the cavernous house, looked in all the rooms, maybe twenty of them, all empty; looked out the front door. A driveway snaked through a long front yard up to an attached garage, which connected to the house through a door in the kitchen. I hit a button beside the doorway and a light came on, the garage door ratcheting up. I hit it again; the garage door went down but the light stayed on. Found a rake hanging on a couple of wall clips, smashed the light with the handle. No point taking any chances when Andrea got here. I walked back through the living room, opened a sliding glass door, and stepped out onto a large concrete deck that jutted over a rocky cliff, maybe fifty feet above the surf. The cool ocean breeze felt good on my face.

Back inside, I found a telephone on a lamp table. I dialed information, got the number of the Las Vegas Police Department, and let the phone company's system make the call. The dispatcher put me straight through to Pick Sanders.

"So, how's the weather in Vegas?"

"It's about fucking time," he roared, not masking the relief in his voice. "You got the case solved? Where do we need to go pick up the pieces?"

I gave him the short version of our trip to LA and where we stood at the moment.

"So you think you're in Malibu? Got an address?"

I gave him the name of the road; the number I'd seen on a piece of junk mail on a coffee table during my inspection.

"You want me to call the regular troops out there? I got a friend I can get, maybe bring a couple of his boys, keep it out of the headlines, if you know what I mean."

"I want to wait for Andrea to play her hand. Gimme the guy's name. I'll call him when we're ready. I think we're safe for the moment. How's Aaron?"

"After about thirty hours without sleep I made him go back to the hotel. We haven't told Devore and Satchley anything yet, by the way. They've been checking in regularly, calls forwarded to the cell phone. We told them we were still looking. Aaron said to wait, thought you'd pop up. He didn't sound much like he felt that would happen, by the way. We didn't know what else to do, and Aaron still wanted to keep the Feebs out of it. When we found the rifle and binoculars and stuff, he figured they'd taken you.

"We tore the house apart, found the basement and escape tunnel after I got one of the department boys to do a little research on the place. We went to the end of the tunnel and saw the tire tracks. Didn't see any blood, so we had to assume they'd taken you somewhere." Pick sounding somewhat apologetic. "I took care of the shooting thing, too. Had Aaron write up your statement like he was you, self-defense and all that, just in case you're worried. Nobody'll be the wiser and the paperwork'll be straight."

"Sounds like you've kept busy."

"One thing we didn't find, by the way, was my piece," Pick said. "You recover it from the goons?"

"I'll ask 'em," I said. I'd forgotten about that gun, suddenly wondering if maybe Andrea held onto the Sig. Added a new dimension to the impending confrontation that I didn't particularly want to think about.

"You hang in there," he said. "We'll come on out there in a little bit. Fairly short hop from here. You call my friend, tell him what you think he needs to know, have him call me.

"And Houston," he added, "Don't be John Wayne. Things get hot, you wait for us."

Pick gave me the Los Angeles detective's name and number before we hung up. I called him and said I might need his services. Detective Sergeant Barry Porter didn't ask any questions; said he would have a couple of officers on standby, and to call when I needed him. I had no doubt he was on the phone to Pick as soon as I hung up.

I went back to the bedroom, ripped the tape off Matthew's mouth, and when I asked him about the Sig, all I got was a blank stare.

"Beats the shit outa me," he said, working his mouth from the sting of the tape. "I put it somewhere in the Vegas house, maybe in the kitchen, last I seen of it. Pussy gun. I don't like 'em."

"You boys better be telling me all I need to know. I've got a long memory and a short fuse," I said, looking at both of them. Matthew's eyes shifted back and forth, but Mark only stared, cold. "You two think of anything, just put your lips together and blow. When you get your lips free of this crap."

I replaced the tape and walked Cissy to the bedroom door, taking the pistol from her and sticking it in a pocket, nearly dragging my pants off my hips. I went back to the bed and noticed Mark was wearing the Gucci belt. Stripped it off and put it where it belonged. Unclasped the Rolex from Matthew's wrist and reclaimed it, too.

"You guys won't be needing these," I said, returning to the door and flipping off the light. "Y'all try to get some sleep."

I told Cissy about my conversation with Pick and that Carson didn't know anything yet.

"He'll be worried sick," she said, though her face seemed to reflect an odd look of discomfort for a second.

"No more worried than he's been up to this point. As long as he believes you're unharmed, which I think he does, he'll just push on," I said. Then, almost as an afterthought, I told her what he'd said to me before we left Charlotte. The message brought fresh tears to her eyes.

"Carson is a lovely man," she said, sobbing. "The best man I've ever known. I don't know if he'll ever forgive me."

"He's already forgiven you," I said. "Let's just put a happy ending on all this and get back home, what do you say?"

"What do we do now?"

"We pick a place to hide and we wait. Andrea might have my gun, by the way. She know anything about pistols?"

"Andrea was an athlete, so maybe. She never really said anything to me about guns, so I couldn't actually say."

"Let me give you another quick lesson," I said, and did. "Remember, shooting this gun is a last resort, to protect yourself. If, by the way, anything happens to me during all this, you get out and get out fast. Just run like hell up the driveway. If there's a gate, there should be an inside release. We're in Malibu, by the way, and there will be other houses."

"Why don't we just call the police and get this over with?"

"We've kept the police out of this up to now, as far as the kidnapping is concerned. I don't want federal agents screwing things up. And," I added, "at this point you might even be considered an accessory to a few things."

She looked at me, confused. "An accessory?"

"You tell a police investigator you had nothing to do with anything, but three people are dead and there's a trail of sorts. Just trust me on this one, okay?"

"Okay." She walked to me and put her arms around my neck, hugging me tight. "I just want to go home." Sounding like a little girl.

"We'll get home, Cissy. I promise."

CHAPTER THIRTY-ONE

I HAD NO IDEA WHERE Andrea had gone or why, and after two hours I was beginning to wonder if she'd be back at all. I had positioned myself in a small sitting room in the front of the house; sat beside the large picture window, watching the driveway. Cissy stayed in the main room, lights off except for one small lamp, looking through the glass wall into the darkness. Not that I thought Andrea would make an entrance up a cliff, but I didn't want Cissy here if the woman was bringing in reinforcements. We checked on the boys upstairs once; both of them appearing to be out like lights.

The waiting brought reflection, me wondering what kind of person I was dealing with in Andrea Dowling Satchley. Early on, the apple of her daddy's eye, terrific looks; mates with an up-and-coming young cleric; they have a kid, then lose him; she goes nuts; spends maybe years plotting some kind of odd revenge on her husband, sees an opportunity with Cissy Devore, and grabs it.

Crazy people are apt to do anything, and I didn't know where Andrea thought she was ultimately headed with all this. Seems she was smart enough to know it would all eventually catch up with her, but crazies typically only analyze the moment, or so I'm told. Not too many people in psychiatric wards known for making long-term plans. Don't often do what you expect them to do, either, and I was very much on edge with that thought.

No, we were hardly out of the woods yet, and I wasn't counting on anything positive happening in the next little while.

—   —   —

I didn't pay much attention to how long I'd been waiting at the window. Watching the clock only made the tedious seem more so. Then two things started to evolve at about the same time.

I heard the air-chopping sound of a helicopter in the distance, and saw a glow toward the end of the driveway.

I ran to the back of the house, found Cissy nodding in the den.

"It's showtime," I said, after jarring her awake. "You go upstairs, stand watch outside the bedroom with Tweedledee and Tweedledum. Remember what I said. If there are any fireworks and you don't hear me, haul ass. Got that?"

She nodded and made her way up the stairs. I went into the kitchen, lights off, half-crouched beside the door leading into the garage, and watched through the six-pane window in the door. In a few seconds, the garage door started its jerky climb; the van's lights illuminated the walls, then pulled in.

Through the door, I could hear Andrea get out of the Chrysler, cursing aloud at the darkness.

"What the hell's the deal with the light?" she said to herself. "Have to get one of the guys to look at it." The van door shut, then I heard the vehicle's back door slide open, the sound of her getting something out. The sliding door again, chuffing home. A couple of steps, then she stopped.

"Matthew?" to the darkness. "Mark?" Footsteps again, a noise like maybe she laid something down. In the stillness of the moment, it occurred to me that the helicopter seemed to be getting closer.

More footsteps, the sound of a door opening somewhere, then nothing. Nothing for several minutes, it seemed like. Shit. Another entrance.

I slowly opened the kitchen door, crept down the short flight of steps in the darkness, pistol held in front, moving it side to side. No sign of Andrea. Just the van, ticking as it cooled, and what looked like a large, plastic shopping bag laid beside it. As my eyes adjusted to the dark, I saw a rectangle in the back corner darker than the rest of the wall, duck-walked over to it. A hidden panel made to look like the paneled wall of the garage. I felt inside and found a switch, flipped it up, and lights illuminated a narrow, tight-fitting wooden staircase leading upward.

Rich people and their paranoia.

I stepped inside, back against the wall, nearly filling the shaft. A shot splintered the wood two feet from my head. I jumped back out and waited, heard footsteps heading away, ran back inside, and looked up. Feet disappearing through what looked like another panel a couple of flights up.

I sprinted back into the house through the kitchen.

"Cissy! Go! Go now!" I shouted, running into the main room. No response. I hit the stairs two at a time, then slowed at the top and rounded the solid banister on my knees, carpet friction burning.

Andrea had an arm around Cissy's neck, the Sig Sauer looking huge against her left temple.

"Well, well, Cash. You're a lot more enterprising than I gave you credit for," Andrea leered. Muffled cries from the bedroom; the chopper getting louder, sounding like it was landing on the house.

"Drop the gun or say good-bye to your sweet little client!" Andrea shouted over the helicopter noise.

I pointed my pistol at Andrea's face; Cissy terrified, eyes widening, locked on the gun, steady in my grip.

"Now what's that going to accomplish, Andrea?" I said, not lowering the Beretta, hopeful.

"It's going to get me out of here, is what," she said, backing up along the landing to a part of the wall swung wide, the hidden garage doorway, dragging Cissy along.

"You hear that noise outside? You won't get far." The chopper sounding like it was settling, maybe in the front yard, I couldn't tell. Had to be the LA guys or Pick, impatient. There'd been plenty of time for them to fly from Vegas.

"That noise, dear heart, cost me two hundred thousand dollars," Andrea said, triumphant, backing through the opening, disappearing out of my line of fire.

- - -

I took the inside stairs two at a time, bounding toward the front door. Better to cut her off than chase. I burst through the door, foolish under the circumstances. The helicopter, a sleek Bell Ranger with, to my great surprise, a television station's number and logo on the side, had alighted about a hundred yards from the house; the shape of someone getting out the sliding side door. Had to be a leased model, since it wasn't likely that anybody's Eyewitless News was already zooming in on the Devore kidnapping.

I could hear the garage door crawling up, so I ran around to the side, backed up against the stucco wall of the house. Plaster and dust flew as another shot ricocheted over my head, causing me to drop to the ground reflexively.

Andrea still had Cissy around the neck, but she'd held out her arm to fire and Cissy apparently saw an advantage, elbowed her sharply in the chest, ducked free, and ran back into the darkness of the garage, leaving Andrea standing alone, dead in my sights.

"Give it up!" I shouted at her, leveling the Beretta, praying I didn't have to squeeze the trigger. "There's nowhere to go, Andrea!"

She didn't respond, just stood there, staring at me; then a slow grin spread across her face and I knew I'd waited too long. The cold steel pressed into my back.

"Drop the gun, sport," the man said, "and raise 'em."

CHAPTER THIRTY-TWO

ANDREA WALKED TOWARD ME, pistol dangling by her side.

"Good timing, Phil," she said as I let the Beretta drop.

"Turn around," the man apparently called Phil said. "Slowly."

I dropped quickly, swinging my right leg low, and caught Phil at the shins, toppling him instantly, his pistol flying into the dark. I rolled on the ground, grabbed my gun, spun around, and squeezed off a shot in Andrea's direction as she vanished into the black maw of the garage.

My knees hurt like hell. I was getting too old for this Bruce Lee crap, but it worked. Phil was sprawled on his back, struggling to get up, looking like a rolled turtle. I stuck the pistol in his face.

"Hate to do this, Phil," I said before bringing the pistol down on his forehead. Feeling around in the dark, I located his gun, a small Smith & Wesson .32 caliber, and stuck it in my pocket. Standard flight gear, I guess.

Back at the front door, I shouted inside, warning Cissy. No reply. Two steps inside and all the house lights went off at once. Somebody throwing a breaker, apparently. Pitch black darkness, only the sound of the helicopter rotor slowly whining to a stop. I glanced toward the aircraft, saw no one else inside. Phil must have flown solo.

I turned and blended in with the shadows of the entry hall, creeping low, one hand sliding on the wall. Dead silence. Would Andrea try to free her bodyguards, or was self-preservation the only thing on her mind right now? I hoped she was being selfish.

I inched forward.

Somewhere inside the house, sounds of walking. I couldn't tell where. Then two muffled thumps, maybe gunshots? I tried to move faster, wishing I'd paid more attention to the layout. A glow told me I was close to the main room and I stopped, crawled the rest of the way, scurrying like a crab.

Shadows playing tricks kept me alert, and as I focused I noticed that the glass door to the deck was open. There may have been a way to escape there, I figured, since the hidden door in the garage had eluded me; but it had looked like a sheer drop on all sides. Under the circumstances, I decided to look.

I belly-crawled across the room, trying to stay behind furniture, feeling exposed, but nothing happened and I made it to the deck. The concrete platform was cold, the ocean breeze picking up, buffeting my face. On my hands and knees I checked the perimeter, looking under the railing, down at the darkness. The deck was suspended over the rocky cliff. No ladder, no stairs, support beams tied back to the foundation of the house.

A noise from inside rose over the wind. A cry. Almost a yelp. I stood up, ran back through the opening, and heard a sound; someone struggling, maybe. I couldn't tell, but it made the hair on the back of my neck stand up. Then a crash, and somebody running.

"Cissy!" Still no reply. I ran into the kitchen; the door to the garage was open. I stepped onto the small stairway, remembering a circuit breaker box on the right. I reached over and started levering breaker switches; lights coming on.

A woman's shout; upstairs, it sounded like. I sprinted through the house, up the stairs, into the bedroom where we'd left Matthew and Mark.

Both men lay on the bed, eyes wide. A hole in each forehead; a pillow, powder-burned and blood-flecked, lay on Matthew's chest.

"Surprise, surprise!" Andrea behind me. I nearly jumped out of my skin, whirled, fired reflexively, the shot shattering the door jamb where she'd stood, then disappeared.

I bolted to the door, stopping, looking outside, seeing the top of her head bounce down the stairs. I followed her, on the way hearing the helicopter engine spooling up outside. Phil must have recovered, either fleeing or getting ready for the Great Escape, but I wasn't in a position to dwell on it. Instead of running for the front door, Andrea took off toward the deck, disappearing through the sliding door.

I followed her, wondering what the hell was going on. At the glass door I stopped. Andrea leaning against the far railing, holding the pistol limp by her side, blood trickling down the side of her face, marring that porcelain skin. I knew I had missed her when I fired, so where did she get the wound?

"I give up, Cash." Madness drew that lovely face into a mask of—what, ferocity? Anguish? She climbed up, straddled the three-foot-high railing, gathering her white pleated skirt tight around shapely legs. Almost like the Marilyn Monroe shot, only with a concrete beam in her crotch.

"Andrea, we can work all this out. I swear to God we can." Desperation. This was not how things were supposed to be happening.

"It's too much, isn't it? I just can't seem to win for losing. The odds, I guess, are always going to be against me." Something like a shadow passed over her face, like an unseen cloud, and for a moment she actually looked like she might have been feeling regret. "You shouldn't take the Lord's name in vain, Cash. Maybe that's what screwed me up."

A sense of dread overcame me, lights coming on in my head. Cissy.

The helicopter sounded like it was lifting off; then the Bell crested the house, hovered over the deck, took off toward the east in a blast of chopping fury.

"Your girlfriend's gone, it would appear. You just can't trust anybody, can you, Cash?" Andrea shouted, looking up. She daintily dropped the pistol over the ledge. "Won't be needing that where I'm going. Frankly, my dear, I'm gone, too," she said, flashing a smile, that other personality returning.

With no more ceremony, Andrea Dowling Satchley leaned out over the ocean, then toppled soundlessly into the darkness, feet disappearing below the rail.

I ran to the edge, looked over at the crashing waves, made out her small, pale figure, limp in the surf, hair spreading outward, arms outstretched like a bizarre, delicate crucifixion as she was embraced by the salty foam.

The helicopter faded in the distance, strobes twinkling until they merged with the stars far, far away.

CHAPTER THIRTY-THREE

THE WORLD MAY NEVER know who dispatched Matthew and Mark. As impossible as it was to grasp, my money'd be on Cissy. Shutting mouths, maybe getting revenge. I didn't know and wondered if, at this point, I even cared.

This case had been nothing but twists and turns, death, and at least emotional destruction. How could I begin to tell Carson Devore what appeared to happen here tonight? Would Charles Satchley calmly accept his wife's plunge into a mental darkness, maybe pray for her soul and get on with his life? I had so wanted to believe the story Cissy told me, but now it really seemed just that: a story. A fable concocted in her head, possibly playing the victim for Andrea while using the woman all the time. Was there a devious side to her personality I was just too blind to see, and was our brief coupling some kind of insurance on her part that I would play my role to the end?

Or had Andrea's insanity rubbed off? Maybe Cissy was just as loony, only handling it better. I thought I knew her, but it appeared that I didn't know her at all. She had me fooled all the way. At least, I think I was being fooled and it wasn't a spur-of-the-moment decision for her to grab the money and hightail it. Andrea would never be telling; and without the bodyguards, I guess nobody would. I suppose that was the point.

But why exact this elaborate price simply to get away? Nothing made sense.

— — —

Aaron and Pick arrived about an hour after Sergeant Porter and his team had marked, tagged, photographed, and scoured the bedroom; removed the two bodies. In the basement of the house, we found an empty silver suitcase, a few stray hundred-dollar bills scattered around the unfinished room. Consolidating the debt, it would seem. One too many suitcases to lug, or a few million already spent.

For an instant I wanted to think that maybe Phil was the wild card. Maybe Andrea had said too much to him, so he decided to take matters in his own hands; but Cissy's absence pointed to something else entirely.

There's an old saying in the South: "The hit dog hollers." A roundabout anecdote that Shakespeare once used as well, and this time certainly seemed to apply. "She doth protest too much."

I'd given a statement to the locals, then handed Porter the Beretta I'd taken from Matthew. Porter doubted I would have to come back, but said he'd be in touch. The helicopter had not filed a flight plan and didn't return to the small private field where it was kept. Phil's gun had been reported stolen from a Los Angeles pawn shop, and Porter's team had tried to find Andrea's in the surf after they'd recovered her body. No luck. They'd also made a half-hearted attempt to locate Cissy Devore, but I told Porter they were wasting their time. He said he'd tag the case unsolved, no immediate suspect.

Without the gun I'd given Cissy, there would likely be no way to officially determine who'd killed the bodyguards, or who didn't.

The shopping bag Andrea had left in the garage contained what Porter said was some kind of high-tech phone equipment "like that kind of expensive crap you get at Sharper Image," probably to set up a scrambling system when she made her calls to Devore. Maybe just an electronic trinket to pass the time. Again I didn't know, again I didn't care.

Aaron, Pick, and I assembled in the kitchen, a somewhat familiar place to share thoughts, "deja vu all over again," to quote Yogi Berra.

"So is this the end of the line?" Aaron breaking the ice first, opening a beer he found in the refrigerator.

"I don't know what else it can be," I said, dull from exhaustion. "It would seem that what has transpired is fairly obvious, wouldn't you say?"

"You mean that Cissy engineered the escape, has disappeared with her husband's money, and there's no point in trying to track down a runaway wife since the 'hostage crisis' appears to be over?"

"That, I suppose."

"Well, don't go buying a hair shirt or flogging yourself unnecessarily. She had us all fooled," he said, patting my shoulder. "I'm inclined to think it was a spur-of-the-moment decision, if that's any consolation."

"But how could you explain Matthew and Mark?"

"Could very well be that Andrea popped them, maybe was planning to pop the two of you, then saw that Cissy was getting away with the goods and decided to throw in the towel, let God be her judge."

"I guess we'll never know."

"Maybe not. I called Carson, by the way," Aaron said. "Didn't go into any detail, but told him to meet us back in town tomorrow, fill them in on everything."

"Did you tell him Cissy wouldn't be with us?" I could envision the disappointment, dismay, sense of loss.

"Figured I'd leave that up to you, being as you're the one who talked to her last."

"And that maybe I'd tell him she needed a little time off, decided to use his bankroll to take a vacation?"

"Whatever."

"I'm going to have to tell him something, and the best I can see is to tell him the truth. Tell them both the truth."

"In all honesty, I had a creepy feeling that Satchley knew it wasn't good news for him," Aaron said.

"Not like he wouldn't be expecting the worst, considering the big picture."

"I just don't know how to close this out. My client's still missing, regardless of the circumstances. My brain's telling me this case isn't over yet, but Carson's apt to tell me it by all means is."

"Maybe she'll send you a postcard. You know, 'Wish you were here,' all that." Aaron was straining to bring some levity to the moment; not succeeding. But his remark did give me an idea.

"Tell you what, Aaron. How about you talking to the husbands and me sticking around for a couple of days, using all my detective know-how, maybe try to find our little lady just one more time before I cash it in, so to speak."

"What would I tell 'em?"

"Tell Charles the facts, tell Carson whatever you want; that I'm still looking for Cissy, making one last-ditch effort to bring it all into the light."

"What you're really doing is trying to justify it to yourself, aren't you?" He looked at me long and hard. "Sounds like a pretty good idea to me."

"Now that's what I like to hear." Pick, speaking up for the first time. "The old team spirit. I'll tell Porter to help you where he can. Maybe you can at least find out where the chopper went; know that much if you don't learn anything else."

"I'd appreciate it. And I'll make sure you get compensated for your time, Pick, I swear," I said.

"Hell, it's been fun, boy. Don't worry about me. Just answer this last big question, then tell us all about it. You still owe me a visit to my house, anyway."

"Done" I said.

We left the house in an unmarked police car piloted by a driver Porter supplied, and after I put Aaron and Pick on separate red-eyes, I began my last quest to solve the Cissy Devore case.

CHAPTER THIRTY-FOUR

FINDING SOMETHING AS BIG as an errant Bell Jet Ranger helicopter proved a more daunting task than I'd expected. Porter had loaned me an office; found me a list of air traffic control towers at a dozen airports in a two-hundred-mile grid around the area.

I talked to most of them, finally finding three who'd reported an unidentified aircraft headed south through their designated space. The path, such as it was, pointed to a little private field just outside San Diego, and with no better ammunition than that, I headed down the coast in a rented Buick.

- - -

Bucks Field was a World War II vintage strip the operator told me had been used for things like glider training during a war he looked plenty old enough to have fought in. Said he'd "Sure enough fueled a chopper just this mornin'. One a them tee-vee jobs, paintin' all over it. Guy just dropped out of the damn sky on me, but that ain't too unusual hereabouts.

"I didn't ask no questions," he said, "jes' like I ain't a-gonna ask you any, and yeah, he had a woman with 'im. Figured maybe she was one a them reporters they got on the television these days, all prettied up.

"Funny thing about it," he added, lighting a filterless Camel cigarette and wheezing out a cloud of smoke, "was she stayed, and he tuck off.""

Like a million old-timers with their protracted tale-telling tactics, it had taken him nearly five minutes to get to that critical point, and he rambled another five before telling me she used his phone, called a cab, and headed into town. I slipped him a fifty, still running on the cash I'd gotten from Carson, extracted the name of the taxi company, and drove into San Diego; booked a room at a La Quinta hotel, and got on the phone.

The cab dispatcher, a marginally amiable guy with a faint Hispanic accent, said he didn't like giving out information on customers over the phone, but after some properly-applied pressure, he agreed to let me look at the log book if I cared to come by, the implication being I should make it profitable for him.

Following his directions, it took me about thirty minutes to get to the Blue Sky Cab Company and, after briefly flashing my private investigator ID and passing a twenty, the dispatcher shoved a stack of paper across the counter; a crude computer printout of what looked like a month's activity.

The cab company was in a cramped, dirty storefront at a strip shopping center that had seen better days. The light wasn't good and there was no place to sit outside the service counter, so I stood there, squinting at the printout while he tried to explain how to read it, pointing here and there with a dirty, tobacco-stained finger.

Between the two of us, we figured out a fare had been picked up at Bucks Field and taken to a resort hotel in Chula Vista, a stone's throw from the Mexican border. I looked at my watch. Cissy had probably been there about five hours, if indeed it had been her in the helicopter.

It took me maybe thirty minutes to get to the resort, a rebuilt 1920s-style affair that rose in peaks and turrets maybe a quarter-mile from the main highway, accessed by a long driveway with a guardhouse, a gazebo-like affair that made me feel oddly like I was entering a Disney World attraction. The complex wrapped around a sun-parched golf course; old men in carts bobbing across the fairways, putting on the greens.

Apparently you had to have a sticker or card or be riding in a hotel vehicle to be allowed past the gate, none of which I had, so a polite uniformed guard with the face and walk of an ex-cop directed me to a parking space alongside the gatehouse, looked at my PI card disdainfully and, after looking at me like he was measuring me for a new suit, asked me to wait in the car.

He said something into a callbox, waited, then ambled back over, directed me to what I guessed to be the employee parking lot; told me how to get to the concierge station inside the grand old building, which now glittered anew with faux twenties decor and subtle modern touches.

"Mr. Cash," the concierge said, straining for respect, probably wondering if my daddy sang country music. "How can I help you?"

I gave him a short version of who I was seeking. He said something into a phone, which they seem to do a lot in the more expensive hotels, then directed me to an office to the right of the huge front desk.

A dapper young woman, all smiles and teeth, stood up behind an antique desk as I walked in; informed me crisply but politely before I could ask that they didn't give out information on clients.

"It's an important investigation, Miss ..."

"Rodriguez," she offered, a little less politely than before. "I understand that you are a private investigator, Mr. Cash?"

"If that's the problem, Miss Rodriguez, I can make it official pretty damn fast," I replied, losing my patience and not bothering to conceal it. It had been a really long couple of weeks. "I can have the homicide bureau of the Los Angeles Police Department give you a call in, oh," I looked at my watch, "five minutes, let's say? Or I can have the CEO of the country's second-largest bank buzz your CEO and ..."

"That won't be necessary," she spluttered, face reddening, probably more from the mention of a CEO than a homicide bureau. She looked at some papers on her desk in what I knew to be a meaningless gesture. "I think we might be able to accommodate you without compromising our records. If you'll just give me a minute."

She disappeared out the door; I took a seat, looking around. A UC Santa Barbara diploma on the wall, some hotel industry certificates, severe decorations; the rigid life behind the walls of splendor. Luxury in this business was obviously reserved for the guests. For employees it was corporate Spartan. She was back in about ten minutes, a computer printout in her hand and an odd look on her face.

"You're welcome to look at this," she said, walking behind her desk, turning and flattening the sheet in front of me. "But you may not have to. It appears that a package was left for you at the concierge station."

She produced a small white envelope, kind of like the ones you get when you make a bank deposit, with my name scrawled on the outside in a feminine handwriting. I opened it and a key fell out, one of those with a plastic end, obviously a locker key. I looked closer and it had a San Diego airport logo embossed in the plastic.

I glanced at the printout, saw that an "A. Satchley" had been pre-registered for today, and had checked out an hour before I got there. Initially part of Andrea's getaway plan, I had no doubt.

I thanked Miss Rodriguez for her time and headed for the airport, wondering when all this chicanery was going to end.

- - -

San Diego's airport was pretty much the same as up-and-coming international terminals all over the world. A lot of people going a lot of places at the same time, most of them looking like they'd just as soon stay home. Transported merrily by moving sidewalks past high-priced shops and snack bars. I wondered if people regarded train stations in the same way a century ago; doubted it. They had character.

Locating the airport lockers wasn't difficult. A helpful terminal porter walked me to the bank of blue metal doors and left me to find which one the key matched, much like a bank teller at a safe deposit vault. It didn't take long to find the locker. I opened it, the key stayed in, and I pulled out a fat, heavy manila envelope. I hefted it, examined the ridges and folds of its bulky shape.

I took the envelope to my car, already knowing at least part of what was in it, feeling the weight and shape of the Beretta. Sitting in the Buick, I dumped the contents onto the bench seat, the pistol falling out with two Number 9 envelopes, one with my name written on it, the other addressed to Carson.

Though tempted to open Carson's, which looked thicker, I decided to open mine, then think about it. Inside the envelope was a four-page letter, written in the curvy longhand of a woman who didn't seem upset, but I was reading too much into it too early.

"Dear Houston," she began. Like writing a boyfriend from summer camp, casual and only vaguely intimate.

"I can imagine what you think at this point, and you would certainly be justified in not thinking too highly of me." An understatement if there ever was one.

"But I need to tell you what happened, what made me make this decision.

"After I broke free from Andrea I went back into the house and found a place to hide. When I didn't hear you right away, I wasn't sure what to do.

"Then Andrea ran into the garage and up the stairs, through that hidden passageway. I think she must have gone straight to the bedroom, and I heard a noise. Two noises, actually.

"I went to the room and found her, standing over Matthew and Mark, a gun in one hand and a pillow in the other. When I saw what she'd done, I freaked, I guess is the best word.

"She told me she had done it for the two of us, that we didn't need any witnesses, that we should go get the money and get away in the helicopter. 'This is the way I wanted it all along, dearest,' she said to me. 'The money is in the basement, through a door just past the room where you and Cash were,' she said. 'We can get it in a minute, slip right out and we'll be gone, nobody else will be hurt and we'll be free, just like I promised you in the first place.

"'Cash won't follow us and I'm certain he won't shoot if he does,' she said. I walked up to her and she opened her arms, tried to embrace me. That's when I hit her with the gun and she stumbled. I suppose it was my frustration and fury coming out all at once, but I didn't care.

"I ran out of the room and didn't know where to go or what to do." Calling out for me might have been a good next step.

"Then I just started thinking about everything that had happened, and that's when I decided to go get the money, get away if I could, sort all this out. Sounds stupid, I know, but it didn't seem so at the time.

"I know you probably won't understand why I would do something like this." Understatement of the century. "But it felt like the right thing to do and wouldn't hurt anybody.

"I got the briefcase in the basement, found the helicopter pilot stumbling around outside, told him I had his money, and told him to get us out of there.

"As we lifted off, I saw Andrea jump, and after thinking about it realized what you might think. That perhaps I had something to do with all this, perhaps I was the one who shot Matthew and Mark." Perhaps, my ass.

"I also knew that you were a good enough detective to follow me, and that's why I'm leaving this package for you. I know my words might not be enough to convince you, and I also know that what we did was something that happened at the moment, and means nothing to you, but it meant something to me. It was a release." So that's what they call it nowadays.

"If you want to read the letter I've written to Carson, I can't tell you not to, but all I said to him was that I need some time alone, need some time to think about us, him and me, and some time to straighten myself out so that another Andrea can't come along and do to me what she did." That'll probably make ol' Carson feel just peachy, particularly the part about the fifteen million.

"Money means nothing to Carson and, quite honestly, doesn't mean very much to me, but it will help me get away long enough to sort things out." I didn't know about Cissy, but fifteen million dollars could help me get away for, oh, the rest of my life, maybe.

"I've enclosed the pistol you gave me so that you can give it to the police, prove to them that it wasn't the one used on Matthew and Mark." For all anyone would ever know, you could have pulled an old switcheroo, Cissy, I thought as I read the letter. No real proof there.

"Please deliver my letter to Carson, whether you read it or not, and please don't think any worse of me for what I did. I suppose I seized on an opportunity at a time I probably shouldn't have, but like I said, under the circumstances, it seems the right thing to do.

"When all this is past us, maybe we can sit down and talk about it.

"Love, Cissy D."

I'm guessing people sign letters with "love" out of habit, because there was none lost between me and my now-former client. I suppose I should have looked at this package as some kind of closure, a final punctuation mark on what had been one of the most frustrating cases of my career to date. But it didn't feel that way as I started stuffing everything back into the folder, angry at having been played for a sap, the question of whether Cissy had been stringing me along the whole time still unanswered, me hoping that wasn't the case, musing that it wasn't possible. Not Cissy.

I would have expected as much from Andrea, all things considered.

It would have been a proper way for her to resolve issues, but from the beginning Cissy had worn an aura of innocence. She had seemed so likely a pawn, and was now turning out to be the deceptive queen in this chess match.

I left Carson's letter sealed, pulled out of the parking deck, and headed for the La Quinta, to grab my stuff and head back to Charlotte. I wasn't looking forward to facing Carson Devore and certainly not Charles Satchley, but the time had come.

CHAPTER THIRTY-FIVE

Few things look better to weary eyes than a glimpse of home, and watching the Charlotte skyline take shape through the clouds as the plane approached the airport gave me a feeling of renewal. At the same time, looking at the imposing sixty-story tower that housed Carson Devore's bank made me realize my current job was far from over. I had to tell the shaper of that mighty institution that, no matter his reach at the board table, his grasp of his own life had failed. I felt my courage ebbing with the plane's descent.

Aaron was waiting at the baggage claim area of Charlotte–Douglas International, helped me lug the three suitcases to his car. He, too, seemed reinvigorated by being back on home turf, a spring in his step.

"How d'you want to do this?" he asked, cutting to the chase after a wan greeting, understanding what was coming.

I had called him; filled him in on my search for Cissy, the letter, the gun—which I'd deposited with Barry Porter in LA, both of us figuring it wouldn't make much difference how the ballistics turned out. Porter also told me Matthew, Mark, and Luke—real names Salvatori, Giancarlo, and Felix Spinetti—had lengthy rap sheets, "so if there's any consolation, it wasn't a great loss," he had said. Pick told Aaron he'd actually had some outstanding warrants on Luke; who, it appeared, had a proclivity toward burglary and thrashing females. All three had done time for fraud, burglary, fencing; all the trappings of the small-time hustler trade. Andrea knew how to pick 'em.

"First things first, I suppose. I'd like to go home, see if it's still there, pet my cat, wash my face so it'll be fresh when it confronts Carson's music. How did Satchley take the news?"

"You know, it was almost like he'd expected it," Aaron said. "They're planning a big funeral at the Primitive Church. No television, though. Then said he'd take some time off, think about things."

"I think from the moment this all started, Charles knew Andrea had something to do with it," I speculated aloud. "Nobody knew her better than him. Not even Rayford."

"Speaking of which," Aaron added a little gloomily, "his body was shipped back to San Fran, donated to a medical college. Turns out he had a will. Apparently expecting the worst at some point in his life. Go figure."

I looked at my watch as we climbed into the Crown Vic. "How about I meet you at your house, we go to Devore's around seven?"

"He wanted me to call as soon as you hit town. I'll delay the call. Fine with me."

Aaron helped me lug the suitcases into the house, Bogie acting like he hadn't seen me in a year, rolling on his back, pawing the air. His antics drew exhausted laughs from both of us.

"Damn cat's nuts," Aaron said, rubbing his belly. "I'll see ya in a couple of hours, then?"

The answering machine showed a double-zero, meaning there were more messages than it could count, so I turned up the volume and punched it as I hung up the Las Vegas clothes, the only souvenirs I'd let myself keep from our adventure. They had been custom-fitted to me, so I didn't see any viable alternative; figured I'd offer to pay for them if necessary.

Two messages were from Eddie, saying Joey was home recuperating, "lookin' okay, considerin,'" one from Frank Malone asking me to call; a few from bill collectors I'd ignored during the past week's hiatus from life; another from Dawn, telling me where to find everything in the house; then one I didn't expect.

"I know you did everything you had to do, and I appreciate that fact," Charles Satchley's voice said. "God guides us all, Houston, and God just called Andrea home.

"If you want to talk about it when you get back, I'll be here. Otherwise, I'd rather my memories of my wife remain as they were. Again, thank you for what you tried to do. The Lord works in mysterious ways, and I hope He'll stay by your side. I'll pray for Andrea and I'll pray for you."

Had to admit he was a stand-up guy.

I punched up Dawn's number; she answered.

"As I live and breathe, it's the wandering detective," she said, feigning levity. "You okay, Beast?"

"I think I'll survive. Not me I'm worried about. Appreciate your looking after things, by the way."

"Just part of the job. And speaking of the job," she said, "I've been green-lighted to go back to work. Got any openings?"

"Are you serious?"

"As a heart attack. I told Jerry what I felt I needed to do, which is to get your ass back on the straight and narrow, though I didn't exactly put it that way to him. We need to get you out of that hole you call an office, into some more respectable digs. Maybe near a modeling school; steer you toward a happier lifestyle."

"Jerry approved this little venture?"

"Nobody 'approves' what I do. It's my choice, like it or lump it. He'll have to like." I tried to imagine how that argument went; couldn't picture it.

"You know I can't pay much."

"Oh, you mean you didn't get the fifteen million? Well, forget it, then," she said with a laugh. "Of course you can't pay much. I worked for you before, remember? How's Monday sound?"

"Like my life's starting over again. See you then."

That bit of surprising news fueled me for the next call.

"Deputy Chief Malone's office," the secretary said.

"Frank in?"

"May I ask who's calling?"

"His favorite private investigator." After a pause, her probably wondering what the hell that was supposed to mean, she put me through.

"Cash?"

"Well, bless my soul. I didn't realize I was your favorite." Sarcastic enough to tell me I was sliding back into a normal routine quicker than I expected.

"We've got to talk about this Farnsworth thing. Am I wrong in guessing there's more to all this than I'll find on a police report?"

"I can't reveal details of a case, Frank. I expect you've got all the information you need ..." If only you knew, I thought, you'd be the happiest man alive. Probably stand on the sidelines and cheer the federal authorities as they trundled me off to Leavenworth.

"All I've got is a fatal accident, an ex-con from Florida who was working for a church, and nobody else that'll tell me much."

"Maybe we'll do lunch and I'll pick your brain, let you graze mine." Slim pickings, probably, I didn't say.

"You and me need to call a truce," he said, shifting gears. "May come a time when we can help each other, if you know what I mean."

"Maybe, Frank. I'll think about it." I couldn't imagine any circumstance where I'd help him, but there was no use at the moment to play games. I was too tired. We hung up more cordial than usual, and I started picking through the pile of mail Dawn had heaped on the kitchen table, gnawing on a pepperoni stick I found unopened in the refrigerator, afraid to look at the expiration date, but it smelled okay.

Bills and junk didn't distract me long. I took a shower, changed into my Sears duds, figuring I didn't need to impress Devore with the Vegas threads. I fed Bogie, played with him a little, then he apparently decided I was home to stay and wandered off somewhere to contemplate cat life.

Aaron showed up on time and we drove to the Devore house, the letter from Cissy burning a hole in my jacket pocket. I looked at the neighborhoods we passed, people living in tidy houses, leading tidy lives. Wondered if maybe I should think about driving a truck, writing a novel.

"Oh, by the way, here's this," Aaron said, reaching under the car seat and handing me my Glock, thrusting me back into the vocation I thought I had so carefully chosen what seemed like a thousand years ago. "Pick took care of everything. You need to make a special trip some day to see his family. Guy really went out on a limb for you."

"I think I'll invite him out for a fishing trip or something, bring the wife and kids," I said, sticking the gun in Aaron's glove compartment.

"You oughta do that."

For the next few minutes, just the gentle rumble of the Ford, then Aaron told me about his conversation with Devore when they got back.

"I didn't set him up for much, other than that she was okay," he said in conclusion. "Told him you'd provide all the details. Funny thing is, he hasn't asked anything about the money yet. Not a word."

"People like that, money is just a part of their lives. He probably knows she's got it," I mused. "I think Carson's genuine, and I think that he'll look at the money as something Cissy'll need, maybe."

"Guess so. You think she'll come back?"

I had to dwell on that one for a minute.

"Who knows. Eventually, maybe. She's one mixed-up woman."

"Think she offed the bodyguards?"

"Based on the time I spent with her, I find it hard to believe. But life's dealt stranger hands. She just doesn't seem like the killer type. My guess?" I looked at him; he glanced back, half-driving, half trying to get a read. "Andrea probably did it, but Cissy didn't stop her, possibly had the chance to."

"Possible. Doubt we'll ever know for sure."

"That's the hell of it. Somebody got away with murder. Not that Matthew and Mark were singing in the choir, but it still kinda gnaws at you."

We pulled into the Devore drive, me thinking, maybe hoping, it would be for the last time. Not looking forward to this at all.

- - -

Carson Devore didn't look much better than the last time I'd seen him, but he was cordial enough, that corporate demeanor easing back into his routine. He guided me and Aaron into the study that seemed almost unfamiliar now, though it hadn't been that many days since I had been in it.

"I'm going to Charles's church for the memorial service Saturday," Devore said, uncomfortable, acting like he didn't want to hear what I had to say. "Sad thing about his wife. Hard to believe, isn't it?" He looked at me with weary eyes, washed-out blue, more lines on his face than I remembered.

"All of this has been pretty hard to believe," I admitted, showing a little reluctance on my own part to relate the obvious.

"So Cissy's not coming back?" he asked, tentative.

"I don't know, Carson. Don't know if I can say that for a fact. She said she needed to sort some things out."

"You talked to her?"

"No. She left me a note. And," I said, reaching inside my jacket pocket, "she left this for you." I handed him the envelope.

He looked at it for what seemed like a long time, turning it in his hands like it was a warrant for his arrest. Then he looked up, fear in his eyes; a man used to plowing his way through billion-dollar mergers, now cowed at the thought of reading a simple letter from his wife. Maybe not so simple, I guess.

"If you two don't mind, I'd like to read this alone," he said, standing up. "I'll be back in a minute. Make yourselves comfortable. You know where the bar is, if you're so inclined."

We weren't, but sat silently.

Devore walked out of the study, tearing the envelope seal as he ambled down the hallway in the general direction of the kitchen. I heard a chair scrape, then nothing. Aaron and I just sat there, staring off into space, not much to say. After maybe ten minutes, Devore came back, eyes red, clutching several sheets of paper.

"So that's it," he said, looking at me.

Not knowing how to react, I simply nodded. "I suppose it is." Dying to know what she had written but too polite to ask. He obviously wasn't going to tell me Cissy's parting words dangling there in his hands.

"I guess I need to go to bed or something," he said absently. We took the cue and stood up.

"If there's anything else I can do …" I started.

"I wish it were that simple, Houston. Here. This is for you." He held out what looked like a check.

"You don't owe me anything, Carson," I protested. *I didn't bring your wife back, safe and sound, like I'd promised,* I didn't add.

"Nothing you can say will convince me of anything but that you saved my wife's life," he said. "Nothing. Take this or I'll have a courier bring it to your office." He folded the check, stuck it in my shirt pocket, patted it fraternally. "I'm a man who built a career on fulfilling obligations, and you've got to let me fulfill this one. Cissy said so," he added, shaking the letter, "and I agree."

Turning to Aaron: "I'm going to take a couple of weeks off, Aaron. Sort a few things out myself, maybe. Get this behind me. Hell, might even retire. Who knows."

"I'll look after the farm," Aaron said, probably hurting inside for his boss, trying not to show it.

"I know you will, and you know I'll look after you." A faint smile. Devore ushered us out the front door, then stood there, waved an arm as we drove off.

"Got anything in the hopper?" Aaron asked after a few minutes of silence, me turning on the dome light, looking at the check.

"Looks like Carson's taking care of my expenses for a while. I might bring Pick out for that fishing trip now. Oh, I almost forgot. Dawn's coming back to the office."

"Best news I've heard all week." Aaron grinned like he already knew. Probably did. "You better take care of her this time."

"She's a married woman."

"I mean treat her like the valuable employee she is."

"You can rest assured I'll do that. Feel like a beer?"

"Bet your ass."

We drove to Billy's and started all over again.

EPILOGUE

I SPENT TWO LAZY WEEKS at Holden Beach with Aaron, Pick Freeman, and his family; rented the beach house the actor Nick Nolte had built, "The Prince of Tides," on the quiet oceanfront. We fished; the grownups played cards while the kids rambled at the local arcade and in the pounding surf. The second week, Dawn and Jerry came, children in tow, and the frolicking reached another level, though Jerry and I stayed politely apart most of the time, him trying to make light of Dawn's return to my fold.

Carson Devore didn't retire, but launched a new merger campaign that swelled his bank's national prominence to first place, I believe, though I'll admit I didn't keep up with such things before, had no intention now.

In late July, Joseph DeMarco Trenton died of cancer. I had never known his middle name until I read the obituary, a glowing, wordy tome that asked for contributions to charities in lieu of flowers. Also didn't know he'd had his hands in so many legitimate businesses until I read the list. The newspaper piece named Eddie as a survivor, and as president of three fairly healthy, legitimate companies. One of them a bicycle manufacturer, and the image of Eddie on a mountain bike just didn't sit.

Dawn, Aaron, and I went to the wake, Eddie promising to be available whenever I needed him. Had a woman with him, a very attractive, middle-aged lady of obvious Italian descent. He looked revitalized, sounded more like the Eddie I'd gotten to know on the field trip to Birmingham.

I got a card from Dee Dee Stancil; wondered how he got my address and remembered, I think, giving him a business card before I left the shop. Said he was reconsidering getting back into mainstream life, so if I ever needed any help on anything, give him a buzz. He listed the names and addresses of three Carolina relatives, said he'd try to drop by when he came back for the family reunion.

Frank Malone and I actually had lunch. He got nowhere with me, eventually closing the case on Claude Farnsworth as an unfortunate traffic fatality. I liked him no better; the feeling was mutual.

Carson's generous check bought me a new office in the more upscale SouthPark area, two doors down from the Evelyn Wilson School of Modeling; Dawn working her magic, fulfilling a promise. The office even had an outer chamber for the secretary, which Dawn decorated nicely and declared adequate and proper for a detective of my stature. Our relationship remained purely professional inside the office, brotherly and sisterly outside, but the sparks are still flying. One never knows.

Charles Satchley resigned from the Primitive Church pulpit after an appropriate period of mourning for his wife, who the papers said was killed in a swimming accident on the west coast. Satchley announced he was starting a new southern prison ministry with offices in Charleston, kind of a holy-owned subsidiary of the parent church. We never had that meeting, and I never really thought he wanted it. Andrea Satchley had been properly eulogized and buried; best things stayed that way.

Cissy's name never even came up in conversation in the months that followed my return from San Diego, until an unseasonably warm Friday afternoon in September when I got a fat package with no return address, postmarked in Anchorage, Alaska, of all the places I'd never expect Cissy to end up.

I took it inside the house, pressed my ear against it. No ticking, so it wasn't a love letter from the Unabomber. I opened it and dumped it on the kitchen table. A bundle of envelopes wrapped with a rubber band fell out, all addressed to me, along with something that surprised me a little. The Swiss Army knife. I thought I'd lost it after the Malibu incident, and hadn't thought any more about it. Wasn't in what the LAPD boys had bagged and tagged, but there was so much going on at the time.

A Post-It note was attached to the envelopes. "I never had the courage to mail these," written in Cissy's curvy script.

I opened the first letter, then worked my way through all of them. Twenty-four, to be exact, I supposed in some chronological order.

For the most part, the letters were Cissy telling me each stop she made as she traveled; first to Mexico, then to Hawaii, then Hong Kong, Tokyo, Europe, Canada, and ultimately, Alaska.

The last letter in the pile was the most interesting. I glanced at it, then read it again, slowly.

"Dear Houston," she began.

"I'm finding that I can't run away from reality. I've actually called Carson a couple of times, just to let him know I'm okay. Though he wanted to, I told him not to call you, no sense in stirring up more questions. I didn't think you would mind.

"I don't know what will happen to the two of us, Carson and me, but the longer time passes, the more I think I'm not particularly good for him. I don't think he agrees, at least not yet. We've had some terrible arguments, but I told him he needed to distance himself from me.

"These letters have been a release for me, confessions of the soul, I suppose." Not too much in the way of confession that I saw, mostly just Cissy talking about how she's beginning to find herself, that kind of thing.

"I shut out most of what happened during that time, but when I do think of it, things seem clearer at times.

"Houston, I wasn't completely honest with you at many points in this, I don't know, charade. Here goes.

"It was Andrea who shot Matthew and Mark, but she did it in front of me, not before I got into the room. You probably thought about that possibility. I watched her do it, and probably could have stopped her but I didn't. I don't know why and may never know.

"I found the pocketknife on the bed, and Andrea said we could leave it there, implicate you in the murders. I almost did leave it, then thought nothing would be accomplished by 'setting you up,' I believe is the term." A term that Cissy might be more familiar with than even she's willing to admit, I thought.

"I'm not telling you this to make you think I'm any better or worse a person, but to let you know that I didn't want to be a party to Andrea's plans. I've sent a letter to the Los Angeles Police Department telling them what happened. They should be getting it about the same time you get this package.

"I may nor may not eventually come back home, but if I do, I want to come with as clear a conscience as I can have.

"Though I'm sure it doesn't make any difference to you, I've actually given most of Carson's money away, at his urging, in part. He said it didn't mean anything to him, that I was all that mattered. It seems there are worthy charities all over the world badly in need of money. Just thought you'd want to know that, too, though it probably doesn't make any difference.

"Carson is probably right. That money had blood on it, and I guess I'm superstitious enough to believe that it could bring only bad luck to whoever has it except those who truly need it.

"This letter is being sent from Alaska, but I don't expect to be here much longer. I don't know where I'll go from here, but wherever God leads me …

"Love, Cissy"

I wondered if I should take the letters to Carson, then decided against it. Sounds like he had dealt with his wife in his own way, still hoping, still holding out for the best in her to guide her home.

I walked over to the kitchen counter, found an old, rusty pot under the sink and held the letters over it, lighting each one with an old Zippo I always kept handy. I watched each letter burn, blacken, and curl, then disintegrate to ashes in the pot.

When I had burned them all, I dumped the sooty collection into the trash can, twist-tied the liner, and carried it outside, dropping it in the roll-out cart. Ashes to ashes, dust to dust.

I put the Swiss Army knife in a bureau drawer in my bedroom and lay on the bed, staring at the ceiling. I tousled Bogie's fur when he jumped aboard.

I tried to remember Cissy's face the last time I saw it, and had some difficulty conjuring the image.

That, I decided, was an appropriate way to end this case.

-THE END-